THE DEVIL'S CHASE

Also by Cap Daniels

THE DEVIL'S CHASE

CHASE FULTON NOVEL #7

CAP DANIELS

ANCHOR WATCH
PUBLISHING
** USA **

The Devil's Chase
Chase Fulton Novel #7
Cap Daniels

This is a work of fiction. Names, characters, places, historical events, and incidents are the product of the author's imagination or have been used fictitiously. Although many locations such as marinas, airports, hotels, restaurants, etc. used in this work actually exist, they are used fictitiously and may have been relocated, exaggerated, or otherwise modified by creative license for the purpose of this work. Although many characters are based on personalities, physical attributes, skills, or intellect of actual individuals, all of the characters in this work are products of the author's imagination.

Published by:

ANCHOR WATCH
PUBLISHING
** USA **

13 Digit ISBN: 978-1-951021-99-3
Library of Congress Control Number: 2019947294

Cover Design: German Creative
Cover Photo: Alexandre Gilliéron

Printed in the United States of America

Dedication

This book is dedicated to…

My dear friend, Steven Ray, upon whom Special Agent Stone W. Hunter, a character in this novel, is based.

I've waited eighteen months since the publication of the first book in this series, or perhaps fifty years, to write this dedication. This, the seventh book in my Chase Fulton Novels series, was to be dedicated to Steven from the start. With "Seven" being our practiced reply to any question for which we don't have a good answer, it's only fitting that this book be in celebration of our friendship.

I've worked alongside Steven for years, and I know, without question, two things about him: First, he's never lied to me. And second, he'd never hesitate to send a bullet over my shoulder and into anyone offering to stick a knife in my back. No one deserves a friend of Steven's remarkable caliber, but I'll forever be grateful for having him in my life. I've never known a man of greater integrity, grit, or fearless honesty. He's taught me the value and purest definition of friendship and talked me out of a great many things that would've ended badly. Steven reminds me daily that simple isn't bad, and rain always ends. He tells me without judgment when I'm on the verge of screwing up, and laughs with me— not at me—when I do it anyway. I've come to trust him more than I trust myself and love him as if he were my brother.

Of the four dozen characters I've created in this series, none could've been Steven until Stone W. Hunter. And of the thousands of people I've encountered throughout my unforgettable life, only one could be Steven Ray: my friend, my brother, and the yardstick against which I will forever measure my own integrity.

Special Thanks To:

My Astonishing Editor
Sarah Flores — Write Down the Line, LLC
www.WriteDowntheLine.com

I can't imagine ever publishing a book without publicly expressing my gratitude to Sarah. She is my teacher, my protector, my literary oracle, and my friend. Her tireless work on both my manuscripts and my craft as a writer makes not only my books palatable, but also makes me a better artist with every stroke of the keys. Without Sarah's involvement in almost every aspect of the creation of these novels, they would be practically unreadable. She is owed as much credit, or more, than me. Making up a story is easy, but turning it into a novel is where Sarah's genius comes alive.

Kay Lynn Westberry
Camden County, GA Historian Extraordinaire

Kay is both a remarkable historian and wonderfully generous hostess. I was fortunate to spend several hours listening to her astonishing stories and trying to absorb the limitless bounty of her knowledge of the history of Camden County. Her direction was invaluable in capturing the beauty and personality of Saint Marys, Georgia. The city is a magnificent place with some of the warmest people I've ever met. My characters seem to enjoy Saint Marys almost as much as I do. Kay plays a major role in my affection for the city and its rich history.

Mary and Mike Neff
Innkeepers/Owners of the Spencer House Inn B&B

Mary and Mike were kind enough to lend me their magnificent bed-and-breakfast for use in this novel. I spent several nights at Spencer House and loved everything about it. The hosts were gracious, welcoming, and entertaining. Their staff is remarkable, and one of them appears in this novel. The property is breathtakingly beautiful, charming, and seems to have a personality of its own. I'll definitely be spending many more nights under their roof.

The Devil's Chase

CAP DANIELS

Chapter 1
Not What You Think

January 22, 2002, my twenty-eighth birthday, found me alone aboard *Aegis*, my fifty-foot sailing catamaran that had been my home for almost five years. In my left hand, I held an envelope addressed to me, Chase Fulton, care of Saint Augustine Municipal Marina. Handwritten in the unmistakable print of a woman, it wasn't my name or address that sent chills racing down my spine. The single name where a return address should have been left me breathless: *A. Fulton*.

Anastasia "Anya" Robertovna Burinkova, a Russian SVR officer who seduced me and almost became my ultimate undoing, took the Americanized first name of *Ana*, and my last name, *Fulton*, when she defected for me.

Anya had been taken back to Russia against her will and held in the Black Dolphin Prison in the city of Sol-Iletsk, near the Kazakh border. It had been Anya's half sister, Captain Ekaterina Norikova of the SVR, who'd facilitated Anya's repatriation back behind the former Iron Curtain. With the help of my partner, Clark Johnson—Army Green Beret turned civilian covert operative—I escorted Captain Norikova back to the former Soviet Union and exchanged her for Anya in a hail of gunfire and explosions at the Black Dolphin Prison.

In the process, I'd not only given Anya her freedom, but also access to a fortune locked in a bank vault in the Cayman Islands. The money had come from the estate of my mentor and Anya's father, Dr. Robert "Rocket" Richter. Nearly two million dollars richer, the gorgeous former Russian spy disappeared into the wilds of Siberia. What she had to say to me in a mysterious letter left me curious and terrified.

Sliding the blade of my pocketknife beneath the sealed flap of the envelope, I paused, thinking of Penny Thomas, the woman who would soon be my wife. Other than beauty, the similarities between Anya and Penny were nonexistent. Penny, the daughter of a liquor salesman, was raised in North Texas, a far cry from the life Anya had lived in Mother Russia, studying for decades to become a spy. I had nothing to hide from Penny, but I was smart enough to know there were more than a few lingering fears about Anya dancing around in her head, so I closed my knife and tucked the unopened envelope in my copy of Bowditch's *Practical Navigator*, where it would remain until Penny and I could open the letter together.

A four-month-old black lab puppy will chew on anything he can fit in his mouth, and our dog, Charlie, was no exception. My favorite pair of boots had become his most recent victim. I'd been wearing boots manufactured by Brill Shoe Industries since the first time I slid a pair on my feet back at The Ranch, where I was transformed from an injured former college baseball player into a covert operative in service to my country. Brill had provided every pair of boots the Israel Defense Forces had worn for decades. If they were good enough for the IDF, they were certainly good enough for me. Charlie's affection, or perhaps hatred for them would soon make it necessary to break out one of the three new pairs I had stored away.

Watching the puppy attack my boot was entertaining, but my eyes kept returning to the unopened envelope. Nothing positive could come from anything Anya had to say to me in a letter, or otherwise. The worst thing she could say was that she missed me and wanted to be back in my bed. That would infuriate Penny and leave me to deal with the aftermath. The best thing she could say was that she was safe, happy, and thankful for what I'd done to free her from the prison. Even that might reinforce Penny's lingering doubts

about any residual feelings I had for Anya. After further considera-
tion, the third possibility would be the worst. She could be involved
in an operation and needed or wanted my help. There was one final
possibility. Perhaps she knew I was in danger, and she wanted to
warn me of an impending doom closing in on me. That's what part
of me hoped. Impending peril had become my playground, so I
could deal with doom. But I had no idea how to manage an angry
Penny.

"Okay, okay. I know you said you don't want anything for your
birthday, and you don't want a party, but it's your birthday, and I
love you, and I want—"

I raised my hands in surrender as Penny continued her verbal
and physical charge into the main salon. "It's a day when I turn a
day older than I was the day before…and that's every day."

The excitement on her face was undeniable. "Yeah, but I love
you, and I want to celebrate the day you were born."

I stood, dragging my boot away from Charlie. "I love you, too,
and we can find all sorts of things to celebrate, but I hate birthdays.
Especially mine."

She narrowed her eyes. "But that doesn't make any sense. You're
supposed to celebrate your birthday."

I wrapped my arms around her in surrender. "Okay, you win.
But first, there's something you have to see."

I handed her the envelope and waited for a reaction. She inspected it, flipping it over several times. "So, it's a letter from A. Fulton. Who's A. Fulton, and why haven't you opened it?"

I took the letter from her hand. "Well, those two questions have
the same answer. I think A. Fulton is Anya, and I haven't opened it
because I wanted you to be here when I did."

"Oh."

What happened next is proof that I'll never understand why
women do the things they do. Penny snatched the letter from my
hand and stuck it beneath her nose, sniffing as if she could detect
some sinister intent within the envelope. Even Charlie stopped his
boot destruction and cocked his head at Penny's action.

Apparently satisfied the envelope contained nothing stinky that would prevent its safe opening, she tore at the flap and yanked the contents from within. A single folded sheet of paper fell into her hand.

Patience would never be one of my strengths, but I did my best to wait for her anxiety to wane before demanding a look. Her eyes devoured the typewritten script I could barely see through the opacity of the paper. I expected a hint of anger or maybe even disbelief from Penny at Anya's audacity to *actually* send me a letter, but neither look developed. Instead, tears formed at the corners of her eyes, and her knees wobbled under her weight.

She thrust the letter toward me as she settled to the settee.

I took the letter from her hand, suddenly more concerned with Penny than with the letter. "What is it?"

"It's not what you think, Chase. It's not from Anya."

Soon, my knees experienced the same failure Penny's had suffered seconds before. I was thankful to feel the settee beneath me when it happened, as nothing could have prepared me for the words I held in my trembling hand.

Son,

Everything you know is false, or at the very least, incomplete. If you're holding this letter in your hands, many things have happened that you never expected, and you've learned far more about your mother and me than you could've ever thought possible. First, above all else, we truly love you and Theresa, and we hope your lives are fuller than they ever could've been if we'd survived. The fact that you're reading this letter is a testament to our death. That part of what you know is true, and you must now embrace your faith that your mother and I are at peace in the presence of God.

Despite our deaths, as you've already learned, you are far from alone. The world in which we lived, albeit not a world you had known existed before our passing, is one of brotherhood beyond comparison. If you've grown to become the man I believed you would, I am saddened that you've been forced to encounter incomparable evil, but I am also proud that you decided to stand in the face of those evils and fight the battles that are the duty of men and women of valor like you—and the people who now surround you.

The purpose of this letter is not to conjure up memories of loss or sadness, but to remind you that you are less alone than you believe. Although our deaths left you and your sister in the hands of strangers, we were not your only family. The remaining family chose lives far outside the world in which you now thrive, but they are family, nonetheless. It is not for us to force our world on them, but since you are reading this letter, the remaining members of your family have chosen to extend their hand from within their world into yours. I encourage you to grasp that hand before it's too late, as it is for your mother and me.

Your Father,

A. Fulton

Chapter 2
Direct and Simple

The look of patience and deep concern on Penny's face spoke volumes about how she cared for me. She had only read the letter's opening line before shoving it into my hand. When I read it, I did so silently, unsure if I had the wherewithal to read the words aloud. I placed the letter faceup on the settee between us and slowly slid it toward her. Her fingertips traced the scars on the back of my hand as she pulled the letter into hers.

The scars were reminders of a life I thought was to be mine, but ultimately, was not to be. They'd been earned on the baseball field in my final game as a catcher for the University of Georgia in the 1996 College World Series. A brilliant career in the Major Leagues had been my destiny, but that injury on that fateful day sent my life in another direction.

The letter in Penny's hand was a reminder of the life that had been my parents', but was now mine. In short, my parents were spies, but on the surface, the world had known them as missionaries. At the hands of assassins, their lives ended on the edge of a rainforest in Panama when I was a boy. From that day, until the moment I read my father's letter, I'd believed I was the last remaining member of my family. My parents couldn't have known, but the assassins who took their lives had also killed Theresa, my baby sister, on that tropical night that would never leave my memory.

When I recovered from my spiral into the past, I watched tears stream down Penny's cheeks. She wouldn't tear her eyes away from the page, though the words were obviously boring holes through her soul, just as they'd done to me.

"Chase, this…this is a letter from your father."

I pulled her against me and felt her breath on my skin. When Penny Thomas cried, she did so like no one else I'd ever known. Her breathing slowed, and her body made a great effort to shrink into itself. I held her as the tears kept coming.

"Yes, it's a letter from my father, but that's not what makes it remarkable."

She leaned back and wiped the tears from her face. "What could be more remarkable than that?"

I pointed toward the paper clenched in her hands. "I'm not the only living Fulton, Penny. All this time, I thought I was the last—"

She placed her palm on my chest. "Your family was never going to end with you, Chase." She tugged at my boot as it continued to suffer Charlie's wrath. "If we can put up with him, a little baby Chase will be a breeze."

Staring at her stomach and admiring the irresistible results of the hours she spent keeping herself in perfect condition, I imagined how she would look as she someday became the mother of our children. "You're not…"

"What if I was?"

I swallowed hard. "But…I mean…we've…."

She smiled. "Relax, Chase. It's just Charlie for now, but who knows what the future will hold for us?"

She held up the paper. "What are we going to do about this?"

I took it from her hand and let myself imagine when it could've been written and how my father could've known what I would become.

"I don't know how to find whoever my father was talking about. What could he possibly mean by 'the remaining members of your family have chosen to extend their hand from within their world into yours'?"

She licked her lips. "I have no idea, but I think we need to figure it out. Don't you?"

"Yeah, I do, and we'll start with whoever sent this letter."

* * *

"Hey, Chase. How are you?"

Dominic Fontana was essentially my boss, if I had a boss. More correctly, he was my handler. He handed down assignments, made sure I had what I needed to complete those assignments, and occasionally scolded me when I took on a job that wasn't officially sanctioned.

"Good morning, Dominic. I'm fine. Listen, I have a direct question, and I need a simple, direct answer, okay?"

"Sure. What is it?"

"Did you send me the letter?"

"What letter?"

I cleared my throat. "Direct and simple, Dominic."

A long, empty moment filled the air. "No, but I know who did."

"Who?" I demanded.

I could hear him moving around his office and the door closing. "Well, I don't know who sent it, but it came from Saint Marys."

I was stumped. "From Saint Marys, Georgia? Like from Judge Huntsinger? Was he my family's lawyer?"

Judge Barnard Henry Huntsinger had been instrumental, to say the least, in the success of my most recent unsanctioned mission. He'd sat on the bench as a federal judge for three decades and currently lived on what remained of Bonaventure, his ancestral plantation on the banks of the North River in the coastal Georgia town of Saint Marys. Dominic had sent me to meet "the Judge," as he preferred to be called, prior to setting off on what had proven to be a mission I'd never forget.

The Judge hadn't known all the answers to my questions, but he pointed me in the right direction to find the men who'd set their sights on me for elimination. Not only had I survived the encounter, but I'd ultimately delivered the Judge's wife's murderer to the lawn of Bonaventure Plantation. I had no desire to know what became of the murderer after I left him at the Judge's feet, but I was headed back to that plantation with an entirely new bevy of questions.

Dominic's voice brought me back. "I don't know, Chase. In fact, I have no idea what's in the letter. The Judge had it, so he's your best option for finding answers to your questions."

My relationship with Dominic had, at times, bordered on contentious, but he'd never directly misled me. He knew more about my family than he'd ever divulge, but he also knew what doses of reality he could administer to keep me upright without driving me over the edge.

"Is that all you're going to tell me?"

"That's all I know, Chase. I swear it. If I knew more, this time, I *would* tell you."

I didn't believe him. After all, he was an old spy; I don't know exactly how old, but somewhere between two or three times as old as me. But his age wasn't his defining trait. The fact that he'd spent his life as a covert operative, and was now a handler of young operators like me, made him a liar of rudimentary necessity.

"Okay, Dominic. I'll go see the Judge. Is there anything else I need to know before I go?"

I could hear his fingertips drumming against the surface of his desk. "Have you heard from Clark?"

Dominic was not only my handler but also my partner's father.

"I was about to ask you the same. I haven't heard from him since he left the country."

His sigh may have been an indication of concern, but more likely, a sign of resolution to say more than he should. "He's in Afghanistan with Brinkwater. That's all I really know. He's not good at saying no when an old friend asks for help, especially when that old friend is former Special Forces."

"I'm sure he's fine, Dom. He's probably kicking in doors and loving every minute of it. Whatever they're doing, you know he's doing it a little harder than everyone else around him."

Dominic almost laughed. "Yeah, I'm sure you're right. Just let me know if you hear from him, okay?"

"Sure, and you do the same."

"Hey, Chase. Don't let the past distract you from the future, all right?"

"What do you mean?"

The fingertip desktop drumming continued. "I mean, you're going to Saint Marys, and you'll probably learn some things that make you consider doing something other than what the world needs of you. It may not always seem like it, but what you do is important to a lot of people who'll never be able to thank you. That doesn't mean they aren't grateful—most of the time they don't know they're supposed to be. And hell, most of them will never know you exist, but that's not the point. The point is that you're good at what you do, and what you do is important. Before you turn your back on the future, remember that the past isn't as shiny as it appears on the surface. We need you, Chase."

He was trying to talk me out of quitting. I'd been told I had options in the past, but until that moment, I never felt I could actually walk away from the world of espionage and clandestine operations. For the first time since the death of my family, I felt maybe I was on the verge of making decisions that would shape my life according to my wants and needs, instead of having those decisions made by someone else for the greater good of whatever.

I swallowed the lump in my throat. "I'll let you know if I hear from Clark. Thanks, Dominic."

I clicked off and turned back to Penny, who'd managed to coax Charlie away from my boot with a bowl of Puppy Chow and a left-over tuna filet.

"You know, you probably shouldn't feed him people food."

She grinned at me. "People food? It's a fish. And Charlie's a dog. Fish isn't people food. Fish is food for everything that eats fish. Besides, it has to be better for him than those hard brown chunks of whatever that is."

I sat on the cabin sole beside the woman I loved and the dog who hated my footwear. "Will it ever be possible to win an argument with you?"

She leaned in and kissed me playfully. "I don't know why you'd even try. Are we sailing or driving?"

I clicked on the marine radio and waited for the offshore forecast to repeat.

Penny beamed. "I'll clear the decks and make ready for sea. You check the engines and stores."

Chapter 3
The Circus is in Town

Convincing Penny Thomas to travel by means other than a sailboat was a wasted effort. Her love of the ocean was one of the many things I loved about her. Since she'd come aboard in Charleston the previous year, she'd become so much more than just the woman I'd soon marry. She was a remarkable sailor and had assumed the role of "master of the vessel" as if it were her birthright. I was reduced to "cabin boy," a role I thoroughly enjoyed.

I think even *Aegis* preferred having Penny's hands on the wheel over mine. Watching my boat respond to Penny's touch was like watching an orchestra under the direction of a world-class conductor. Penny's face of an angel and body of a goddess made the sight even more irresistible for me. Although it was her looks and larger-than-life personality that originally drew me to her, I'd come to respect and adore her for what lay beyond the facade. The way she cared for me as if we were one living soul baffled me. How could anyone look at me and see forever? I was little more than a boat bum who occasionally chased bad guys across the globe. I was physically battered, with a right hand that looked like it had lost a wrestling match with a meat grinder, and I was even more damaged inside. What did I have to offer a woman like Penny Thomas? Perhaps she was a gift to me from a benevolent God who knew I'd never survive without her. Or perhaps God knew I could never truly become what I was meant to be without the stability and undying love Penny brought to my life.

On that day, I was meant to be a sail trimmer, so I trimmed as if I'd never wanted to do anything else.

Penny studied the headsail. "Ease the genoa, would you?"

At her command, I opened the clutch and unwound the first wrap of the genoa sheet from the winch, allowing the line to slide ever so slowly against the pull of the gargantuan headsail.

"Perfect!" She released the wheel and sat back in the captain's chair, watching the thirty-thousand-pound boat settle into her stride. "Look at that. Twelve-and-a-half knots of boat speed on sixteen knots of wind."

I couldn't let her get away with it. "Yeah, but three of those knots of boat speed belong to the Gulf Stream."

She slid her sunglasses down her nose and winked across the rim. "Yeah, but it's still boat speed."

Charlie had begun to get his sea legs, but I still wasn't a fan of him running around on deck while we were underway. There are no better swimmers in the canine world than black labs, but drowning wasn't my fear for the little guy. His twenty-pound mass would make a tasty morsel for any subsurface predator waiting for a snack in our wake. I lifted him from the deck of the cockpit and deposited him on the cabin top near the helm station—one of his favorite spots on the boat when we were at sea. The wind sent his ears flopping and flying and made him impossible to ignore.

Penny tossed him peanuts, and he clumsily snapped at them, occasionally catching one, much to his and her delight. I started to offer the people-food argument again, but just as before, I knew I'd lose.

Penny ran her fingers through her long hair in a futile attempt to manage the mess it always became at sea. "Does the Judge know we're coming?"

"I suspect he knows, but I didn't call. Do you think I should?"

She bounced a peanut off my nose. "It's not polite to just show up."

* * *

"Good morning, Chase. The Judge said you'd probably call," said Ben Hedgcock, one of the young legal protégés.

"It's about the letter," I said, covering the mouthpiece against the wind.

"The Judge didn't say what it was about, but he told me to make sure you knew the depth at the dock is six feet at low tide, and that we have plenty of bedrooms for whomever you bring with you."

"We're content on the boat," I said.

Ben was quick on the draw. "You can take that up with the Judge, but if I were you, I'd plan to wake up in a bed that isn't floating."

"Thank you, Ben. We'll be there before dark."

Penny grinned. "So, I guess they're expecting us, huh?"

"Yeah, you could say that. I don't like being predictable."

She was back at the task of trying to manage her hair, and again, she was losing the battle. She finally settled for a ponytail holder and UGA baseball cap. That should be an event in the Miss America pageant instead of the swimsuit or evening gown craziness. If there's anything sexier than a beautiful woman in a baseball cap, I have no idea what it could be.

Content with her new utilitarian look, she said, "You're not predictable. You're reliable."

"I'm not sure those things are mutually exclusive."

"Regardless of why the Judge had that letter or why he chose to send it today, he knew you'd figure out it came from him. You proved to him that you aren't great at letting the past dangle in the wind without getting involved, so of course he knew you were coming. He's probably expecting the whole entourage, though. Clark, Skipper, and us two."

The mention of Clark's name sent my mind back to the scene of my partner in a hasty fighting position atop a dune on the Marquesas as we fought it out with a gang of kidnappers. The sick feeling in the pit of my stomach when I heard Clark's rifle go silent came flooding back as I thought of him in the Afghan mountains without me. He never would've let me go without him, but I wasn't on the guest list for the operation. The idea of him under fire without me pulling a trigger beside him didn't set well with me. We'd saved each other's lives more than once, and I had no doubt we'd be doing it again.

"Dominic said Clark is in Afghanistan."

Penny frowned. "Afghanistan? What's he doing over there?"

I held up my palms. "Search me, but if I had to guess, I'd say he's leaving a trail of destruction in his wake."

She looked beyond me and across the rolling sea. "You wish you were there leaving your own trail of destruction, don't you?"

"I don't know if that's it. I don't really want to be over there, but I don't like the idea of Clark being there alone."

"He's not alone, is he?"

"Well, no, but I don't like him being in harm's way without me there to have his back. I guess I'd rather have him here with us than me over there with him."

She ran her fingers through mine. "You're a good friend, Chase Fulton. He's lucky to have you."

I wiggled the bill of her ball cap. "I'm lucky to have you."

"You're darned right you are. Now get ready for the approach into Saint Marys."

I glanced over the cabin top and saw the buoy marking the entrance to Saint Marys and Fernandina.

Penny pointed across the bow. "That yellow buoy belongs to the Navy. The submariners use it to mark...something."

I laughed. "Something? Well, that's pretty technical, Captain Ahab."

She launched a water bottle at my head. "Watch it, smarty-pants. What do you know about what the submarines do up here?"

I pointed toward the buoy. "I know they use that yellow buoy for...something."

That earned me a silent finger-point warning.

We turned downwind and began our run into the inlet. *Aegis's* stern danced more spiritedly than I liked, and Penny spun the wheel trying to get the squirming stern under control.

I grabbed an overhead handhold to keep from falling. "What was that all about?"

She shut off the autopilot and tightened the wheel friction. "That's a nasty little following sea. Easterly winds and an incoming tide. I should've expected it, but you had me distracted."

I tossed the water bottle back toward the captain. "Oh, I had you distracted, did I?"

"Yes, you did," she scolded. "Now, make ready for steaming, and stop distracting me."

"Aye, aye, captain."

The diesels gulped their first breath in hours and purred like kittens—albeit really big kittens—beneath our feet as I furled the genoa. "Do you want to leave the mainsail up?"

She glanced at the wall of white sailcloth still capturing the late-afternoon sea breeze. "Yeah, we'll leave it up for now. There's a turning basin in front of Fort Clinch. We'll come about and bring it down once we're in there."

We continued our progress into the mouth of the Saint Marys River, and Fort Clinch came into view off the port bow.

I pointed toward the cannon atop the massive red brick ramparts. "That would be an imposing sight for a blockade runner. Don't you think?"

Penny looked up at the stronghold. "I'm not sure those cannons ever fired on any ships in this inlet, but if we don't figure out a way to overcome this tide, we're going to look like we've been fired upon."

The tidal current was pushing us into the river at seven knots, making steering a nightmare. Sailboats steer by means of oversized rudders hung beneath the stern. Beneath *Aegis* we had a pair of rudders that resembled barn doors in size, if not in design, but even rudders the size of ours had one functional requirement: water had to be flowing past them from bow to stern to have any effectiveness in steering. The current's speed reduced the flow of water across the rudders to less than one knot, making steering sloppy at best, and sometimes nonexistent at worst.

Penny eased the throttles to maximum rpms and turned the wheel hard-to-starboard. "I'll get her to come about and stick her bow in the wind. Do your best to get that sail down as soon as the wind is on our bow."

I scampered up the ladder to the upper deck and the main boom as *Aegis* began her slow, lumbering turn to the north. I wasn't sure we'd make it through the hundred-eighty-degree turn, and if we did, I doubted the engines had the power to overcome the incoming tidal current. Inside the rock jetties, the massive tide was funneled down to less than three-quarters of a mile wide, significantly increasing the speed of the current. Even if we made the turn and got the mainsail down, there was no chance of exiting the mouth of the river back into the North Atlantic. We were committed to the river, and we'd found ourselves in a precarious situation.

Despite my haste to do everything I could to get the mainsail down and stowed, I noticed two scenarios playing out, each of which had great potential to put a damper on our arrival to Bonaventure Plantation. The first was a pair of shrimp boats a quarter-mile in trail of us who were also caught in the same tidal current. Their engines were far more powerful than ours, but their rudders were a fourth of the size. They could power around us and hopefully avoid a collision, but they weren't the greatest risk.

A commotion to the west quickly garnered my full attention. Beyond the first major turn in the Saint Marys River Channel buzzed a pair of Navy gunboats, two massive support vessels, half a dozen tugboats, more Marine police than I could count, and a bevy of smaller vessels that looked like vultures circling roadkill. Lights of every color flashed, filling the sky with coursing rainbows against the backdrop of the purple and orange sunset above the town of Saint Marys. Orders from loudspeakers echoed through the air, adding a staccato soundtrack to the chaos. At the center of the mayhem, the shiny, black, rounded prow of an American nuclear submarine jutted from the shallows of Cumberland Sound near the southwestern tip of Cumberland Island.

"Get it down!"

The urgency in Penny's voice echoing from below brought me back to our problem at hand. I wrangled the seven-story-tall mainsail into its lazyjacks and bound it inside its cover. *Aegis's* engines roared at full power, and Penny did her best to keep the boat pointed into the wind. It was a battle she could win in the short term, but ultimately, we were destined to continue into the river. Hopefully, we'd do it under control without a shrimp boat piled on top of us.

"Sail's in the bag!"

Before the words fully left my mouth, Penny let the bow fall off to starboard, and fifteen tons of fiberglass and aluminum performed a sharp about-face that would've made any Marine drill instructor proud.

The instant my feet hit the deck at the base of ladder, I heard, "What the heck is going on over there?"

Before I could answer, a pair of heavily laden shrimp boats flanked *Aegis* on either side, black smoke pouring from their stacks, determined to plow through water faster than the tide and make it back to the dock in one piece.

I repositioned my sunglasses on my face. "It looks like the current got the best of a nuclear sub—almost like it did to us. Maybe they could've used you at the helm."

Penny laughed, placed one hand on her hip, and did a little look-at-me dance. "Do you really think they want *me* on a submarine?"

I tipped my hat to her performance. "I think a boatload of sailors stuck in a metal tube for months at a time would kill to have you on board, but you'd cause a lot more commotion than a simple grounding in the sound."

She feigned modesty. "Oh, shucks.... Little ol' me?"

I continued surveying the action ahead. "Does little ol' you have a plan to get around that mess?"

"Here, take the wheel. I'll go up and have a look."

She surrendered the helm and climbed the ladder. As the mouth of the river widened, the current slowed enough to give *Aegis's* rudders something to bite. I steered well south of the waterborne circus, wanting nothing to do with an operation involving dragging part of the country's nuclear arsenal off a South Georgia sandbar.

"I don't think we're getting around that. It's a train wreck."

"Oh, it's far worse than a train wreck. It looks like a dead end to a formerly promising naval career for some poor sub skipper."

She pressed her lips into a thin line. "I don't envy that guy."

"Neither do I," I admitted. "How about Fernandina for the night? We can head up to Bonaventure in the morning after the Navy is finished playing in the sand."

A wicked grin consumed her face. "I have a much better idea."

Chapter 4
The First Lie

Penny's idea was indeed much better than a night in Fernandina Marina with a hundred other boats, noisy halyards rattling against masts, and a sky full of yellow light from mercury-vapor bulbs atop aluminum poles.

We dropped anchor in sixteen feet of water before high tide on a sandy-bottom anchorage called Little Tiger North. The anchorage was in the northern mouth of the Amelia River, south of the convergence with the Saint Marys. Fort Clinch State Park consumed the northern tip of Amelia Island, so the absence of artificial light made for a perfect location to spend the night. Although the lights and loudspeakers of the naval commotion upstream were still pulsating in the distance, the anchorage was beautiful. With eleven casts, we caught four perfect whiting that turned into succulent filets on the grill.

Penny came from the galley with a pair of wineglasses in one hand and a bottle in the other. "I've been saving this for a perfect evening, and this one just might qualify."

I pulled the cork from the bottle of French Chardonnay and poured each glass a little over half full. We touched glasses and shared a moment of silent appreciation as we watched each other over the golden wine.

Penny looked up sheepishly. "I have some exciting news."

I knew there was a reason she broke out a bottle she'd been saving for months. "Let's hear it."

She blushed, something I'd rarely seen her do. It was a rare glimpse into the little girl who lived inside the magnificent woman.

Almost as if she were embarrassed, she whispered, "I sold my screenplay."

"That's spectacular! When? I didn't even know you were shopping it around. In fact, I didn't know you'd finished it. Penny, that's great news. Congratulations!"

Her eyes widened. "Calm down, Chase. It's not that big of a deal. It's an option offer, really. A production company wants to buy the first right of refusal to produce it if it ever goes that far, so it won't be a movie anytime soon or anything."

"Still, that's amazing. I'm happy for you, and I'm so proud of you. You know, that's the first real thing I knew about you?"

She looked confused. "What are you talking about?"

"The night we met in Charleston, the first thing I learned about you was that you were a writer. Remember? You gave me a copy of your screenplay to read."

She smiled. "Of course I remember. That was when I believed the first lie you ever told me."

I felt the color drain from my face. "What?"

She sighed as if I were supposed to know what she was talking about. "You told me you were a writer when we met, and I believed you. That's why I wanted you to read my screenplay."

Suddenly, the whiting didn't feel so good in my stomach. "Penny, I couldn't—"

Her hand landed on my forearm. "Chase, I understand now. I wasn't trying to deflate our moment. I understand. Really, I do."

I couldn't meet her eyes. "I'm sorry that was necessary."

"It wasn't necessary," she said. "You could've told me the truth or nothing at all. I still would've fallen in love with you."

I bit my lip, knowing I was about to tell yet another lie. "I've never lied to you since that night."

She tilted her head and continued her girlish smile. "Of course you have, Chase, and I understand. Omission is the worst lie. You're involved in so many secret operations, I know you can't tell me everything."

"I'm not trying to hide anything from you."

She squeezed my arm. "Stop. I want you to know that I love you no matter what the truth is, no matter how much you hurt inside over the things you have to do when you go away. I'll always listen, even when you're not talking."

My inability to meet her gaze vanished, and suddenly, I couldn't look away. Penny was the most astonishing woman I would ever know, and she was begging me to let her love me completely. The problem was, I had no idea how to say yes.

I had no explanation for what came out of my mouth next. "What am I going to learn at the plantation tomorrow?"

Her smile melted into a somber look, and she lifted her glass to her lips. After a mouthful of the wine, she looked up at me. "I don't know, but whatever it is, *we* will find out together, and *we* will deal with it together...no matter what it is."

"I've been alone for a long time, Penny."

She slowly shook her head. "No, you haven't. You've *believed* yourself to be alone, and that isn't the same thing. You've got me—all of me—and Clark and Skipper. And if that letter means what we think, you have a family beyond us."

I wonder if she realized how wise she actually was, or if self-awareness evaded her. She was impossible not to admire. I'd been enamored by her from the moment we met, and the feelings had only grown stronger with time.

"But if I do have a family—whoever they are—they turned their backs on me."

"What do you mean?"

"If my father's letter is any indication, they knew about me, but they didn't want to be part of our lives."

She wrinkled her brow. "No, that's not what the letter said. Your father wrote that it wasn't right to force the way you live on the rest of the family, and now they're reaching out. Otherwise, the letter would have never come."

Perhaps she was right, but it was all too much for me to piece together in one night. "I don't know, but no matter what, my real family—the family that matters to me—is you, Clark, and Skipper. The three of you chose to be my family when there was no bloodline binding us together. Family isn't about genetics. It's about locking arms when the rest of the world turns its back on you. You are my family."

Before she could respond, my phone chirped, and I recognized the number as the Bonaventure Plantation. I answered the call on speaker so Penny could hear.

"I'm sorry. I should have called. There's a submarine sideways in the channel, so we anchored out in the mouth of the Amelia River for the night. We'll be there first thing in the morning."

The voice that came from the tiny speaker surprised me. It wasn't the voice of either of the young lawyers at the Judge's plantation. Instead, a female voice said, "That's what we assumed, Chase, but grandfather insisted that I call to check on you. How many places shall I set for breakfast? Is Clark with you?"

Maebelle was Judge Huntsinger's great-granddaughter and well on her way to becoming a world-class chef. And for some reason, young women always wanted to know if Clark was with me.

"Thanks for checking on us, Maebelle. I'm looking forward to your breakfast. We'll be there at eight, if that's okay. It's just the two of us—Penny and me."

"Aww, no Clark? Where is he?"

Penny covered her mouth, stifling a giggle, and I stuck my finger to my lips in a useless effort to keep her from laughing. "He's overseas doing some work, but I'm sure he'd much rather have breakfast with you."

I could almost hear her blush through the phone. "Yeah, well, I'd fix him breakfast anytime."

I didn't know what to say that wouldn't result in either Penny or me bursting out in laughter. "So, eight o'clock's okay?"

"Sure, eight will be fine. We'll see you then. Oh, and Chase? Thanks for coming. It means a lot."

I was taken aback by her comment. "Sure, Maebelle. We'll see you in the morning."

I cast a look at Penny. "That was strange."

She laughed. "No, it wasn't. Maebelle is a twenty-year-old girl, and you know how they fall at Clark's feet. He just has this thing about him."

I frowned. "Yeah, I know that thing, and I've gotten used to it. I meant her saying it means a lot that we'd come. What do you think that's all about?"

"The Judge is old," she said, "and he probably sees it as some last responsibility to tell you about your family. I heard you ask Dominic if the Judge was your family's attorney. What did he say?"

"He said he didn't know. All he knows is that the letter was sent from Saint Marys. I can never tell if he's telling me the whole truth. Either he truly doesn't know what's going on, or he's not going to tell me. Either way, the answers I'm looking for are a few miles up the river, and I have a feeling that tomorrow those answers may start pouring out faster than I can take them."

* * *

Penny and I lay on the trampoline at the bow of the boat and watched the night sky glisten with a billion tiny points of shimmering light. We counted seven shooting stars and made a wish on every one. My wishes were always the same, but Penny—being a famous screenwriter—was a little more creative with her wishes.

"I wish this night would never end," I whispered for the fourth time as a meteor streaked so close it felt like we could touch it.

Penny traced her fingers down the bridge of my nose. "I wish we had ten thousand more nights like this, but each one better than the last."

Uttered seconds after the last shooting star vanished over the horizon, her final wish left me breathless.

"I wish your father could see you now."

Chapter 5
Homecoming

The sun rose over Fort Clinch as it had done since long before the Spaniards showed up, but something about this particular morning felt different than any I'd ever experienced. I felt like I was going home, although "home" was a concept altogether foreign to me. Since the death of my parents and sister in Panama, I'd slept in the dormitories of a private school and a grand Southern university, the bunkhouse of The Ranch, and aboard two sailboats. To say I ever really had a home during the past fifteen years of my life would be a farce.

"Good morning." Penny yawned, stretched, and then sat beside me on *Aegis's* upper deck.

I pointed my coffee cup toward the rising sun. "Isn't it beautiful?"

"Yes, it is," she murmured, "but not as beautiful as a cup of that coffee would be."

I handed her my mug and started down the ladder. When I returned, she was lying facedown with her chin propped on the backs of her folded hands. When she saw me topping the ladder, she smiled and pressed her fingertip to her lips, then pointed toward the bow. On the prow of the portside hull sat Charlie, completely mesmerized by a pair of dolphins playing ahead of the boat. We watched in silence as his head tilted from side to side in wonder.

I placed the fresh mug of coffee on the mat beside Penny and joined her, waiting to see what happened next. We didn't have to wait long. Although still a bit shrill, Charlie's voice was slowly changing into the baritone it would become. He reminded me of how I sounded during puberty. He barked, in constantly changing tones, at the frolicking pair of dolphins I assumed to be mother and calf. Charlie seemed to be propelled by his barking, his body lunging forward with every yelp.

Penny lunged toward the puppy. "Oh, my God. He's going to jump!"

I patted her arm. "They won't hurt him if he does."

He'd never threatened to leap from the boat before, so I had no reason to believe he'd do it that morning, but I was wrong.

He took four or five running strides and leapt as gracefully as twenty pounds of fur, razor-sharp puppy teeth, and blubber could leap, and landed with a splash a few feet from the dolphins. As quickly as Charlie had launched himself from the boat, Penny was on her feet and sliding down the ladder. I didn't want to miss whatever the show was about to become, so I didn't move. My inaction was soon rewarded.

The dolphin calf surfaced inches from Charlie's nose and chirped at him. Charlie returned the sound, and the two were instantly old friends. Charlie gave chase every time the dolphin dived beneath the surface and barked excitedly when it resurfaced.

I'd almost forgotten Penny had been on a mission to intercede in the morning's festivities, when I heard an unexpected splash to the left of the boat. When I saw her long, toned back surface a few feet from Charlie and the dolphin, I was pleased to see she'd doffed her shorts and T-shirt prior to her plunge.

The commotion startled the dolphin calf and his mother, and they both quickly disappeared. Again, Charlie gave chase. Even Penny's athletic stroke couldn't keep pace with the pup whose webbed feet made him the far superior swimmer, so she gave up and decided to call his name instead.

"Charlie, get over here. What are you doing?"

For a moment, he was torn between his desire to rejoin his new friend or swim back to his primary source of food. Ultimately, instinct—and hunger—won out, and he paddled toward Penny.

I was back in the cockpit by the time the drenched duo made it up the sugar-scoop boarding ladder at the stern. I handed Penny a towel and pulled out the shower nozzle for Charlie. Rinsing him off was the easy part since he loved everything to do with water, but drying him off was another story. He was having none of that. Penny lifted the deck-mounted shower nozzle and allowed me to watch her rinse the brackish water from her skin. Unlike Charlie, she offered no resistance to my offer to dry her off.

"We're going to be late for breakfast if we don't get going," I said.

The only place I wanted to go at that moment was back to our cabin, but my advances were shunned.

"Not now, silly boy. But I will have to shower again sometime, and you'll be welcome to get as involved as you'd like."

That was a raincheck I could support.

The anchor came out of the sand at the first tug of the windlass, and we were soon headed across Cumberland Sound toward the town of Saint Marys.

I laid *Aegis* alongside the Bonaventure Plantation dock at ten minutes before eight, and Penny tied us securely to the cleats. It was a floating dock, so there was no need to be concerned about the massive tidal flow raising or lowering my boat away from the dock.

Judge Barnard Henry Huntsinger was sitting alone in his gazebo and rose to greet us as we walked up the riverbank. "Welcome back to Bonaventure. It's so good to see you both. Won't you come in?"

I shook the old man's rugged, twisted hand, but Penny got a hug.

The Judge pointed toward the dock. "That's a fine piece of boat you've got there. It looks like you had better luck in the pass than the Navy did last night."

I glanced back at *Aegis*. Seeing her always made me proud. I was thankful Penny had kept her off the sand and shoals the submariners didn't miss. "Thank you, Judge. It's good to see you again. Rumor has it there's a gourmet breakfast being served around here."

He laughed. "Every meal that girl makes is gourmet…especially her breakfasts. Thanks for comin', Chase."

"I had to come, Judge."

He pulled a bandana from his hip pocket and wiped at his face. "I know, son, but we'll have time for all that after breakfast. Let's go see what Maebelle's got on the table."

The spread was nothing short of spectacular. Biscuits the size of saucers were piled on a platter big enough to land a small plane. Fresh fruit of every imaginable variety overflowed from bowls that had to be older than this country. Where she got fresh fruit in January was beyond me.

Maebelle appeared with a platter of steaming-hot omelettes. "Hey, guys! We'll have formal hellos later. For now, sit, sit. I've whipped up something I think you're gonna love."

The Judge, Penny, and I found seats at the table as Maebelle looked around the room as if she'd lost something important.

The thundering sound of the Judge's boot striking the floor of the dining room brought Ben Hedgcock and Jeff Montgomery bounding into the room.

"Boys, when Miss Maebelle serves a breakfast this fine, you don't make her wait. You hear me?"

I tried not to laugh at the Judge's scolding, but Penny made no such effort. "Hey, guys. It's good to see both of you again. Is he always this way?"

Jeff, the less serious of the two young lawyers who'd spent the last several weeks under the tutelage of the Judge, adjusted his tie. "Hello there, Penny. It's great to see you and Chase again. And no, the Judge isn't usually this pleasant. I think he's on his best behavior to impress you."

The Judge slid his glasses up his nose. "Keep it up, son, and you'll be eating Pop-Tarts on the front porch."

Maebelle slid an omelette onto each of our plates, and the serving dishes made their rounds. We piled our plates high with biscuits that felt like clouds, gravy, roasted potatoes, fruit, and strips of bacon that smelled like heaven.

The first bite left me in awe. "Is this salmon?"

Maebelle smiled as if she'd been waiting a lifetime for someone to ask. "It's fresh rainbow trout, believe it or not. I got them from Seth, a friend of mine who works downtown at Spencer House. He brought the fish back from Tennessee last night. He's a rock climber, and oh, my God, he's gorgeous. Anyway, he goes all over the place climbing, and he always brings me back something special to cook for him. This time it was the trout. He told me he caught them after his climb, though he's probably lying. I think he bought them, but I don't care."

As much as I wanted to hear her story, I couldn't stop forking the breakfast into my mouth. "Well, I'm sorry he's not going to get any of his own trout, but I'm certainly thankful he brought them back. This is amazing."

She blushed. "There are two more left out in the kitchen, so he'll get those for lunch. I plan to broil them with some new potatoes and cherry tomatoes with rosemary, thyme, and lemon butter."

The Judge cleared his throat. "Girl, that boy's just using you for your cooking…and God knows what else."

Maebelle locked eyes with him. "No, Granddaddy, I'm using him as a taste tester for every new recipe I come up with—and God knows what else."

Ben and Jeff didn't dare chuckle, but Penny offered a high five to Maebelle. "You go, girl!"

"Well, I guess we oughta have some dessert, Maebelle."

"Dessert?" Penny and I echoed.

The Judge scoffed. "Absolutely. When I tell you my granddaughter's a chef, I don't mean just a meat-and-potatoes chef. She's every kind of chef there is…especially the pastry kind."

Before we knew it, a plate of some culinary masterpiece landed before each of us. The Judge poked at his with a fork. "Tell us what it is, darlin'."

"It's a brown sugar coffee cake, of sorts, but with a little extra kick. I'm serving it with a maple, bourbon, and roasted pecan sauce with a pineapple slice for a little acidity."

Maebelle had a bright future ahead of her, wherever she and her chef's hat landed.

When there wasn't a crumb to be found on anyone's plate, the Judge leaned back in his chair and wiped his chin with a linen napkin. "Have you ever had a better breakfast than that?"

I mirrored his motion with my napkin. "No, sir, I have not. And Maebelle, yours is a talent beyond words. Breakfast was truly remarkable."

Even though the smile and tilt of her head was more than adequate gratitude for the high praise, she whispered, "Thank you. I'm so glad you enjoyed it."

The Judge stood and tossed his napkin onto his empty plate. "Good. I'm glad you agree with my assessment of Maebelle's cooking. That's part of the reason you're here. Now, let's go out back and have a talk."

Penny pushed back her chair and rose. "I'll help Maebelle clean up. It's the least I can do for such a wonderful meal."

"Hogwash!" the Judge roared. "You'll do no such thing. Maebelle doesn't have to do any cleaning up. We've got people for that. And besides, this is a talk for all of us—not just the menfolk." He turned his stern gaze my way. "That reminds me. Have you married this pretty girl yet?"

I shot a glance at Penny. "No, sir. We've—"

I didn't have the opportunity to finish my defense before the Judge pointed at Ben. "You get the clerk over here and have her bring the marriage license book. We'll be out back by the cannon."

Chapter 6
Not by My Hand

The cannon had been recently relocated twice. I'd moved it for the first time in nearly two hundred years when I pulled it from the muddy bottom of Cumberland Sound with the help of Captain Stinnett's Research Vessel, the *Lori Danielle*, and his top-notch salvage diving crew. Before that move, the cannon had been aboard either a British man-o'-war or a warship captured by the British during the War of 1812. A ragtag bunch of plantation hands and U.S. Army troops under the command of Captain Abraham Massias of the 43rd Infantry Regiment had burned and sank the ships while the British were pillaging the town of Saint Marys during the war. I retrieved one of the dozens of sunken cannons as a gift to the Judge. When I delivered my gift beside his gazebo six weeks earlier, a mafia hit man named Loui Giordano was handcuffed to it. Giordano was the *real* gift. He was guilty of dozens of murders over the previous thirty years, the most important of which, at least to the Judge, was his wife, Mildred Huntsinger, who'd fallen victim to Giordano in her own kitchen at Bonaventure Plantation in 1978. I delivered Giordano alive, and I would never ask what became of him.

The second time it had been moved was accomplished by hands other than mine. Apparently, those had been the hands of master craftsmen. The three-century-old weapon of war now sat inside a beautifully constructed pavilion, resting upon a carriage that could've passed for an authentic eighteenth-century warship. The gun was poised with the muzzle directed toward the rising sun over the North River. It was easy to imagine smoke roiling from the heavy gun as it lobbed balls downstream at northbound aggressors.

"I like what you've done with the gun, Judge."

The old man laid his hand atop the relic and stroked it as if he'd cast the weapon himself. "Thank you, Chase…not just for the cannon, but for…"

"You're welcome, Judge. That's not something we ever need to discuss."

He motioned toward a collection of Adirondack chairs near the back of the pavilion. "Let's have a seat."

Penny rubbed her hand across the arm of one of the Adirondacks. "I love these chairs, Judge."

He did the same. "They're made of pecan wood grown right here on this very ground. You know, Miss Penny, there's a bull-malarkey story about how pecan trees showed up here in Saint Marys. There's even a historical marker about it if you can believe that. It's just down the road. I'm sure you'll wander across it, but I 'spect you'll wander across a great many fascinating sights here on the riverfront. Don't always believe everything you read…especially on historical markers. History, as they say, is written by the victors, but I don't think that's entirely true. I think history is written by the people who want you to *think* they were the victors. The stories of the vanquished are often far closer to reality than those told by the scribes of the victorious."

Penny glanced at me. "I don't know how long we'll be staying, but this is certainly a beautiful place. I look forward to seeing more of the town and learning the history."

The Judge picked at imaginary lint on his pants. "That's what we need to talk about. I know you came up here so I could explain that mysterious letter, but I won't be doing that."

I frowned at his declaration, but he held up a hand.

"What I mean is, I won't directly be explaining that letter, but it'll all make sense before we climb out of these dad-blasted chairs that'll trap an old man." He squirmed in the seat and motioned his drawn, liver-spotted hand toward his granddaughter. "Maebelle here is the last remaining direct descendant of the Huntsinger family, and by all rights, this place is hers, you see. But this town is a small, inconsequential place most people have never heard of, and my beautiful, talented granddaughter is grander than any forgotten little port town in southeast Georgia. Hell, you've eaten her food more than once now. You know a place like this can't hold her down. Why, she belongs in Paris or Madrid or maybe New York. She went to school at the CIA, for Pete's sake."

As if the Judge didn't already have my full attention, the mention of Maebelle attending a CIA school kicked me in the gut.

The Judge let his words hang in the air as he watched me try not to react. "That's right. You heard me. The CIA. The Culinary Institute of America is the finest cooking school in the country. It's right up there with Le Cordon Bleu…even though they don't know how to spell *blue*."

The color left my face as I realized I'd fallen right into his trap, and I waggled my finger at the Judge. "The CIA…"

He held up his palms in feigned innocence. "Hey, that's what it's called. I didn't name the place."

I nodded. "Go on. Don't let me interrupt you. But how does this have anything to do with the letter from my father?"

"Patience, my boy. We're getting there."

Another squirm and shuffle by the Judge in the Adirondack chair made it clear he would rather be sitting on a rock, so I hopped to my feet. "I'll be right back."

Jogging along the marshy bank of the North River, I tried to imagine where the Judge's story was going, but it wouldn't come together for me.

I shouldered one of the weathered oak rocking chairs from the gazebo and returned to the cannon pavilion. "Here you go, Judge. I think you'll be more comfortable in this. It looks like that Adirondack is kicking your tail."

"Thank you, son. Those things are beautiful, but they're definitely not for a ninety-three-year-old ass. Pardon an old man's language if you will, Miss Penny."

Penny waved a dismissive hand. "I live on a boat with a sailor, Judge. Your language is never going to offend me."

He settled into the rocker as if it had been custom built for his ninety-three-year-old body. "Where was I? Ah, yes. The CIA. How could I forget?"

A wink followed in the wake of his jab, but I did my best to remain stoic.

"So, as I was saying, Maebelle is destined for things far beyond these old stinky marshes that I love so much. It breaks my heart to lose her to the great broad world, but I understand."

He paused, apparently waiting for a reaction, so I obliged. "Maebelle's going to take the world by storm no matter where she lands. You should be very proud."

"Oh, I am. The only thing that'd make me prouder would be seeing my old house turned into her first restaurant, but there simply aren't enough mouths to feed 'round here. So, that brings us to your father's letter."

I felt a lump swell in my throat, leaving me incapable of speaking.

"That letter has been in my safe for over twenty years. I've never read it, but there's still enough electricity bouncing around in my old head to guess what it must have said."

I found my voice. "I have the letter if you'd like to read it, Judge."

He pursed his lips in animated, deliberate thought. "No, I don't think that's necessary. Let me tell you why I think you're here, and if that doesn't cover it, maybe we'll take a look at the letter before lunch. How's that sound?"

I nodded in silent approval of his suggestion, but my brain was screaming, "Get on with it!"

"Your mother was a niece of mine by marriage. Now, I don't know what they taught you over in Athens about familial law and genealogy, if anything, but by my reckoning, that makes me your great uncle—or maybe twice great uncle. I've not studied the tree as thoroughly as perhaps I should have. Regardless of the greats involved, I'm your uncle somewhere up that tree, and that makes you an heir to what little fortune I have."

Every hair on my body stood immediately and decisively on end. The goosebumps covering my flesh were almost painful in their intensity, and once again, I found myself without words. Penny, on the other hand, made a sound I'd never heard her create—a combination of a groan and a gasp veiled beneath a delicate sob. I ached to turn to her, but I couldn't unlock my eyes from the Judge's.

"Would you like a drink, son?"

I squeaked, "No, sir."

"Okay, then. Shall I go on?"

I nodded, still locked steadfastly on his eyes.

He cleared his throat. "I know I should've told you this the first time we met in November of last year, but for reasons that are of no consequence to this discussion, I chose to leave our family ties where they'd been for a quarter-century: locked away in confinement within a dark, soulless vault."

He again retrieved his red bandana from a pocket and wiped at his lips. "I've delivered many an oration in my near century on this muddy earth, but I can't recall ever having been less prepared for a speech than I am for this one, so I'd truly appreciate your interaction…if for no other reason than to make it easier on an old man."

I stammered, "Judge, I…I don't know what to say." The words simply wouldn't come, no matter how desperately I grasped for them.

"I know, son. You have a lot of questions, and most of 'em don't have any answers—or at least not answers that would satisfy your well-deserved curiosity. Here's the skinny of it all, as we used to say in the courts. Your mother married your father, and they became—or already were—agents of the federal government of this great nation—much, I suspect, as you are now."

I forced an exhalation. "I'm not.…"

"Relax, son. I'm not making any accusations, and I don't want to know what you are, be it a spy or diplomat. It makes no difference to me. That's between you"—he motioned to Penny—"your wife, and your God. I play no role in any of that, and that's exactly how the family felt about what your parents chose to do with their brief lives. Their decision cost them the privilege of seeing their children grow into adults, and it ultimately cost them everything. Our family, that is, *your* family, chose two different paths. Most of us chose a life of ignorant complacency, while a few—your parents primarily —chose a life of action in defense and preservation of what they believed to be a worthy endeavor; that endeavor being the great experiment of capitalism, freedom, and liberty. Noble, indeed, was their decision, but not conducive to the rearing of a family."

I gathered my wits and stood. "I'm going to need a moment, Judge." Penny stood with me, but I held up my hand, silently insisting that she stay while I try to digest what I'd just heard.

Twenty minutes later, I returned from *Aegis* with my most prized possession and stuck the tip of my machete into the wooden plank decking of the pavilion, only inches from the Judge's feet. "That's the knife that slaughtered the butchers who murdered my parents and my sister, Theresa. It wasn't done by my hand, but by the hand of a man who loved and respected them as if they were his own blood. Family, I've learned, has far less to do with genetics than it has to do with choices."

The Judge slowly surveyed the machete. "Wisdom flows from only two fountains, my boy: the first being the Almighty God, and the second being experience. The latter is a gift from the former, and it would appear you've been given that gift in abundance. That's evident in your eyes, son, for those are the eyes of age in the body of a young man who has seen too much. I imagine you've witnessed men doing unspeakable things in the name of greed, hatred, love, or a thousand other motivations—none of which justify their atrocities. I see the indecision in your eyes. I see the way you look at Miss Penny and how she looks at you. I know the life you want to give that girl, and I know the tireless pull you feel from what you consider to be a duty to your parents, and to all of us who rely on men like you to keep us safe and free."

I faced the woman who'd chosen to walk away from the comfortable, carefree life she'd known and step into my world of utter chaos.

"Our lives are the sum of our choices." I heard my father say those words long before I was old enough or wise enough to understand their genius and absolute truth.

As if he believed he'd given me enough time to swallow the pill I'd been handed, the Judge said, "Now you have one more decision before you, and this one may be the greatest of your life…or perhaps the most foul."

Penny's eyes left mine, and I followed her gaze back to the face of my uncle.

"Bonaventure Plantation represents approximately one-third of my wealth, and ninety-three years represent nearly one hundred percent of my life. I'll soon draw my final breath on this Earth and move on to join the soul of my beloved wife in what lies beyond that blackest of veils. The bulk of my estate will rightfully fall to Maebelle to ensure she lives to see the fullness of her dreams play out wherever she chooses." The Judge looked out over the marsh and then back at me. "And my son, Bonaventure Plantation is yours."

Chapter 7
The Ride

There are few things I've ever truly hated. Horses are one of those things. Penny, a lover of every living thing, couldn't stop grinning as the four of us ambled away from the stables, mounted atop four quarter horses, mine—not surprisingly—named Pecan. Maebelle had described Pecan as "gentler than a carousel horse." We'd see about that. Prior to that day, I'd ridden, or attempted to ride, exactly four horses, and I'd been thrown exactly nine times. Based on my track record with beasts of burden, I was about to make double digits.

"This used to be the paper mill. What a rancid odor that place put out." The Judge waved his hand over a corner of the plantation that looked like the end of the industrial world. "I leased this piece of land to the mill instead of selling it when they approached me. It was good for the local economy while it lasted. We put a lot of local folks to work in the mill, but like most things, it was temporary, and the land reverted back to me when they closed the plant. The environmentalists who're paid to declare such things tell me this section of the ground has some environmental concerns." He made a show of installing air quotes around "environmental concerns."

I hadn't expected a tour of the plantation that morning, and certainly not on horseback, but the Judge insisted, and in my limited experience with him, the man got what he wanted.

"Over here, to the northwest, is the airport, but like the paper mill, the old airstrip may be drawing its final breaths. The Navy doesn't particularly like having a civilian airport that close to a nuclear submarine base, but that's not the primary reason the airport's failing. The economy is struggling and may not be able to support it much longer. Do you know anything about airplanes, son?"

Pecan may be the gentlest horse to ever live, but I was, without a doubt, the worst equestrian in history. If I wasn't falling to one side or the other, I was leaning forward in a clumsy effort to remain aboard. "I know they're a lot safer than horses."

That's when Pecan started bucking like a rodeo bronco. It was like trying to ride a psychotic kangaroo on a trampoline. I've been in a gunfight with a loose grenade rolling around inside a shipping container on a Chinese cargo vessel sunken in the Panama Canal, but I've never been more frightened than I was that day on Pecan. I was getting thrown, and there was nothing I could do to stop it. I just prayed Pecan would let me decide how and where I would land. Those are the moments when otherwise rational humans begin to broker deals with God, and I was no exception. Although I'll never remember the precise deal I was negotiating with Him, it ended with, "…and I swear I'll never get on another horse again."

I remember a Bible verse from Sunday school that said many people have entertained angels unaware. Although Maebelle may not be the typical name that comes to mind when thinking about angels, she became my guardian that day. Through my blurred, bobbing vision, I saw her horse galloping toward me at a Kentucky Derby pace. The closer they came, the more I thought a collision was about to end all of our lives, but at the last second, Maebelle extended her right arm, grabbed Pecan's reins, and by some wizardry, cast out the demons that had possessed my horse. Pecan calmly lowered his head, swished his tail, and began chomping at a tiny tuft of green grass.

I saw Maebelle's lips moving, but I was too busy trying to catch my breath to hear what she was saying.

"Do you have your phone in your pocket?"

"What?" I yelled over the pounding of my heart.

"Do you have your cell phone in your pocket?"

I reached for the pocket where I typically carried my phone and patted the material. "Yeah, I've got it."

The greatest chef I'd ever met began laughing like a hyena. When she finally regained her composure, she said, "I forgot to tell you, but Pecan hates ringing cell phones."

"Oh, really? You couldn't have mentioned that thirty minutes ago when you were telling me how gentle he is? I seem to remember some BS about a carousel horse being more spirited than Pecan."

She grinned sheepishly and shrugged. "Sorry. I forgot."

I turned to Penny for support, but she was convulsing from uncontrollable laughter. Obviously, I was on my own.

Dismounting my trusty roller coaster of a horse, I yanked my phone from my pocket and thrust it toward Maebelle. "Here! Do something with this thing. I'm not risking another of those episodes."

She stood in the stirrups and pocketed my phone, which to Pecan was the most disturbing device in all of Christendom. "Hey, you missed a call, but Pecan already let you know that."

Relieved to be on the ground and in one piece, I took the phone back and discovered it was a satellite call from a number I didn't recognize. Three seconds into the voicemail, my heart stopped for the second time in one day.

"Uh, Chase, Marvin Malloy. You remember me...Mongo? I worked with you on the Russian thing last year. We've got a situation. I don't know what time zone you're in, so I'll call again at seventeen hundred Zulu."

I shot a glance at my watch. Seventeen hundred Zulu would be noon, Eastern Standard Time. I had over an hour until I'd hear from Mongo again. The urge to try calling the sat-phone back was overwhelming, but if Mongo was with Clark in Afghanistan, there was a high probability that a ringing phone could get them discovered and even killed. I wasn't willing to risk that, so I'd have to wait the seventy-eight minutes for Mongo to call.

Penny recognized the look of terror on my face and realized its source was far more sinister than the out-of-control horse. "What is it, Chase? Who was that?"

"It was one of the guys from Brinkwater Security. Marvin Malloy. I think he's with Clark in…" I paused and glanced up at Maebelle and the Judge still situated in their saddles.

My uncle—great or otherwise—nodded once. "Come on, Maebelle. Let's have a look at this fence. It may need a little work."

Penny's raised eyebrows told me she couldn't wait another second, so I continued. "He's one of the guys on the team with Clark in Afghanistan, and he says there's a situation. He didn't leave any details on voicemail, but he said he'll call back at noon."

She hopped down from her horse. "What's going on over there? Is everything all right? Is Clark hurt?"

I took her hand. "I don't know any more than I've already told you."

"Well, how did he sound on the phone? Did it sound bad?"

I handed her the phone. "Here. Listen to the message for yourself, but let's not jump to any conclusions. We'll wait for the call."

With the phone pressed to her ear, she listened as if she were waiting for tumblers to fall inside the door of a safe. "Oh, Chase. That doesn't sound good. I know you don't want to hear this, but that's the call I'm afraid of hearing every time I answer the phone while you're off on an operation."

"Relax. There's no reason to worry yet. He'll call back, and we'll get to the bottom of it all. I know it's hard not to think the worst, but let's just wait."

She hugged me. "He's gonna be all right. I know it."

I held her tightly against my chest. "Yeah, I know. I just don't think I could ever forgive myself if he got hurt, or worse, and I wasn't there."

"Don't think like that."

I cautiously climbed back into Pecan's saddle, making certain the cell phone stayed with Penny. Now that Pecan's demons had been exorcised, he was once again as docile as a lamb. We caught up with the Judge and Maebelle as they pretended to be inspecting a fence.

"Judge, I'm sorry to cut this expedition short, but that was an urgent message from overseas. I have to answer when they call back in an hour. Can we continue the tour this afternoon?"

"Of course we can. The nickel tour can wait. Your work is important."

I pinched the bridge of my nose between my thumb and index finger. "It may not be work, Judge. It may be bad news about Clark."

With nothing more than a somber look and a single nod, he let me know he shared my concern.

Maebelle said, "Let's get the horses back to the stables. Wanna race, Chase?"

Not to be outdone by a horse—or chef—I did as I'd watched the jockeys at Belmont Park do on my first assignment out of The Ranch. I raised myself slightly out of the saddle, leaned forward, and gave Pecan a slap on the rump with the ends of the reins. As it turned out, the only thing Pecan hated worse than cellphones was being slapped with reins. My count for getting thrown from a horse hit double digits, and it was a long walk back to the barn.

* * *

The Judge and Maebelle joined us in the main salon back aboard *Aegis*, where Penny offered to make drinks, though Maebelle insisted she would take care of everything. Minutes later, she'd made tea and lemonade and put together a tray of cheese and crackers.

"Where did you find all of this stuff?" I asked. "I didn't know we had cheese *or* lemons onboard."

She grinned. "That's why I manage the kitchen and you do whatever it is you do, cowpoke."

Before I could put together a witty retort, my phone chirped, and I grabbed it almost immediately. "Chase here."

I hopped down the stairs and into my cabin where I could speak freely and hear better.

"Chase, it's Mongo. Thanks for picking up."

"What's going on? You said there's a situation."

"Yeah, that's right. I didn't know what else to call it. We're going to need some help."

"What do you mean you need help? Don't you have onsite support?"

The connection crackled, but I pieced together most of what he was saying.

"Shot up...Khyber Pass...eighty clicks...Jalalabad."

"You're breaking up, Mongo. Can you get a better line of sight with the satellites?"

"Okay...How about now?"

"Yeah, that's better. So, you got shot up on the Khyber Pass, eighty clicks out of Jalalabad. Is that right?"

"Yeah, but it's worse than that. Clark's in pretty bad shape, but he's alive. The problem is, we don't have any support. We're on our own out here, and nobody's coming to get us."

I tried to keep my emotions in check and force my mind to stay focused on the mission details, but Clark was hurt, and I was ten thousand miles away. "What do you need from me?"

"We need a way to get Clark and Singer out of here. I'm pretty sure Clark's back is broken, and Singer's got a busted leg. The rest of us can survive and hum our way out, but Clark's critical. I'm thinking forty-eight hours at best before he starts tanking."

I took a long, deep breath. "Is he conscious? Can he talk?"

"He's got his eyes open some of the time, but we've got him tucked away in the back of a cave where there's no chance of the sat-phone working. Look, man. I know you want to talk to him, but really, we need to get him a dust-off outta here double-quick."

I immediately started gathering mission-critical data. "How many hours of battery life do you have for the sat-phone?"

"We can solar charge."

"Souls remaining?"

"Five. Clark, Snake, Singer, Smoke, and me."

"Casualties?"

"One dead, one critical—that'd be Clark. Two walking-wounded —that's Singer and Snake. Me and Smoke ain't hurt bad enough to say."

"Supplies?"

"We're good on ammo and cold weather gear. There's plenty of snow to melt and drink, and we've got enough rations for a week. What we don't have is a doctor or a ride home."

"Coordinates?"

He read off their latitude and longitude, and I read it back twice to make sure there was no chance of screwing it up.

"I've got it, Mongo. Check in every three hours for now, and I'll get to work. Oh, and tell Clark I said to embrace the suck. I'm on my way."

I took a moment to gather my thoughts before going back topside.

Every eye was laser-focused on me when I climbed the stairs back to the main salon, but Penny was the first to speak. "Is Clark all right?"

I swallowed hard. "I'm going to Afghanistan."

Chapter 8
I'm All You've Got

"Judge, I'm sorry, but I have to go to work. Clark's gotten himself in a jam, and we have to go get him."

Maebelle's face shone full terror, and she gasped. "Is he all right?"

I summoned the courage to look into her eyes. "I'm going to make sure he is."

For the first time that day, the Judge rose with the agility of a man half his age. "Well, Maebelle and I will be getting out of your way. If you need anything, it's yours, Chase. Absolutely anything."

Maebelle took my arm. "Please don't let anything happen to him."

I forced a smile, and the Judge encouraged her to leave the boat with him.

She turned back. "Please, Chase."

"I'll bring him home, Maebelle. It's what I do."

Ten minutes later, *Aegis's* main salon had been converted into the war room, and Skipper was on speakerphone.

"Skipper, listen closely, and don't ask questions until I'm finished. Got it?"

"Yes, Chase. Go on."

I was not looking forward to breaking the news. Skipper, who the rest of the world called Elizabeth, was the closest thing I had to a sister after the death of my own. She was the daughter of my UGA baseball coach. After I'd graduated from the university, as well as The Ranch where I became an operator, Skipper had made some less-than-stellar decisions that left her in the hands of some particularly nasty characters in South Florida. My partner Clark and I rescued her and returned her to her family in Athens, but as they say, you can never go home. Skipper was living proof of that. She'd seen too much of the worst of humanity to ever be the ponytailed, teenage daughter of Coach Bobby Woodley and his wife Laura's all-American family. Inside and out, she'd healed aboard my boat and slowly turned her anger and disgust for humanity's bottom feeders into a career as one of the best young operational analysts in the business. She was an invaluable asset to me and a true friend to Clark.

"Clark's hurt."

She sucked in a crisp breath but didn't speak.

"He's part of a five-man Brinkwater Security element in the Khyber Pass, and they were ambushed. He's alive but nonmobile. We're going in to get him out."

I finished the briefing, filling her in on every detail I'd gathered from Mongo. The sound of her scribbling furiously on the pad told me she was already planning and plotting. When I exhausted the data I knew, I asked, "Questions?"

Her first question was the first one I should've asked. "What were they doing on the Khyber Pass in January?"

"I have no idea," I admitted.

She sighed. "Okay, I'm on it. I'll find assets in the region, and we can put together a plan from there, but, Chase...there's a problem."

"What is it?"

"I'm alone. Ginger's on a blackout assignment, and I have no way to reach her. I'm all you've got."

"You're all I need, Skipper. Call me in an hour."

Ginger was Skipper's trainer. She'd taken Skipper under her wing following a mission in Central America and declared her to be the finest operational mind she'd ever seen. Skipper had never worked a mission of this magnitude without Ginger's oversight, but fate had kicked her out of the nest, and it was time for her to fly.

With a pencil clenched between my teeth, I started pacing. Penny's eyes were transfixed on me with every stride, and I knew she had a thousand questions, but I needed time to think. Nothing was coming to me. I had no idea how to get Clark off that mountain, and the clock was ticking.

"We need to start a timeline."

Penny looked up, obviously confused. "What?"

I threw a legal pad toward her. "Start writing down everything we know and what time we learned it. Zero-hour is forty-eight hours from noon today. That's the outside limit of when Mongo thinks Clark's going to crash."

She started writing at a feverish pace and then froze. "Is today Saturday?"

"No, it's Wednesday the twenty-third."

She frowned. "Why did I think it was Saturday? Never mind. That doesn't matter." She dived back into the timeline, and I could hear her whispering as she wrote. "Forty-eight hours from noon today. That's just two days. Wednesday, so that'll make it Friday. Why did I think it was Saturday? That's bizarre. Two days isn't long enough."

I was still pacing and chewing on the pencil with my mind roaring through options that all ended the same way: in utter disaster on top of a mountain in Pakistan. Time was running out, and I was growing more frustrated by the minute. Penny's incessant whispering was on the verge of driving me mad, and I was prepared to ask her to stop the whispering, but her lips weren't moving. She wasn't making a sound, but her breathy words kept pranging inside my skull.

Two days...Saturday...bizarre...that's bizarre...Saturday...two days...bizarre...bizarre two days after Saturday...

"That's it!" I grabbed her face in my hands and kissed her madly. "You're a genius! I love you. I need a map of Southwest Asia!"

"What the hell's wrong with you? What are you talking about?"

"A map. I need a map. Now!"

She spun the computer screen around, showing me a map of Afghanistan, Pakistan, Western China, and Tajikistan. I drove my finger into the screen. "There! That's the answer. Two days after Saturday, Bazaar, Tajikistan!"

She stared at the screen in utter confusion. "You're losing it. What on earth are you talking about?"

I couldn't stop grinning. "It's the only thing I learned in World Geography. They used to have a bazaar—you know, a market—every Monday in a little town in Tajikistan, and it was called the Dushanbe Bozor. *Du* means two days after, and *Shanbe* means Saturday. *Bozor*, of course, means bazaar. The name of the town became Dushanbe, and they have an airport...a big, long, international airport."

Her eyes lit up. "Oh, yeah! I've heard of that. It was in *Spies Like Us*."

"What?"

"The movie from the eighties. *Spies Like Us*. Come on, Chase. You're a spy, and you've never seen *Spies Like Us*? They were on the road to Dushanbe in the movie."

I shook my head. "I'm not a spy."

She rolled her eyes. "Whatever."

"I've got to talk to Skipper. Has it been an hour?"

Penny twisted her watch from the underside of her wrist. "Almost, but, Chase...don't you think we should tell Dominic about Clark?"

I collapsed to the settee. "Damnit. Of course we've got to call Dominic, but how am I supposed to tell a man that his son has a broken back and is pinned down on the top of a mountain in one of the most inhospitable places on Earth?"

She grimaced. "You've got to tell him. Maybe he can help."

I dialed his number from memory and glanced at Penny. "I'll need four minutes with Dominic. In three minutes, get Skipper on the phone. Got it?"

She nodded and checked her watch again.

"Dominic, it's Chase. Listen. We've got a problem. Clark got caught in an ambush up on the Khyber Pass. He's alive, but for some reason, Brinkwater left them up there without any support. He's with four other guys. They're all shot up, but Clark got the worst of it. He's immobile. I'm going to get him. Dushanbe looks like the best way in, but I'm going to need a lot of help."

Dominic sighed. "That's what I was afraid of. They were an escort detail aboard an ammo supply train across the pass. There's usually too much snow up there for the trains to run, but this one had to go."

"Why didn't you tell me this when we talked yesterday?" I demanded.

"It didn't matter yesterday, but today it does."

I couldn't argue with him. "Okay, I've got Skipper compiling a list of assets in the region. Can you do the same?"

"Sure. I'll get right on it. What else can I do?"

I exhaled. "I don't know, Dominic. Pray?"

"Go get my boy off that mountain. Whatever the cost, whatever the stakes, just get him back."

"I will."

I hung up as Penny pressed the speaker button on the secure line with Skipper.

"Hey, Chase. Do you want to talk first, or do you want me to go?"

"You go," I said.

"Okay. The closest American military assets are in Kabul. It's an Army Ranger platoon, but re-tasking them is next to impossible. The Brinkwater guys are operating out of Dubai, a thousand miles to the southwest, but they're denying that they ever had a team on the Khyber Pass. What's that about?"

I clenched my teeth. "Hmm, I don't know, Skipper, but it sounds right in line with what Mongo and Dominic told me. There's more to this than meets the eye. We'll deal with that along the way, but our focus has to be on getting Clark off that mountain. Did you find anything we could use?"

Her voice cracked. "I'm trying, but after the World Trade Center last year, that place is a mess."

"It's okay. Just keep trying. I think Dushanbe is our best in and out. It's only three hundred fifty miles from the top of the pass. I just need to get there, find a pilot, a helicopter that has the range to make the pass, and a few in-country trigger-pullers."

"No, that's only half of what you need. Getting to Clark isn't the mission. Getting him back off that mountain and into a hospital before he dies is the mission."

Penny put her face in her hands. The situation was hard on all of us.

"Yeah, I know, Skipper. You're right. Get back to work, and get me booked on something to Dushanbe today."

"Okay, I'm on it. Does Dominic know?"

"Yeah, I just got off the phone with him. He's putting together an asset sheet, as well. Give him thirty minutes, then check on his progress. Call me in an hour. I'm supposed to hear back from Mongo in ninety minutes."

Skipper's confident tone was back. "You got it, Chase. Talk soon. Out."

I brushed Penny's hair out of her face and kissed her forehead. "We're going to get him out of there."

She nodded, trying not to cry. "I know. It just feels impossible right now."

I lifted her chin. "Everything is impossible until somebody does it. We've got this."

"Chase, we don't even have a plan yet. I mean, what if you get there and the weather's too bad to fly? What if you're too late? What if whoever ambushed Clark gets to you? I know you're good at this, but he's a Green Beret, and look what happened to him."

I didn't have any answers, but I knew she didn't really need any. There was no way I wasn't going to the Khyber Pass. I might not come off the mountain alive, but I'd never let Clark Johnson die in the back of that cold dark cave without spilling every drop of my blood trying to save him.

The cabin that would've been the third bedroom on my boat was built out as a storage room and workshop. I kept spare parts for almost every system on the boat, as well as tools and manuals, but the most important items were my go bags. I had one for almost every area of operation I could be called upon. The one I never wanted to use was about to get dusted off.

"I need to check my cold weather bag. I'll be right back."

My boots, parts of which were well on their way through Charlie's digestive system, would be useless in the Spīn Ghar mountains, so a new pair came off the shelf. I wasn't looking forward to breaking in a new pair of boots in some of the roughest terrain in the world, but Charlie's chewing obsession left me no other choice.

Fear isn't what operators experience when picturing an upcoming mission. It's mental preparation more than dread. We never go into a scenario thinking we're going to fail, but I was digging deep for any shred of hope I could pull from my soul for what I was about to face.

What I saw when I climbed back up to the main salon immediately erased my anxiety over the coming mission, and I knew everything was going to be all right.

Chapter 9
First Things First

Penny had abandoned the tasks at hand and sat in silent awe of the book before her. Judge Huntsinger stood with a satisfied smile set broadly across his face as he ran his finger down the page, reading the names written on every line.

"What's this?" Penny peered up at me with a look of timeless, childlike wonder. Her eyes glistened, and her smile was unlike any I'd ever seen her wear. "Chase this is your family's Bible. It was printed in England in seventeen sixty, over two hundred years ago. Look at this." She traced her finger down the page just as the Judge had done. "Look at these names. This the most amazing thing I've ever seen."

I sat beside her and let my fingertips drift across two centuries of my ancestors' names written in beautiful script—the earliest of them barely visible. "Judge, this is astonishing."

He slowly nodded and closed the book. "The last time this Bible was on a boat, it was making its way from the Old World to the new one. That may be what you're doing, son. If you'll care for it and protect it the way I have—and read it to your children the way I did—this is my wedding gift to both of you." He patted the worn cover of the Bible. "I don't know what's going on right now, but it has you and Miss Penny in quite a fit. Knowing where you came from and the foundations you were built on can be a powerful thing, especially when the whole world seems to be crashing down around you. But I'm just an old pecan farmer. What do I know?"

Seeing Penny Thomas cry was a painful sight to behold, but with her arms wrapped around Judge Barnard Henry Huntsinger that afternoon, they were some of the most wonderful drops of water I'd ever see.

I joined Penny in thanking him for the priceless treasure. He didn't cry, but I think he made his exit before the tears came. That was a powerful moment in my life. In the midst of crisis, a man who barely knew me changed my life with a five-minute visit to my boat with a two-hundred-forty-two-year-old Bible.

I held Penny as if I'd never see her again, and she squeezed me as if her heart believed the same. "Chase, I'm not asking you to quit, but I need you. When you come home with Clark, I need you to be home…with me."

I looked into her eyes. "What do you mean?"

She wiped the tears with the back of her hand and looked up at me. "I need you to be mine for a time. I don't know how long. Maybe a few days, or maybe a year. I don't know. But when you come home, I need us—you and me—to forget about everything else in the world and just be together. Can you give me that?"

"I can't think of anything I'd rather do, but I have to get Clark home. You understand that."

She squeezed her eyes closed. "Yes, I understand. I do, but Clark's not the only one who needs you."

I shook my wrist, twisting my watch into view. "Come with me. There's something we have to do."

I led her off the boat and up the slope toward the house, where we found the Judge conducting a constitutional law class from his favorite rocking chair. Jeff and Ben were like mesmerized little boys listening to their grandfather tell stories.

As we walked up the steps, the Judge slowly began to nod as if he'd been expecting to see us come up the stairs for hours. He removed his hat and smiled. "Miss Penny…Chase. I thought you might be making your way up here pretty soon. Will these two boys do?"

Penny stared at me with wonder and uncertainty, but I tried to ignore her.

I looked at Ben and Jeff. "We should probably get Maebelle out here."

The Judge nudged Ben with the toe of his shoe. "Go get Maebelle, and tell her to bring a camera."

Ben leapt to his feet and soon returned through the door with Maebelle on his heels. She handed a small, worn leather Bible to the Judge. "I guess you were right, Granddaddy."

"Yeah, baby. When you've been on Earth as long as I have, you get pretty good at predicting what people are going to do next."

Penny was still baffled, and I was in awe of the Judge's insight.

He stood and placed his hand on my shoulder. "Take a knee, son."

Penny watched me kneel beside her, and the afternoon sun over her shoulder shone in her golden hair, making her look like an angel from where I knelt. I'd never seen a more beautiful woman, inside or out, and I'd never love anyone more than I loved her.

The Judge cleared his throat. "Before the eyes of God, and in the company of these friends and your family, Chase Daniel Fulton, do you vow on your very soul to love this woman, protect her from all harms she may ever face, honor her in all that you do, and keep only her in your heart until the Almighty God takes the last breath from your chest?"

"Yes, sir, I do."

He turned to Penny, who stood motionless beside me with her bottom lip trembling. "Miss Penny, reach down and take your man's hand."

As I remained on my knee at her feet, she reached out for my hand. I slid mine into hers, and I could feel her pulse beating through her skin.

"Nicole Thomas, likewise, before these friends and those who will soon be your family, do you vow upon your immortal soul to give yourself in love to this man who has pledged the same to you? Do you vow to love him, care for him, guide him when he strays, and help him back to his feet when he stumbles? Do you pledge your faithfulness, mind, body, and soul to this holy union?"

Penny beamed as she smiled down at me. "I do."

"Stand to your feet, Chase, and take your bride's hands."

I followed his instructions as he dug into one of his pockets and held his weathered hand toward me. "Take this ring. Place it on her finger, and tell her you love her."

I took the simple antique silver ring from his fingertips and slid it onto Penny's finger. "I love you, Penny Thomas."

We turned back to the Judge, and he pulled the band from his left hand.

Penny said, "No, Judge. We can't take your ring."

He pressed the worn silver band into her palm. "You can give it back later, but right now, you need it more than I do. Take it and put it on your husband's hand. Tell him you love him."

She did as he insisted and slid the ring over the first knuckle of my ring finger. It wouldn't go further, no matter how hard she tried, and she chuckled. "I love you, Chase Fulton."

The Judge placed his hand on top of ours. "May God bless and keep you both, and may you live a life of service to each other, and to Him, as faithfully as you are able. By the power vested in me by the great State of Georgia, you are now, by both the blessing of God and by my lawful pronouncement, man and wife. You may, of course, kiss your bride."

This kiss was the best of my life, and the woman in my arms was the best of a thousand lives.

We thanked and hugged the Judge and Maebelle. Jeff and Ben weren't huggers, but they were full of congratulations.

Maebelle said, "I know you guys don't have time to…well, you don't have time to do anything else, but I did make a little cake for you, and maybe you could have a little bite before you go do whatever it is you have to do."

I didn't feel good about eating wedding cake while my partner was lying in a cave with a broken back, halfway around the world, but we took five minutes.

The Judge signed the license the clerk had delivered. "How on earth do you get Penny out of Nicole Bethany Thomas?"

She laughed. "It's a long story, Judge, but I promise to tell you about it as soon as all of this is over. Thank you so much."

He squeezed her against his chest. "You're part of the family now, and on behalf of the few of us left, I'd like to say we sure are proud to have you, Mrs. Fulton."

Chapter 10
Wheels-Up

Skipper's call was right on time. "Okay, I have a schedule. Let me know when you're ready to write."

I scrambled for a pencil. "Okay, Skipper. Let's hear it."

"You're on an Air Force C-5 tonight at twenty-thirty out of Charleston to Frankfurt. Can you make that?"

I checked the time. "Yeah, no problem."

"Good. You'll be connecting commercial to Dubai and then to Dushanbe."

"Nice work, Skipper. How about local aerial assets out of Dushanbe?"

I could hear her flipping through pages of notes. "I'm still working on that, but we do have one possible option so far. I don't speak whatever that crazy language is, but there's a guy with at least one, and maybe two helicopters in Dushanbe. He thinks I'm insane, and I'm completely certain he is, but his English got much better when I started talking about payment in American dollars."

"He sounds like my kind of guy. Does he have a name?"

"Yeah, but I'll have to spell it for you. Let me know when you're ready."

I sat with my pencil poised above the page. "All right. Let's have it."

"First name, S-e-p-e-h-r. Last name, maybe, S-o-r-o-u-s-h."

"Got it. Thanks. Penny and I got married. Oh, and the language is Tajik. It's—"

"What! Married? Without me? What the hell, Chase?"

I laughed. "It was a quick decision and a very long story. We'll tell you all about it when this is over, but the Judge married us this afternoon at Bonaventure."

"Wow. That's...anyway, get on that plane, and call me from Frankfurt. And congratulations."

"Thanks, Skipper. You're the best. Talk soon."

I hung up and turned to my wife. "I guess she wanted to be a bride's maid."

Penny's grin was unquenchable. "I can't believe we did that, but I love that we did. And now you're going on the honeymoon without me."

I pointed toward the map of the Afghan mountains. "You're welcome to come along if you want, but you'll want to pack a scarf and an automatic weapon."

"Sounds like my kind of place, but I'll pass this time. But that doesn't get you off the hook. You owe me a real—and I mean *real*—honeymoon when you get back. Got it?"

"Yeah, I got it. A *real* honeymoon. None of that fake honeymoon stuff."

"I need to talk to the Judge about getting to Charleston. Do you want to come?"

"To Charleston? Or to talk to the Judge?"

"Well...both, I guess."

She pursed her lips and turned her gaze toward the sky. "Uh, no to the Judge, and yes to Charleston."

I found the Judge just where he'd been before our ceremony, sitting on the porch and still teaching class.

"Judge, I'm sorry to interrupt again, but I need to get to Charleston as soon as possible. Can you recommend a way to accomplish that?"

"Why, sure. Crip at the airport will run you up there. He gets two or three hundred bucks an hour to run people wherever they want to go. He's got a nice little twin engine of some kind. I'll have one of these boys set it up for you. When do you want to leave?"

"You're a lifesaver, Judge. I'm ready as soon as Crip can get to the airport."

Everything was falling into place, and my confidence was growing until I heard Mongo's voice on the phone.

"Uh, Chase, he's startin' to tank. His temp is over a hundred and two, and he's having trouble staying awake."

My blood ran cold. "Keep him pumped full of antibiotics and IV fluids. I'm on my way. I'll be in Dushanbe in eighteen hours and knocking on your door after that."

The fear in his voice was palpable. "We're thinking about racking him up and carrying him outta here."

I held my breath, trying to imagine what conditions must be like in that cave. "I can't make those decisions from here, Mongo. You're on the ground. Who's in charge?"

"Smoke's officially in charge. At least he was when we worked for Brinkwater. We're startin' to feel like the A-Team right now. We've been left out in the cold to fend for ourselves, so I'm not sure we're answering to any outside command at this point."

"I'll be there ASAP. Keep your head down and our boy alive. Fire up the sat-phone five minutes before the top of every hour for ten minutes, and I'll call you as soon as I get into Europe."

He grunted. "Okay. Um, Chase…. Have you got a plan?"

"Yeah, Mongo. I've got a plan."

Penny's look of concern was back, and I had nothing encouraging to tell her. "Clark's getting worse, isn't he?"

"Yes," I admitted. "He's got a nasty fever, and he's having trouble staying awake. They're thinking of strapping him onto a makeshift backboard and hiking him out."

Her eyes widened. "Where would they go?"

I shrugged. "I don't know. East, I guess, into Pakistan, but that terrain is tough enough when it's seventy degrees and sunny. Carrying a man with a broken back through the snow, down the Khyber Pass, doesn't sound like a good option."

She shook her head. "You've got to get them out of there."

"I know, Penny, and that's what I'm going to do. The Judge is arranging our flight to Charleston. He'll be ready to go in a few minutes. Are you coming?"

"Yeah, I'm not leaving you alone until the last second. How can I help you get ready?"

"I need some cash. Grab fifty thousand out of the safe, the sat-phone, and four batteries. Throw some granola bars and a couple bottles of water in a bag...please."

As she went to work on my list, a voice came from the dock. "Chase!"

I stepped into the cockpit and saw Maebelle standing beside the boat and peering up.

"Chase, Crip says he's ready to go. I can run you up to the airport whenever you're ready."

Back in the boat, Penny stood with a dry bag over her shoulder. "We're ready now."

* * *

Crip wasn't what I expected. I pictured him in his seventies for some reason, but I was way wrong.

"Hey, yo, man. What's up? I'm Crip."

Before I could respond, Crip's full attention fell on Penny. "Hey, baby. What's your name?"

"My name is Mrs. Fulton, and *his* name is Mr. Fulton, and he shot the last person who called me *baby* right in the face. Twice."

Crip held up his hands. "Hey, man, I was messing around. I didn't mean nothing by it. I'm sorry."

I locked eyes with the young pilot who looked like he belonged on a skateboard, not at the controls of an airplane. "That didn't really happen. I only shot the guy once in the face." I thudded the center of Crip's chest with my index finger. "The other shot went right here."

Again, his hands went up. "Like I said, man. I was messing around. It won't happen again. You two need to get to Charleston, right?"

"Yeah, Charleston. How much?"

Crip began calculating the trip in his mind. "It'd normally be seven-fifty, but five hundred for you, man. I didn't mean—"

I patted him on the shoulder. "Seven-fifty will be fine. She'll pay you when you drop her back off tonight after you've kept your hands to yourself."

"Yeah, man. You've got it. That's cool."

We climbed aboard his Twin Comanche and blasted off. The flight lasted over an hour, and Crip turned out to be a far better pilot than I expected.

I checked in with base operations, and just as Skipper had promised, my seat was reserved, and they were expecting two hundred pounds of gear in three bags.

I stood on the ramp with Penny as she tried to hold back her tears.

"Please be careful, Chase. This one is the hardest yet. I know everything you do is dangerous, but this…"

I played with her hair and lifted her chin. "I'll be home in less than a week. I promise."

She shook her head. "You can't make promises like that. You don't know…."

Her hands trembled as I took them in mine and kissed each one. "Listen to me. I'm going to be careful. I'll be home in less than a week, and then I'm all yours for the honeymoon."

She tried to smile. "So help me, Chase…. If you get killed, I'll never forgive you. I'd suck at being a widow."

"You don't suck at anything, Penny, but I'm not going to get killed. I'm getting Clark and the guys off that mountain, and I'm bringing them home."

She put on her business face and sighed. "What do you need from me?"

I tried to put together a checklist for her, but I was too focused on what I'd be doing in the coming days. "Keep an eye on the weather up on the Khyber Pass. Coordinate with Skipper and Dominic to make sure they're keeping each other in the loop. I'd like for you to stay at Bonaventure until I get back. I'll check in at least once every twenty-four hours and keep you up to date the best I can. Skipper will always know where I am, and I'm sure she'll keep you posted."

She wrapped her arms around me and buried her head in my chest. "I love you, Chase. I'll see you in a few days."

"I love you, Penny Fulton."

The rear ramp of the C-5 cargo plane closed seconds after I made my way into the massive interior. I'd been aboard a lot of airplanes, but that was my first time inside a C-5 Galaxy. I was amazed at the sheer volume of the plane.

"Sir, I'll take your gear, and you can make your way upstairs."

A clean-shaven, lean man in his twenties reached for my bags. He was wearing a green Air Force flight suit with a tab that read: "Staff Sergeant T. Willoughby."

"What does the T stand for, Sergeant Willoughby?"

"Thomas, sir, but everybody calls me T-Willow."

I smiled. "T-Willow. I like it. Can you make sure to keep my bags together? I'll be in a hurry when we get to Germany."

He slung my bags across his shoulder. "Sure thing, sir. Do you mind if I ask you a question?"

"Sure. What is it?"

He looked around as if he didn't want anyone to hear. "Are you really a CIA agent?"

I laughed. "Where'd you get that idea, Thomas? I'm just a guy catching a ride to go check on his brother overseas. That's all."

T-Willow smirked a half-smile. It reminded me of Clark's mischievous grin when we were about to do something less than legitimate. "Whatever you say, sir." He pointed to a pallet with two heavy plastic bins. "Your bags will be right here."

He placed my gear inside one of the containers and stretched a piece of green duct tape across the top. The man produced a blue sharpie from his pocket and wrote "007" on the tape. He glanced up at me. "You know...like James Bond."

I smiled. "Yeah, shaken...not stirred."

The seats upstairs in a C-5 face rearward. I've heard it's because the Air Force believes it's a more survivable position in a crash. I have no idea if that's true, but once we were wheels-up and level at forty-one thousand feet, none of us could tell if we were facing forward or aft. It was a smooth, quiet ride on one of the world's largest flying objects.

I wanted to sleep, but my mind wouldn't let me. I pictured Clark, beaten and battered, in the back of that cold, dark cave, and the rest of the Brinkwater team awaiting my arrival and standing guard in shifts over him. They were men of action, warriors, so waiting to be rescued had to be the worst feeling in the world. I imagined how badly everyone had to be itching to pick Clark up and hike down that mountain, killing every bad guy they encountered along the way. Their instinct to keep moving forward, no matter what obstacle stood in front of them, had to be almost irresistible. Nothing about the coming days would be easy, but seeing my partner broken and helpless was the thing I dreaded most.

My second thought was consumed with Sepehr Soroush, the Tajiki pilot. Skipper said he was motivated by American dollars, and that was a solid enough motivation for me. I could satisfy his greed as long as he could satisfy my need to get Clark off that mountain.

I ran a mental inventory of helicopters that could be in Dushanbe, but I couldn't come up with any with the range and cargo capacity to fly three hundred fifty miles, pick up five men and their gear, then fly three hundred fifty miles back to Dushanbe without refueling. Such a helicopter didn't exist. I prayed Sepehr had some ideas.

Apparently, my body demanded that my brain let it rest because our touchdown in Frankfurt roused me from my sleep.

T-Willow tore the tape from my bin and helped me get my gear bags back over my shoulders. "Good luck checking on your brother, Mr. Bond."

I slapped the loadmaster on the shoulder. "Thank you for the ride, Thomas Willoughby. I'll be sure to tell M what a good job you're doing."

The cold night air hit me like a freight train. It was only a small taste of the weather to come on top of the Khyber Pass, but it was still completely unwelcome. I found a quiet spot in the corner of the passenger services terminal and dialed Penny's number. "I'm safe in Frankfurt, and I'll be headed for Dubai soon. Do you have anything new for me?"

"Oh, Chase. I'm so glad you called. I know I was overly dramatic, and I'm sorry. I worry about you, but I know you'll be careful, and I know you're really good at...well, that sort of stuff. Everything's fine here. Skipper has some more information for you, but I'm sure you've already called her."

"No, actually, I called you first. She's next."

I could almost hear Penny's smile. "I love you, Chase. Be careful."

Penny was right. Skipper did have some new information, and it was some of the best news I could've dreamed of getting.

"Do you remember Bimini, the woman from the boat in Greece?"

I thought for a moment. "Sure, she was Dennis Crowe's girlfriend, and they took us from Greece to Israel. Though she was more than just a cute girl in a bikini."

Skipper chuckled. "She's a lot more than just a cute girl in a bikini. In fact, she's a defense intelligence agent, and she's on her way to Dushanbe right now. It turns out she speaks that freaky language."

I couldn't believe my luck.

Skipper rattled off Bimini's sat-phone number, and the good news kept coming. "She'll be on the ground before you get there, so she'll get the ball rolling. That's all I've got for now. Do you have anything for me?"

"I don't know how you do it, Skipper. Please check on Penny every day if you don't mind. She's worried about this op more than any of the others, and I'm not sure why."

Skipper sighed. "Yeah, well, she sorta has every reason to worry. You're going solo into a part of the world where almost everyone would love to kill you. And she's your wife now."

"Okay, I get it. Hey, I need one more thing..."

"Just one?"

"Well, one for now. I need you to find out where the Brinkwater tactical operations center is in Dubai. I need to pay them a little visit."

The clicking of her tongue against her teeth said she didn't approve. "Uh, Chase, are you sure that's such a good idea?"

"I need to know why they left that team, out in the cold, on top of that mountain."

"I know what you mean, but now's not the time to start making new enemies...especially with those guys."

"Just find their TOC, Skipper. I'll worry about the rest."

Chapter 11
Admit Nothing...Deny Everything

Dubai isn't like the rest of the Middle East. It's one of the seven territories that make up the United Arab Emirates on the coast of the Persian Gulf. They may hate Western culture, but they don't have any qualms about taking Western money, and there's no shortage of people throwing plenty of that around the emirate. The few blades of grass that exist in Dubai cling to life only by means of groundskeepers who feed, water, and nurture them meticulously. The rest of the landscape is dominated by the most plentiful element in that part of the world: sand.

Except for the spawning resorts on the coast, the whole place looked like a beach with no ocean. The future would see Dubai turn into a wealthy tourist mecca of sorts, but in January of 2002, it was still a city trying to get a footing in the barren Arabian Desert.

I made my way through the Al Maktoum International Airport and found an alcove where I believed I could have two minutes of privacy. Escaping the security cameras wasn't possible, but I could at least get out of earshot of most English-speaking nosy nellies.

Skipper picked up on the seventh ring. I assumed it had something to do with the thousands of miles the sat-phone signal had to travel before reaching Silver Springs, Maryland, where Skipper had set up camp. My assumption was wrong.

"Yeah...hello."

Her still-asleep voice made me laugh. "Sorry to disturb you, Sleeping Beauty, but wakey wakey. I'm in Dubai. Where oh where could Brinkwater be?"

"Sorry, Chase. I was catching some sleep. I was awake for two days."

"It's fine, Skipper. We all have to sleep. Did you find the Brinkwater TOC?"

She cleared her throat. "Yeah, their ops center is in the Lufthansa facility south of the international airport. It seems they have quite the cozy relationship with the Germans."

"I knew you could do it. Remind me to talk to your boss about getting you a raise."

"Yeah, about that. Since you're the boss and all…"

"No time for that now, Skipper. I have to make a social visit down at Lufthansa and then jet off to Dushanbe."

I hung up before she could try talking sense into me. Brinkwater may have been one of the world's biggest security contractors, but they weren't exempt from responsibility for letting five men rot on the Khyber Pass, especially when one of those men was Clark Johnson.

Security at Lufthansa was tighter than Langley. I'd made short work of getting into the office of the deputy director of operations at CIA headquarters, but getting past Hans at the first checkpoint in the Lufthansa facility was turning into a nightmare. My German wasn't bad, but it wasn't good enough to convince him that I belonged to the anointed group allowed beyond his locked door.

As I was about to convert courtesy into aggression, two unmistakably American men in typical security contractor dress strutted through the door behind me and flashed laminated ID tags toward the German guard. I caught the name Guffey on one of the badges. A buzzer sounded, and the two men pushed their way through a heavy metal door leading into the depths of the building…exactly where I needed to be.

An idea sprang to life, and I slammed my palm on the counter in front of the guard. "*Danke für nichts, Arschloch. Auf Wiedersehen.*"

Outside the facility were two dozen empty parking spaces and eleven vehicles. I played the odds that the empty spots would be filling up soon—hopefully with Brinkwater vehicles.

My patience, such as it was, paid off. Thirty minutes before I had to be back in the passenger terminal, a blacked-out Suburban pulled up. I could make out the shape of two men through the windshield, but I couldn't see into the back. At least four men were what I needed to make my ruse work, but I had no time left to wait for the perfect bait.

As they'd been taught and practiced hundreds of times, the two men in the front seat checked the mirrors carefully before opening their doors. Once the doors were open, the mirrors were useless, and I planned to take full advantage of that weakness. Breaking cover from behind the electrical transformer I'd been hiding behind, I sprinted toward the back of the SUV. To my delight, one of the back doors opened as I skidded to a stop near the rear bumper. Three players would have to do.

As the third man stepped from the back seat, I showed myself from behind the vehicle, holding up my wallet in front of me. The only thing visible inside my wallet was a fake ID that wouldn't fool a bouncer at a strip club, let alone three tier-one operators, but I didn't let that slow me down.

I continued my confident approach. "Jim Bond, CIA. Which one of you is in charge?"

The man's face showed instant surprise, but his well-trained reflexes kicked in almost immediately. His pistol cleared its holster and rose menacingly as I closed the distance between us. Before he could get his front sight aligned with my chest, I caught the pistol in my left hand, threw the cred-pack into his face, and ripped the gun from his grip. Thankfully, he hadn't covered the trigger with his index finger yet, so the weapon didn't fire. Continuing into him, I dropped the magazine from the Glock and racked the slide, sending the chambered round arcing through the air. With the slide locked to the rear and the pistol completely harmless, I shoved the polymer frame of the Glock into the man's face.

"If you ever pull a pistol on me again, I'll shove it up your ass. I identified myself as a CIA officer in the middle of a parking lot. You've got to be some kind of jackass to pull a gun on a CIA agent. Now, which one of you is in charge?"

The man swatted at the Glock in a wasted effort to get me out of his face. There was no chance I was stepping away from him until I knew his two buddies weren't going to pull their weapons. I needed him as a shield in case my crazy plan went south.

Thankfully, the man who'd been in the front passenger seat spoke up. "I'm in charge. What the hell is this all about?"

"I'll tell you what it's about. It's about one of your men getting one of my men killed downtown last night by running his mouth. I thought you guys were supposed to be professionals."

"What are you talking about? We haven't gotten anybody killed."

"Oh, is that so? Your man Guffey was running his tequila-drunk mouth about one of my men and blew his cover. Now I have to explain to my boss, the DDO, why one of *your* men was drinking in public in the emirates and running his mouth about one of *my* men, who is now on his way back to the States with a flag draped over him."

With no further need for my human shield, I shoved the man away from me and approached the guy who claimed to be in charge. "So, are you Guffey's supervisor?"

The man showed a look of bewildered concern. The thought of one of his team getting a CIA operative killed in an alcohol-related incident in the United Arab Emirates was not helping the man's ulcers. "No, Guffey doesn't work for me, but let's go inside and work this out. There has to be some mistake."

I didn't lower my tone. I needed him to believe I was still steaming. "Fine, but there better be somebody in that building who can answer my questions. Otherwise, this whole operation is going straight to Hell with me stomping it down."

The man held up his hands defensively. "Relax, man. We'll get to the bottom of this. Just save it. The ops chief is inside."

He motioned for me to follow him, so I let him believe he was escorting an American CIA agent into the high-security tactical operations center inside the Lufthansa facility on the edge of the Arabian Desert.

As we approached the first checkpoint, the German guard who'd kept me at bay rose and began to protest my second arrival, but the Brinkwater man shut him down. "Relax. He's with us. Now, open the door."

The buzzer sounded, and we pushed our way through. The man who'd drawn his pistol on me was still holding his bloody nose and cursing every breath. One more checkpoint gave us access to the plush Brinkwater ops center.

The man I was following forced open a door, stuck his head inside, and growled, "Guffey, come with me now!"

Guffey, who had no idea what was going on or how he became involved, slowly rose to his feet and fell in line with the rest of us. Forty paces down the corridor, we entered an office that looked like it could belong to a bank president...one who had an affection for automatic weapons and maps of the Middle East.

The man who'd led me into the office said, "Jerry, this is Jim Bond. He's with the CIA and says Guffey got one of his men killed downtown after a few rounds of tequila shots."

The man behind the desk raised his eyebrows and skeptically looked me over. "Is that so?"

I ignored his question. "Are you in charge?"

The man glanced at Guffey for an exaggerated moment and then back at me. "That's right. I'm Jerry Beard, the operations officer. And you said your name was Bond. Is that right?"

I shook my head. "No, I didn't say that. Your man said that."

Beard's eyes locked onto the man who'd led me to his office. "What the hell is this all about, Hal?"

Hal pointed at me. "He showed us a CIA cred-pack, identified himself as a CIA agent, disarmed Chip, and demanded to see the man in charge. That's you, Jerry."

Beard turned back to me, inquisition in his eyes.

I held up my palms. "I don't have a cred-pack. Have one of your cowboys search me if you'd like. Here's how I see it. I just disarmed and overpowered one of your men, convinced one of your lieutenants to escort me right past two German high-security checkpoints by convincing him my name was Secret Agent Bond. On top of all that, I pulled poor innocent Guffey into the whole mix with me. I did all of that without firing a shot or throwing a punch."

Hal reached for his pistol, and I lifted a stapler from Beard's desk. "If you pull that pistol, I'll staple your eyes to your kneecaps, and you know I can do it. So, relax those hands right back down by your sides, and leave that useless pistol where it is."

"What is it you want?" Beard demanded.

I smiled. "Finally, we get to the real question. Thanks for keeping up. What I want is for you to understand that I'm the type of man who gets exactly what he wants. After all, I got in here in less than fifteen minutes. Now that you know what I am, it's important for you to know what I'm going to do next."

Beard leaned back in his chair. "And what is that?"

I let my smile dissolve into a look of stern consternation. "I'm going to rescue the five men you abandoned and left for dead on the Khyber Pass, and then I'm going to watch your congressional budget dry up and blow away while you beg for crumbs under the table."

I glanced at my watch. "I'll be checking in with my boss in eleven minutes. If I don't make that call from the phone number he's expecting…. Well, do you really want to know what'll happen if I don't make that call, Mr. Beard?"

Beard rose from his chair and stuck a well-manicured finger in my face. "You listen to me, you little…"

I pushed his hand away and glanced back at my watch. "Ten minutes."

Beard's face turned the color of blood, and he growled. "Those men went rogue up on the pass. They knew what they were getting into. They knew what would happen if they got caught. They knew the risks."

I cast another glance at my watch and shrugged. "Nine minutes. And now I know you willingly left those men up there to die. Keep in mind, Mr. Beard, if I can sashay into your office, I can do the same right into your bedroom some night while you're dreaming of that next big contract payment. If those men on the pass are dead when I get there...sweet dreams."

I pecked on the crystal of my watch. "I think I should go make that call now, don't you?"

I made it out of the Lufthansa facility and back to the passenger terminal just in time to make my flight to Dushanbe. My little side trip to see Jerry Beard had eaten up more time than I'd planned, but I had a point to make. Someone once warned me about pissing in a hornet's nest, but sometimes it's worth getting stung to eradicate hornets like the ones at Brinkwater.

Chapter 12
Language Barrier

She wasn't wearing a bikini this time. When I stepped from the plane into the terminal at Dushanbe International Airport, Bimini was wearing cargo pants, a flannel shirt hanging open over a Harvard sweatshirt, and a University of Georgia Bulldogs baseball cap.

"Nice hat. I didn't know you were such a Bulldogs fan."

She grinned. "Thanks for noticing. I didn't want you to miss me when you got off the plane. I figured the hat might make a nice homing beacon. How was your flight?"

"Long. Thanks for your help on this one. You know, I knew you weren't just a tagalong on Dennis Crowe's boat last year."

She continued grinning. "No, you didn't, but you're sweet for saying so. And you're kinda cute, so I couldn't resist lending a hand. That analyst of yours is pretty sharp."

"Yeah, Skipper's got it together. She's still learning, but she's going to be something special."

Bimini furrowed her brow. "Skipper?"

I laughed. "Yeah. She's Elizabeth to the rest of the world, but I call her Skipper. It's a long story."

"They all are," she said. "Now I suppose you're ready to hit the ground running. Am I right?"

I snatched the largest of my packs from baggage claim and headed for customs and immigration.

Bimini grabbed my elbow. "Follow me."

I looked toward the immigration line and then back at her. "I haven't checked in."

"Yeah, I know, and you're not going to."

Moments later, we were in a Toyota Land Cruiser, leaving the airport through a demolished chain-link gate.

"Where are we going?"

She kept her hands on the wheel and eyes on the road. "Trust me. There's someone you want to meet. I've been laying some groundwork. After all, you don't want to get caught over a barrel... especially a barrel of jet fuel."

"What are you talking about?"

"You'll see. Just sit back and enjoy the ride. We'll be there in five minutes."

She was spot-on with her prediction. Five minutes later, we slid to a stop in front of a building that looked like it could have once been a metal foundry.

We stepped from the truck, and I surveyed the dilapidated building. "What is this place?"

She motioned for me to follow her. "Who knows? Today it's a contract negotiations office. Mr. Soroush is patiently waiting to spend your money."

We found the pilot smoking a cigarette and drinking hot tea from a metal cup. Physically, he was the Tajik version of Leo from the Central American jungle, and that made my heart happy.

I stuck out my hand. "Mr. Soroush, my name is—"

He slapped my hand away. "*Nomi şumo ci guna ast? Ojo şumo pulro ovarded?*"

Bimini spoke up. "He says he doesn't—"

"Let me guess. He says he doesn't care what my name is as long as I brought American dollars."

The weathered pilot laughed. "You speak Tajik, young man?"

"No, Mr. Soroush. I speak dollars. I understand that's a language you and I have in common."

He crushed out his cigarette, and the stream of white smoke swirled above his dark hand like a halo. His English wasn't bad, but he thought about every word as it left his lips. "The…uh, lady, and me…We, uh, put fuel on mountain. Du thousand liters. That much fuel…uh, is, uh…how you say…expensive."

I pulled a banded stack of hundred-dollar bills from my pack and placed it on the table. The man's dark eyes locked onto the cash as if it were a cobra, and I slowly pushed the stack toward him. "That's ten thousand American, Mr. Soroush. Thank you for the fuel. That's all we'll be needing. Goodbye."

His body froze in place, but his eyes darted back and forth between Bimini and the fortune on the table. "*Ammo, man fikr kardam, ki şumo воjad pilotro talaв kuned.*"

"English, Mr. Soroush."

Bimini came to his aid. "He said he thought you needed a pilot."

I picked up the money and tossed it toward him. "We don't need a pilot anymore. We have one. We just needed your fuel. That's all."

He caught the bills and held them close to his chest. "But…uh, I will do it…uh, how you say…cheaper…and better."

I placed my fists on the table. "How much?"

His eyes were still darting wildly. "Twenty thousand."

I pounded on the table and smiled broadly. "Done. Twenty thousand it is. You have ten in your hand, and you'll get the other ten when you deliver us back here safely after the mission."

He began to twitch, and his already wide eyes grew even wider. "No…uh, I mean…twenty thousand more."

I turned to Bimini. "See, I told you he was too expensive. The other guys said twelve thousand."

Without a word, she turned back to the pilot with an expectant look on her face. "*Duvozdah hazor,* Soroush."

He nodded in sharp staccato motions. "Okay, okay, twelve thousand. *Duvozdah hazor.* Okay."

I knocked on the table in front of the old pilot. "Listen closely. If you have trouble understanding me, she'll translate, but I want you to look at me. Got it?"

Soroush nodded and set his eyes on mine.

"Good," I began. "My brother is at the top of that mountain, and he's hurt. You are going to take me to the top of the Khyber Pass, and you're going to wait by the helicopter. You're not going to leave, and you're not going to fall asleep. Got it?"

He continued nodding. "Yes, no sleep, no go away."

"Exactly. We're going to put my brother on your helicopter with four other men. Soldiers. Understand?"

"Yes, yes, five men. One is hurt. Is your brother."

"Good, you're tracking. Now, you're going to get us safely back to Dushanbe. That's when you get paid."

"No, is not good. I get half now and half when finished."

I leaned in. "I just gave you ten thousand dollars American because I trusted you when you said you staged five hundred gallons of fuel on that mountain. That's trust, Soroush. You get paid when everybody is safely on the ground here in Dushanbe. That's the deal. No negotiation. Take it or leave it."

I turned to Bimini. "He takes the deal, or we walk. I've got two more pilots lined up who want this job. Make him understand."

She leaned down and spoke to the old man in rapid-fire Tajik. I couldn't understand a word, but the pilot's expression and body language told me all I needed to know.

When the chatter stopped, I said, "I want to see your helicopter."

Without a word, he stood, motioned for me to follow, and headed for the back of the building. He led us down a long dark corridor and finally through a heavy steel door. Sitting a hundred feet away was a hideous desert camo Russian MI-17 Hip helicopter.

If the MI-17 was airworthy, it certainly had the capacity to carry thirty men off the top of the mountain, but it looked like it was on the verge of falling apart.

My confidence was waning, and I turned to Bimini. "Have you been up in that thing?"

"Yeah, I helped stage the fuel. It's ugly, but it flies."

Having no other options, I reached for Soroush's hand. "Tomorrow morning. We take off one hour before sunrise."

He shook my hand and nodded his agreement.

As Bimini and I drove away, she said, "You don't really have two other pilots who want this job, do you?"

I tried to suppress my smile. "No, but your friend back there didn't need to know that."

"One more question," she said. "Is Clark really your brother?"

"Brother is just the beginning of what Clark Johnson is to me."

"That's what I thought. You look like you could use a shower, some grub, and a good night's rest."

"You read my mind. I also need to make some phone calls, preferably privately."

She tossed a key onto my lap. "I've got a safe house here. It's been swept, by me, so I know it's clean. Your calls will be as private as if you were in a skiff at Langley. There's food in the kitchen, a hot shower, and three beds. I'll drop you off."

"Where are you going?"

"I've got some work to do, but I'll be back at the house in a couple of hours. Don't shoot me when I come in."

I held up my hands. "I don't have a gun."

She motioned toward the keyring. "The small key opens the safe behind the medicine cabinet in the master bath. Help yourself. You can bet your ass everybody we encounter on that mountain will be armed to the teeth, so we'd be wise to follow suit."

"We?"

"Yes, we. You're not going up there without an extra set of eyes on your six. Besides, how many of the local languages do you speak?"

I was impressed with Bimini, but a mission with flying bullets was not the place to get to know a new partner. "No offense, but I'm going to get in a firefight on that mountain, and keeping an eye on you is not where my focus needs to be."

She hit the brakes, and the truck slid to a stop, angled slightly in the traffic lane. Horns blared and curses flew as cars swerved to miss us on the busy street. "Why? Because I'm a woman?"

I glanced in the mirror, anticipating being rear-ended at any moment. "No, you being a woman has nothing to do with it. I don't know anything about you. I don't even know if you can shoot. So far, all I know is that you can sail, cook fish, speak Tajik, and drive like a maniac."

She pulled her sunglasses from her Mediterranean tanned face. "FBI sniper course. Top of my class. I'm thirty-four years old, and if tomorrow goes as you think it will, I'll have been in one firefight for every year I've spent on Earth. Over a hundred confirmed kills and only two bullet holes in me. If you go up that mountain alone, I'll be coming up to rescue your shot-up ass in a couple of days, so let's save ourselves a lot of time and heartache. I'm going, and you don't have to worry about keeping an eye on me. I'm a big girl, and you're going to need all the help you can get."

I'd clearly bitten off more than I could chew with Bimini. "Fine, you're coming. Now, can we please get moving before somebody plows over us?"

She returned her sunglasses to her face and accelerated back to highway speed. Ten minutes later, we arrived in front of a house that could exist in any American cookie-cutter subdivision. It was unassuming, but clean and blended in perfectly with the neighborhood.

"Well, here it is. Make yourself at home, and I'll be back in a couple of hours. No one will be coming through the door except me, so don't shoot. Do you want me to call before I come in?"

I surveyed the house and shook my head. "No, it's your house. I won't shoot, but I will probably be asleep, so try not to make too much noise."

The inside of the house looked a lot like the outside. Everything about it was typical of a suburban starter home. Just as she'd described, the hidden safe was all but undetectable behind the medicine cabinet, but the contents were anything but typical.

I'd expected to find a few handguns and maybe a sniper rifle, but the small space was a virtual arsenal. An M-249 squad automatic weapon immediately caught my eye. Despite its weight, the SAW was definitely going flying with me. I selected a Beretta M9 9mm and an AR-10 chambered in 308. What wasn't in the safe was ammunition. I suspected Bimini had a stash, but I'd have to wait for her arrival to find out.

I could feel my eyelids closing, so I crammed a sandwich down my throat and crawled into bed in the master. In addition to being farthest from the front door, the master was the only other room in the house—apart from the living room—with an exterior door. Bimini believed no one would come through the front door besides her, but I'd learned to always leave myself another way out when unexpected things started happening. And those happened far more often than I liked.

Merciful sleep came quickly and thoroughly. When my eyelids finally allowed the light back in, I discovered I had slept for almost six hours, and the sun had disappeared somewhere over the western horizon.

I found my hostess curled like a cat in an oversized chair facing the front door of the safe house. "I didn't hear you come in. How long have you been home?"

She looked up over the back of the chair. "Oh, look. It's Rip Van Winkle. I've been back awhile. I'm not surprised you didn't hear me. I tend to make very little noise. It's a skill that tends to keep people like me alive."

I sat opposite her, primarily so I could pick out signs of deception. "So, where'd you go after dropping me off?"

She looked up and offered a quarter smile. "I wondered how long it would take for the inquisition to start."

I didn't react, so she laid the book she'd been pretending to read on the table before letting her gaze settle on mine. "I couldn't tell my bosses I was coming to Tajikistan to help rescue a team of private security contractors, now could I?"

I opted to continue my silence.

"So, I've been nurturing a relationship with a local informant."

I raised my eyebrows just enough to be noticed, but I still didn't speak, and that did it. She looked away and almost blushed.

I chuckled. "I see. Nurturing a relationship sounds like something you enjoyed. Does Dennis know?"

"Dennis grew bored with me. I haven't seen him since after we took you to Israel last fall."

"Is that so?"

She smirked. "Well, I've seen him, but he didn't see me. In addition to coming and going almost silently, I'm pretty good at watching without being seen."

"You're full of surprises, Bimini. I assume that's not your real name. How long have you been with the DIA?"

"I came over to Defense Intel in ninety-eight. Before that, I was with the State Department."

I relaxed and crossed my legs. "We could do this all night, but why don't we cut to the chase?"

She lowered her chin. "You're the chase, Mr. Fulton."

"Okay," I said. "Stop me when I get off track. You're DIA, formerly of State, which means you *were* CIA, and they wouldn't let you do the fieldwork you are clearly qualified to do, so you jumped ship and ran to DOD at the age of thirty. That means the CIA recruited you out of college."

She slowly shook her head.

"Oh, you weren't recruited out of college, so that means you were military. You're wearing a Harvard sweatshirt, but you'd never advertise your real alma mater, so that means you're an academy grad. Either Navy or Air Force."

She smiled.

I squinted, remembering the sail from Greece to Israel. "You were good on the boat, but not Naval Academy good. So that means you're a Colorado Springs graduate and former Air Force intelligence officer."

She repositioned in her chair. "Don't stop now, Secret Agent Man. You're doing fine."

"Okay...let's see. You did your time in a blue uniform. I'm guessing six years." She smiled, so I continued. "That would have been ninety-five or ninety-six. You probably applied to every government agency under the sun...except the CIA. Nobody who applies directly to the CIA ever gets hired by the Agency, so they plucked your resume from somebody else's database and knocked on your door."

She grimaced. "That's not exactly how it happened, but you're still doing fine. Go on."

To buy myself enough time to piece together her more recent story, I excused myself. "I'll be right back. I'm going to have something to drink. Can I get you anything?"

She looked at her watch. "Really? A drink? We're flying in eight hours."

"Just a glass of water. Get off my back."

She laughed. "Yeah, I'd love a glass of water. Thanks."

I poured two glasses from the filtered pitcher in the refrigerator and returned to the living room. When she took the glass from my hand, her index finger lingered against mine a second longer than it should have.

Most people in the intelligence business live lonely lives. Bimini was attractive enough to catch the eye of most men, but she was trying a little too hard, and that was enough to send my radar into overdrive.

Half emptying my glass, I said, "Where was I?"

"They came knocking."

"Oh, yes. So, you jumped at the chance to become a spy, and they sent you off to the Farm where you excelled, but you were still heels and a skirt in a loafer-and-slacks world, so you didn't get to play grown-up spy with the boys."

She frowned. "Ouch. That wasn't nice."

"The truth rarely is."

She shrugged.

"So, you became an analyst, and occasionally they let you play in the field when they thought you couldn't do any harm, but you wanted to play in the big league. You wanted a clandestine services post, but they wouldn't let you out of the kiddie pool. That's when DIA dangled a little bait in front of you, and you couldn't resist biting. So, here you are, working Southwest Asia and northern Africa all by yourself."

She lifted her glass from the table and inspected it. "Not bad. You missed a few details, but you did a pretty good job of hitting the high spots."

"Thank you. Does DIA know you're freelancing?"

She placed her glass back on the coaster. "I'm sure they know, but it's not like I hung up a shingle saying 'Spy for Hire.'"

"They'll fire you if you get too far off the reservation."

"Maybe, but I've got a few insurance policies tucked away, so I'd have to stray pretty far afield before my bosses would raise much of a fuss. As long as I don't cause any international incidents, I can keep drawing my DOD check and playing in the big leagues with guys like you, Chase Fulton."

I raised my glass. "Here's to playing in the bigs."

She returned my salute, and we finished our drinks that would've been much better had they been distilled spirits, but the water in Dushanbe wasn't as bad as I expected.

She stole a glance at the clock on the wall behind me. "Well, I guess you'd like to have some bullets for your weapons of choice. Nice choices, by the way."

Chapter 13
She Can Shoot

The second safe—the one I hadn't noticed—was artfully disguised as a water heater in a kitchen closet.

"That's clever."

She curtsied. "Thank you. I designed and built it myself."

I nodded with respect. "I'm impressed."

"This won't be the last time you're impressed with my handi-work."

She let the comment hang in the air like a high slow curveball, but I didn't swing on it. I took the pitch and let the umpire call it a ball. I couldn't tell if she was disappointed or impressed that I didn't react.

"Here's a couple cans of five-five-six linked for the SAW, a can of three-oh-eight for the AR, and how much nine-mil do you want?"

I took the ammo cans as she lifted them from the water heater safe. "Three hundred rounds and six magazines should be more than enough…I hope."

She bent at the waist and leaned into the safe, giving me ample opportunity to see what she clearly believed was her best side.

"Here's two hundred rounds and four mags. That's all I have, unless you want forty cal."

I ignored her backside. "No, I'll stick with the nine-millimeter. I'm sure they'll have five-five-six, three-oh-eight, and nine-mil in the cave with them."

She stood up, stretching her back and baring her midriff. Maybe I was overthinking her behavior, but it appeared to me as if she were working hard to get my attention. I was far more interested in her ability to keep me alive when the bullets started flying the next day than I was in how good her abs looked. Besides, I had all the woman I could handle back in the States. It was going to take far more than Bimini to distract that part of my brain.

With the safe once again looking like a water heater, we staged the ammo and weapons so loading would be efficient. Having the neighbors seeing us carrying an arsenal to our vehicle in the wee hours of the morning would not be optimal. I double-checked my gear bags and laid out my clothes and boots for the morning. Bimini did the same.

I noticed her checking out my gear as I was giving hers a cursory glance. She held up one of my boots. "Breaking in new boots on an actual mission isn't the best plan, super-spy."

I yanked my boot from her hand and feigned anger. "Give me that. I lost my last pair in a desperate battle with a wild animal, so I had no choice."

"A wild animal, you say?"

"Yes, he's a fanged beast of almost twenty pounds named Charlie. He was sort of an engagement gift for my wife."

Her eyes widened in surprise. "A wife *and* a wild animal. I didn't have you pegged as the domestic type. I thought more of a playboy, perhaps."

"Sorry to disappoint you, but my playboy days are well astern."

She smiled. "Oh, I'm not disappointed. I've been shaking my ass at you all night trying to find out if you're going to take the bait or treat me as an equal. I hate when guys get all chivalrous and try to protect the poor, defenseless maiden when bullets and blood start flying. That's not the time for chivalry. Just do your job the same as I'm going to do mine, and you can hold the door for me when we get home. Out there, we're soldiers. I like knowing you feel the same."

"Everything's a test, huh?"

She shook her head. "No, not anymore. The tests are over. Now we go to work. Let's brief the mission, then get what sleep we can."

We sat at the kitchen table with a map of the Khyber Pass spread out in front of us.

She pressed her finger into the map about eighty miles from the top of the pass. "Here's where we staged the fuel. It's not particularly easy to defend, but it's remote, so there's not much chance of an ambush."

I studied the terrain and tried to find the cave where Clark and the rest of the team were holed up. There was no obvious location on our map, but the grid coordinates Mongo had given placed it within one mile of the highest elevation on the pass.

"I like it. I agree it would be tough to get a force of any size into position for an ambush, even if they knew we were coming. Do you have any reason to believe anyone saw you staging the fuel?"

She shook her head. "No, we flew several passes and didn't see anything other than a few goats. The landing zone is only about four hundred feet across and maybe five hundred long, but the Hip can get in and out without any problem, even fully loaded."

My confidence was starting to build, but even the best of plans rarely survive first contact with the enemy. Of course, I wasn't certain who the enemy was at that point. Anyone we encountered could've been considered a foe. We'd be flying a Russian helicopter through the Pakistani mountains into a pass that had historically seen more fighting than any other piece of ground within a thousand miles. It was ludicrous to expect the operation to go smoothly.

I ran through the plan in my head before trying to lay it out for Bimini. "Okay, so we'll load up every drop of fuel the chopper can carry and be airborne an hour before sunup. We'll fly nap of the Earth, staying below any active radar and out of sight as much as possible. That Hip is loud and makes a big target if it's well above the tree line. How's Soroush's flying?"

"He's good," she said. "Very good. Maybe one of the best I've ever seen. I know you've got some concerns about the helicopter, but it's a lot better than it looks, especially in his hands. He can do anything you ask, and even a few things you'd never think to ask."

I continued picturing our winding course up the side of the mountain. "Okay, that's good. We'll set down as close to the grid coordinates as we can get. It's essential that we spend no more time than necessary on the ground. There's nothing more important than getting Clark and the others on the Hip and airborne as quickly as possible. I want Soroush in the helicopter with the rotor turning the whole time."

She visually followed my finger up the mountainside. "I agree. If we don't encounter any resistance, and they have Clark strapped up, we should be on the ground in less than five minutes."

I continued studying the terrain at the top of the pass. "It's too wide open up there. There's no way we're getting in and out without being spotted and drawing fire."

My watch showed ten o'clock local, so I pulled my sat-phone and dialed Mongo. He answered thirty seconds later.

"I've been waiting for this call," he said.

"Me too, Mongo. How's the patient?"

"He's hanging on, but this is the last night he's going to survive on this mountain. We're low on morphine, and he's in trouble if we don't get him out of here soon."

I swallowed the lump in my throat. "We'll be there after first light in the morning. I'll call you when we're fifteen minutes out, and I'm going to need a signal. Can you mark the LZ?"

"Yeah, I'll pop white smoke when I hear the chopper. What kind of bird do you have?"

"A Russian MI-17 Hip."

The line went silent for several seconds. "Well, I can't say I've ever looked forward to seeing a Russian helicopter coming, but there's a first time for everything, I guess. We'll have Clark packed and strapped. It's pretty wide open up here, so you and the pilot pull perimeter security. We'll be approaching from the southwest. Kill anybody who ain't us. Got it?"

"Yeah, Mongo, I got it. You're the only friendly on the mountain."

"If you do make it and we get lucky enough to get on the Hip, where are you taking us?"

I traced the perilous nap-of-the-Earth route down the mountain with my fingertip. "Back to Dushanbe."

The sat-phone connection was good enough for me to hear him scratching at his beard. "Can that chopper make it up here and back without a fuel stop?"

"No, but we've already solved that problem. We've staged five hundred gallons about eighty miles down the mountain from your location. We'll pick you up, run for the gas stop, and then back to Dushanbe."

He sighed. "Okay, whatever you say. You're the only bus out of town, so we'll go wherever you take us. Listen, though. If you get spotted and they figure out you're not really Russians, they're going to shoot. Are you armed up?"

Bimini spoke up. "There's a pair of seven-six-two door guns on the Hip, and we're bringing plenty of lead."

"Who the hell is that?"

"Oh, I forgot to tell you. That's our interpreter, the OGA local liaison."

"OGA liaison? What do we need with an interpreter and another government agency liaison? Chase, what's going on?"

I expected him to be nervous about a woman on the mission, but I should've known he'd object to any government agent along for the ride. "It's okay, Mongo. She's with me, and she's essential. It's not like she's on the clock for this one."

There was still hesitance in his voice. "All right, man. If you say so. But can she shoot?"

"Yeah, she can shoot."

"Okay. Anything else?"

"No, I think that covers it. I'll see you after sunup."

"Hey, Chase. Thanks for coming."

I tried to sound unconcerned. "Are you kidding? I wouldn't miss it for the world. Out."

"Well, that went better than I expected," Bimini said.

"Yeah, me too. I've got a couple more calls to make, then I'm going back to sleep if you don't have anything else to discuss."

She stood, rolled the map, and winked. "Tell your wife I said hey and that she's a lucky girl."

I gave my gear one final check and headed for the bedroom, where I called Skipper and briefed the plan as Bimini and I had done. The weather report was fair, but not perfect, so the earlier we got off the mountain, the better. Snow was likely in the early afternoon, and the cloud cover would eliminate any satellite coverage, so we'd be moving without an oversight and no backup if something went wrong. Skipper didn't like it, but Clark's condition prevented any possibility of delaying the mission. The tiny weather window we had would have to do. There was no other option.

Penny answered almost before I heard the first ring. "Chase? Is that you?"

"Hello, Mrs. Fulton."

"I've been worried sick. Are you okay?"

I slid beneath the cover and relaxed against the pillows. "Yeah, I'm good. Just settling down for some sleep before we fly in the morning."

"Oh, good," she said. "I was hoping you could get some sleep. Is everything...well, you know. How...I mean..."

"Everything looks good. There's no reason to worry. We have a good pilot, a good helicopter, and a good plan. If everything goes as planned, we should be back on the ground in Dushanbe by midafternoon with Clark and the rest of the team."

"Please be careful, Chase. And let me know as soon as you're back on the ground and safe. Please."

"I promise to call as soon as we're down and safe. Everything will be fine, and I'll see you in a couple of days."

"Okay. I love you."

I swallowed hard, trying to hide my uncertainty behind a confident tone. "I love you, too, Penny. I'll see you soon."

I plugged in the sat-phone to charge and closed my eyes, wondering if I'd just heard my wife's voice for the last time.

Chapter 14

I'll Fly Away

No prying eyes peered through the predawn darkness as Bimini and I loaded our gear into the truck. Even though the city would come to life in a matter of hours, it would've been easy to believe she and I were the only people awake within a hundred miles.

There was little doubt that as the sun rose over the mountains, the peaceful solitude of the morning would dissolve into chaos. The lives of five abandoned warriors rested heavily in my hands, and I had no intention of letting another day end with those men holed up in that cold dark cave atop the Khyber Pass. I'd bring them home or perish in the effort. No other option existed.

Bimini seemed to sense the intensity of the moment just as I did. We barely spoke other than to check and double-check our gear. I watched her silent professionalism as she performed function checks on every weapon in our arsenal and carefully packed each piece of gear in the back of the truck. Her experience was evident as she moved with silent efficiency through the darkness.

We passed fewer than a dozen cars on our twenty-minute ride to the warehouse. The gate stood ajar when we pulled into the gravel-lined alley beside the dilapidated building. As she let the truck roll to a stop, I dismounted and hefted the clanging gate across the muddy ground until there was just enough room for the truck to roll through.

As I turned to drag the gate closed, I paused, considering our departure. When we made it back to the ground with Clark, I didn't want any hurdles between me and the hospital. In an effort to make our egress as clean as possible, I left the gate open and climbed back into the truck.

Bimini's eyes scanned the mirror. "Good thinking. Every second is going to count when we get home."

Our headlights swept across the nearly ten-ton helicopter that looked more like a robotic grasshopper than anything that could be capable of the mission I demanded of it. Soroush was untying the lines that had been securing the rotor blades against the wind. To my surprise, a second man was crouched on top of the machine with a small flashlight in his mouth and both hands plunged deeply inside the engine cowling.

Bimini backed the truck to the ramp of the chopper as Soroush tossed the tie-downs into the cargo bay.

I stepped from the truck and pointed to the man on top of the aircraft. "Who is he, and what's he doing here?"

My accusatory tone widened the pilot's eyes. "He is…um… *muhandisii zarurī*. I cannot fly without."

"English, Soroush. What is *muhandisii zarurī*?"

Surprises are unavoidable, but keeping them to a minimum is what makes nearly impossible missions possible. An extra human suddenly thrown into a mission as potentially fraught with probable failure as this one was one surprise I could not overlook.

Soroush began making twisting motions with his hands and stuttering gibberish as his eyes darted between the other man and me.

I held up my hands in the universal signal for calm down. "Just stop talking and wait."

Bimini arrived as if on cue.

I pointed toward the man above us. "Find out who and what he is, and make Soroush understand we are not adding additional personnel to this mission at the last minute."

The two of them dived into an incomprehensible rapid-fire conversation, and I found myself obsessed with watching the man with the flashlight in his mouth. I needed neither his distraction nor his delay.

Bimini's hand landed on my arm. "Chase, listen. The man is a flight engineer. Soroush can't fly without another pilot or an engineer. That means either *you're* in the front seat"—she pointed upward—"or he is."

I closed my eyes, inhaled the cold morning air, and let the sudden change of mission parameters bounce around inside my head. After a long moment, I took Soroush by the collar. "Listen very closely to me. I am not the type of man who wastes time with empty threats. Do you understand?"

The pilot nodded sharply.

"Good. If your engineer does anything—and I mean anything—to endanger this mission, there is no limit to the lengths I will go to make sure both you and he pay dearly for the rest of your very short lives. Is there anything about what I just said you don't understand?"

He slowly shook his head. "He is my son, my own blood, and he will not fail."

I locked eyes with him. "Failure means death for all of us and for five men on that mountain. That is *not* an option."

He never blinked as he held my gaze. "We will not fail."

Twenty minutes later, the gear was loaded, strapped down, and the massive rotors began to turn. Soroush and his son managed the start-up in practiced perfection as if they'd done it thousands of times. Perhaps they had.

I expected the Hip to lumber from the ground, but the machine leapt into the air with the agility and power of a pouncing cat.

The sun had not yet breached the eastern horizon, but the city was coming to life as we climbed out of the metropolitan maze. Head-lights and taillights dotted the grids of the roads, and the building windows flickered to life with the light from within.

The next time I saw Dushanbe, I would have Clark on a stretcher at my feet and four warriors of immeasurable valor in the webbed seats of the chopper. Blood would spill, and lives would end on the mountain in the coming hours. I prayed the lives that would reach their end would not be those of my team. Everyone on the chopper was a volunteer who didn't have to be on the mission. Everyone other than me could've been sleeping soundly in their beds, but I had no choice other than to do everything in my power to bring Clark and his teammates to safety. I was committed by duty and love for the man who'd fought beside me when lesser men would've walked away in fear. If I were the one lying injured and near death on top of that mountain, the one thing I would know above all else is that Clark Johnson would come for me, and I owed him nothing short of the same.

The MI-17 Hip was quieter and a much smoother ride than I expected, but as the sun came up, the view outside was anything but reassuring. With the city of Dushanbe well behind us, we flew down the western face of the Spīn Ghar mountain range. The sun shone off the snowcapped peaks in blinding beams that reminded me of the Rocky Mountains…if the Rockies were littered with combatants who wanted to kill anyone who looked and sounded like me.

The air inside the cargo bay of the Hip was decreasing as our altitude climbed, but I barely noticed. Soroush's son turned from the cockpit and motioned for us to come forward. When we stuck our heads into the cockpit, Soroush turned sharply to the east and pointed the aircraft into a winding mountain pass that looked barely wide enough for our rotors.

He glanced over his shoulder and smiled. "*Parvozi havopajmo ва şalloq meaftad.*"

The look on Bimini's face told me she was working on a translation I could understand. She finally pointed into the mountains. "To fly there is to chase the devil."

The nose of the chopper came up, and we entered the pass. We were making one hundred ten knots, and Soroush was flying mere feet above jagged rocks that could easily tear the helicopter to shreds. I braced myself against the bulkhead and kept my eyes focused on ahead.

Bimini sat perfectly relaxed as if she were out for a Sunday drive. "I hope you don't get airsick."

"Flying doesn't make me sick, but crashing makes me want to throw up. I'd like to avoid that."

"If we hit the mountain at this speed, we'll never feel our stomachs...or any other body part for that matter."

The old pilot's skill at the controls was impressive. He flew the heavy chopper as if it were a nimble craft less than half its size. For the first time, I was glad I'd elected to have his son in the front seat instead of me. There was nothing I could've done to contribute to the safety of the flight.

An eternity after beginning to chase the devil, I spotted the remains of what must have been a two-thousand-year-old structure. We'd reached an area that didn't qualify as a plateau so much as a less-rugged area of the mountains. The structure was the prominent feature of the landscape despite the dramatic peaks and endless crags.

"What's that?" I asked as much with my outstretched finger as with my voice.

"Taimoor Fort," came Soroush's instant reply, almost as if he were proud of the remains, as if, perhaps, he'd built the original structure with his own hands.

I nudged Bimini. "Ask him how far we are from the coordinates I provided."

She leaned into the cockpit and spoke with the pilot who'd visibly relaxed after having survived the treacherous mountain pass.

"Ten minutes!" Bimini said.

I moved away from the cockpit and withdrew my sat-phone from my pack. Seven minutes later, we saw a plume of white smoke rising from the grenade Mongo had released to mark the landing zone and to indicate the speed and direction of the swirling mountaintop winds.

I pointed toward the smoke. "There's your LZ."

Soroush and his son busied themselves setting up for the approach and landing in an area the size of a postage stamp. Bimini pulled her rifle from the webbing of the seat, and I double-checked the M249. Second only to sitting on the ground, we were entering the most vulnerable position the chopper could be in. Flying low and slow on an approach to a critically small landing zone left almost no room for deviation and made the massive aircraft little more than a sitting duck.

As I moved to the window to cover our approach, a buzzer sounded from the cockpit, and the lumbering chopper pitched up and banked to the right in an exaggerated and violent maneuver. Unable to keep my footing, I slammed into the bulkhead and nearly lost control of the squad automatic weapon in my arms.

When I finally clawed my way to the window, the tell-tale white smoke trail of a surface-to-air missile painted a jagged line across the sky. We were still in the air, and no pieces were falling off, so we hadn't been hit.

Following the white smoke trail to an outcropping of jagged rocks amid patches of snow, I saw four men with rifles raised and one with the empty tube of a shoulder-fired rocket launcher in his arms. Bracing the forearm of the SAW on the sill of the window, I poured a wall of 5.56-millimeter lead onto their position. Dust, rocks, and pulverized debris filled the air around the fighters as they melted to the ground.

Soroush brought the chopper around to the right to reattempt the approach, and Bimini leaned from the opposite window with her rifle trained on the area I'd swept seconds before.

Over her shoulder, she yelled, "Get that SAW over here!"

I pulled the muzzle back inside the chopper and crossed the cargo bay.

She pointed to an area just behind the bodies of the fighters who were having their first face-to-face with Allah. "There's a stash under that camo netting. See it?"

I focused on the area and finally saw what had her attention: Several wooden crates, presumably more missiles, were stacked haphazardly beneath brown and white blankets.

I trained the SAW on the stash and opened up, demolishing everything in sight with fifteen seconds of full-auto fire.

When Soroush rolled back onto the approach, two of Mongo's teammates spread out, forming a perimeter defense. Both of the men were moving in obvious pain, completely unlike they'd moved in Russia. There were obviously hurt far worse than Mongo had indicated during our first conversation three days before.

Mongo's size made him easy to identify, but the other men were all so similar, it was impossible to identify any of them. He said Smoke wasn't hurt badly, so I assumed he was the man carrying the foot-end of the stretcher holding the motionless form of my partner.

Seconds before touching down, Soroush's son leapt from the cockpit and sent the ramp at the rear of the cargo bay on its way to the full-open position. As the wheels of the chopper touched the snow-covered rocky earth, Bimini, the engineer, and I poured through the opening with weapons raised.

My yearning to run to Clark was almost too much to overcome, but I had to provide cover for the rest of the team to move to the chopper.

Singer, the Southern Baptist sniper of the group, dragged himself toward the chopper with agony consuming his face. His left leg was splinted and bandaged in a heavy dressing, and despite the obvious pain, he moved beside the stretcher and shuffled backward, protecting Clark from potential incoming fire.

Snake, one of the best tactical drivers in the world, carried his left arm in a makeshift sling with his hand stained black with blood. He held an M4 rifle like a pistol in his right hand and mirrored Singer's movements.

Mongo held the head of Clark's improvised stretcher in his enormous hands and shuffled toward the helicopter, dragging Smoke behind him like a ragdoll.

The ground around Smoke's feet erupted into a cloud of dust and flying debris, and I immediately began scanning the high ground in search of the gunmen who'd opened up on us. If I couldn't find them, we'd soon be cut to shreds, left for birds to pick the flesh from our bones.

The unmistakable report of an AK47 fired full auto, and I hit the deck, rolling toward the only cover I could see: a pair of small boulders near a snowdrift. As I made the roll, I looked up to see the last thing I expected. Soroush's son was kneeling with his Russian Kalashnikov rifle, pouring lead into the overhang two hundred meters to the east. I trained my SAW on the same spot and crushed the trigger. Lead poured from my barrel at a rate far greater than the AK in the Tajik's hands, turning the mountainside into a torrent of lead, snow, rocks, and sand. The fighters who'd occupied the position and fired on us dissolved into pink mist sprayed across the face of the rocks.

I scanned the environment for additional threats and rose to a kneeling position. The motion sent waves of pain through my abdomen as if a mule had kicked me where no man ever wants to be kicked. I caught my breath and suppressed the urge to vomit. When I looked up, the muzzle of Bimini's M4 swung toward my face, and I watched orange fire belch from the weapon. I slammed my body and head into the snow and rolled onto my back. Less than ten yards behind me, Bimini cut down a pair of gunmen with a barrage of fire. The sickening pain in my bowels was still there, but it was less severe than a bullet in the back of the head would've been if Bimini hadn't picked off my attackers.

Mongo's team had positioned themselves in a semicircle behind the chopper, and their bullets continued cutting through the mountain air. Bimini, the Tajik, and I scampered toward the aircraft, never taking our eyes off the surrounding cliffs. We ran up the ramp, and Bimini and I took our positions at the windows, with our weapons protruding through the openings. The Tajik dived into the cockpit beside his father, and the rotors began to roar above our heads. As the landing gear and ramp left the ground, Singer and Snake rolled on board while Smoke and Mongo laid on the ramp to cover our departure.

We cleared the small ledge at the southern end of the landing zone, and Soroush lowered the nose, accelerating down the slope. Clear of the dust, smoke, and gunfire, and through the ringing in my ears from battle, I heard Singer belting out "I'll Fly Away," and I couldn't resist joining in the chorus.

Chapter 15
Fill 'er Up

Mongo laid his massive hand on my shoulder. "Go see to Clark. I'll take the SAW."

I handed the weapon to him and marveled at how small the gun looked in his arms. Kneeling beside my partner, I laid my hand on his chest. His colorless face looked like that of a corpse. His eyes were partially open, but lifeless, and I felt the panic rise in my chest as I thrust my fingertips toward the flesh of his neck. Desperately, I felt for a pulse but could only feel my own heart pounding in my fingertips. The man who'd taught me to stay alive above all else lay lifeless and cold beneath my hands. The contents of my stomach rose into my throat, and an anger I didn't know I possessed swelled inside my skull.

Snake rested his hand on my arm. "It's okay, man. He's alive. We've just got him pumped so full of morphine he can't feel a thing. We knew the exfil was going to be hot, so we couldn't have him awake. If we didn't knock him out, he would've insisted on joining the fight. You know how he is."

Bimini tossed a stethoscope from the med bag, and I caught it midair. Over the thump of the rotors and the roar of the wind in the cargo bay, I could hear my partner's heart beating every two seconds like a clock keeping half-time.

Snake hung an IV bag and connected the line to the catheter taped to the inside of Clark's arm. He rechecked Clark's vital signs and made a note inside a small green book he pulled from my partner's pocket. "You saved his life, Chase. He's gonna be damned glad to see you when he wakes up."

I shook my head. "You guys saved his life. I just found him a ride home."

"Speaking of home…" Snake said. "Where are we going?"

"We'll be making a fuel stop any minute now and then back to Dushanbe."

"A fuel stop? Up here in these mountains?"

I laughed. "Yeah, I had a couple of friends build us a gas station not far from here. Snake, meet Bimini—door gunner and gas station builder extraordinaire."

Bimini looked down at the filthy, bearded warrior. "It's nice to meet you, Snake."

He looked up, surprise evident on his face, "Forgive me, but I didn't realize you were—"

She handed him a bottle of water. "You didn't realize I was what? Left-handed? A chick?"

He looked at me for help.

I shrugged. "I didn't realize she was a lefty either."

We continued introductions until we felt the chopper's nose rise and the big bird slow down. Without a word, everyone moved to a defensive position to cover our approach to the site where Bimini and Soroush had staged the barrels of jet fuel.

The instant the landing gear hit the ground, Soroush's son was out of the cockpit and hammering the caps off the fuel barrels. Seconds later, he had a pair of electric fuel pumps with pickups in the barrels and hoses leading to the Hip's tanks.

The rest of us exited the chopper and set a perimeter defense. We were as vulnerable as we'd ever be sitting on the ground with fuel hoses and electrical lines like spaghetti strung to and from the helicopter. In my estimation, the refueling took far too long. I didn't like being a sitting duck, even with a team of tier-one operators at my side.

After too many minutes on the ground, the Tajik dragged the pumps and hoses back aboard the Hip, and we mounted up. Back in the air without another firefight, we closed the rear ramp in a wasted attempt to keep the cold air outside.

We settled in for the remaining two hours of the run back to Dushanbe, and Bimini spread out the contents of the med bag. "Come here, Singer. Let's have a look at that leg."

We rotated through shifts as door gunner while Bimini redressed wounds and passed out protein bars and bottles of water.

I leaned into the cockpit, trying to recognize familiar terrain. "Are we going back the same way we came?"

Soroush looked up at me, and I watched his eyes as he tried to piece together what I'd asked. Finally, he said, "No. Different. We fly high and fast now."

On the one hand, high and fast sounded good, but I didn't like the idea of showing up on anyone's radar scope if there were radar antennas on the Pakistan-Afghanistan border.

I got Bimini's attention. "Soroush says we're flying home high and fast. How do you feel about that?"

She smiled. "We'll be in Afghan airspace most of the way, and we're in a Russian military helicopter behaving exactly as a Russian chopper should behave. Nobody's going to mess with us."

"If you say so. You're the regional expert. I'm just a knuckle-dragger."

A hearty round of grunts and growls went up as the Brinkwater team—or former Brinkwater team—echoed, "Knuckle-draggers!"

During the gunfight and exfiltration, the backs of Bimini's hands had taken quite a beating, leaving them scuffed, dirty, and bleeding.

Mongo took her hands in his. He said, "You may be the regional expert like Chase said, but it looks to me like you qualify as a knuckle-dragger just like the rest of us."

She smiled. "Now, that's a club I'm proud to be part of."

An hour southeast of Dushanbe, I dialed Skipper's number.

She answered without ceremony. "I wondered if you were ever going to call. Tell me what's going on."

"We've got Clark and the team on the chopper, and we're less than an hour from Dushanbe."

"Oh, thank God. How was it?"

"Not too bad," I said. "We ran into a few snags, but we're better shooters than they were."

"How's Clark?"

I looked down at my partner. "He's not good, but he's alive. Can you see about getting us into the hands of some first-world medical care once we're on the ground?"

"I can do better than that," she said. "I've got you a medivac from Dushanbe to Frankfurt with a trauma team onboard."

"How did you pull that off?"

"It's a long story, but the plane belongs to the Air Force, and the crew is made up of Air Force reservists called up to active duty for the fighting in Afghanistan."

"Skipper, you're incredible."

She scoffed. "Yeah, I know. I deserve a bonus and a raise."

"You deserve more than that, but we'll deal with it when I get home. Is the medivac on the ground now?"

"It will be in twenty minutes."

"You're the best, Skipper. Do me a favor and call Penny. Let her know our status, and tell her I'll call as soon as I can."

"You got it, Chase. Oh, and hey…nice job. I knew you'd pull it off."

I couldn't suppress my smile. "I'll see you in a few days."

I poked my head into the cockpit. "Take us to Dushanbe International. We'll have a medivac waiting for us on the ground."

He typed the new destination into the GPS in Cyrillic, and I chuckled. "*Ty govorish' po-Russki.*"

Soroush smiled at me. "*Da.* I speak Russian. We did not need woman after all."

I glanced back at Bimini as she took her turn on the gun in the window. "Oh, yes we did, my friend."

* * *

We landed at Dushanbe International Airport forty-five minutes later and taxied up between a pair of jets. The one on the left was a C-9 Nightingale and bore U.S. Air Force markings with a red cross painted on the tail. The second jet was a Gulfstream G550 with Belgium registration.

We'd packed away our arsenal of weaponry before landing since automatic rifles are rarely welcome on the tarmac at international airports, but there was no way to hide the combatants in the Hip. No one would believe we were anything other than soldiers. Thankfully, the Nightingale was only steps away.

When the ramp was lowered, I was surprised to see a pair of stretchers with accompanying medics waiting on the ramp. Two of the medics were in Air Force flight suits, while the other two were in white scrubs bearing the Brinkwater Security Services logo on the sleeves. Standing beside the medics in the Brinkwater scrubs was none other than Jerry Beard, the operations officer from Dubai.

Beard pushed his way past the Air Force crew and met me at the bottom of the ramp. "Mr. Fulton, how nice it is to see you again. We had every faith you'd deliver our team back to safety, but our search and rescue forces were only minutes behind you. Of course, that doesn't matter at this point, but we'll take it from here, and we'll see that you are compensated handsomely for your effort."

Thundering strides came down the ramp behind me, and I didn't have to look to know whose feet were making the sound. Mongo's anvil-sized fist landed with a cracking thud, and blood from Beard's nose and lips sprayed through the air. The man collapsed to the ground like a felled oak.

The man I knew only as "Hal," who'd led me into Jerry Beard's office two days before, came toward us at a sprint. Mongo grabbed the chrome rail of the gurney and lifted the heavy bed as if it were a child's toy, hurling it through the air, directly at Hal. The man's attempts to dodge and block the flying gurney were a wasted effort. The seven-foot-long mechanical rolling bed sent Hal to his back on the concrete of the airport parking apron. His eyes were wide open, but he was out cold and taking a nice swim through the spirit world by the time the flying bed came to rest on the tarmac.

Mongo called out, "Anybody else want to try telling me how much you missed us? Huh?"

With no one else to receive his wrath, Mongo grabbed one of the medics and lifted him off the ground. "You left us up there to die, you son of a bitch!"

The medic's eyes went wide, and terror filled his face. "No, sir. It wasn't me. I'm just a paramedic. I didn't do any of that."

Mongo threw the trembling man toward his partner, sending both men crashing to the ground. Snake and Smoke came down the ramp, intent on getting the big man under control, but they were too late. Mongo had already grabbed a pair of landing gear chocks—two wooden blocks tied together with a three-foot-long length of rope—and sent the chocks careening through the air toward the Gulfstream luxury business jet.

I had no idea how far Mongo would go toward destroying the Brinkwater jet, but I had no intention of stopping him. The company had abandoned him and his team in one of the most inhospitable places on Earth, and it was time to make somebody pay for that atrocity.

The landing gear door beneath the left wing was Mongo's final victim. His shoulder twisted the metal beyond recognition, rendering it unusable.

Snake was the first to think of a way to call off the huge man and at least temporarily postpone his retribution. "Mongo! Give it a rest. We've got to get Clark out of here."

The admonition froze the giant in his tracks. The Air Force medics seemed oblivious to the melee and rolled their gurney up the Hip's ramp. Moments later, Clark was aboard the C-9 Nightingale, and the remainder of the team was climbing the ramp into the medivac.

Soroush and his son hadn't left the cockpit, so I pulled a stack of banded bills from my pack and knelt between them in the front of the Russian chopper.

"Thank you, Soroush. I couldn't have pulled it off without you. This is for you." I laid two packs of ten thousand dollars beside his arm on the console, and I laid the third stack of cash on the engineer's leg. "Thank you for what you did today, and I'm sorry for the way I treated you this morning. You're a good man and a true warrior."

He looked up at me like a confused child and mumbled something that could have been "Thank you."

My remaining ten grand found its way into Bimini's pack without her noticing, but I couldn't simply walk away. "Thank you for everything. None of this could have happened without you, and my friend would be dead on top of that mountain if you hadn't agreed to help. I hope this isn't the last time I see you."

She smiled the smile of an exhausted warrior. "No, Chase. That's not true. You would've found a way without me. That's what you do. I'm glad I could help, and thanks for letting me tag along. As if you had a choice."

She stepped toward me and extended her arms. We hugged in silent understanding of what it means to put yourself in harm's way to save the life of a fellow fighter.

"Don't worry about any of this, Chase. I'll take care of everything here. You go with your brother, and let me know how he's doing. Elizabeth, who you seem to call Skipper for some reason, knows how to reach me."

My words were too weak, but I offered them anyway. "Thank you for...everything."

She slugged me on the shoulder. "Get out of here, you big dumb jock. It's a long way to Germany."

I watched Dushanbe disappear behind me for the second time in less than nine hours, and I couldn't stop thinking that good luck and God were on my side that day. The humming engines of the modified DC-9 sang me to sleep with my hand resting on Clark Johnson's arm.

Chapter 16
Old Familiar Wounds

The heart monitor the Air Force flight nurse connected sounded a regular tone with every beat of Clark's heart. The beeping and the slow rise and fall of his chest were the only signs that he was alive. X-rays confirmed his back was broken at the fifth lumbar and first sacral vertebrae, but that was far from the extent of his injuries. Several fractured ribs, including one driven deeply into his left lung, were the most obvious injuries detected.

"Although impossible to survive without medical intervention, none of Mr. Johnson's injuries are what we would consider life-threatening." Lieutenant Colonel Franklin Rush was a board-certified emergency medicine specialist and trauma surgeon whose day job found him in the emergency rooms at two of Chicago's busiest hospitals. "The Air Force paid for medical school, so I still serve as a reservist. I'm proud to answer the call when they need reserve physicians on temporary active duty."

I was in awe of Dr. Rush's patriotism, as well as his confidence in Clark's ultimate recovery.

"I don't know how to thank you for what you're doing for my partner, Dr. Rush."

"You don't have to thank me," he said, "but I'm a little unclear about who you are exactly. Are you with Delta Force or the SEALs?"

"Something like that," I said. "Thanks for taking such good care of all of us."

The doctor made the rounds, examining every member of the team as we continued our six-hundred-mile-per-hour progress ever westward toward Germany. Holding up an X-ray in front of Singer, he said, "I'm not sure how you were walking on this leg, but as you can see, the fibula is shattered. That's the smaller of the two bones in your lower leg."

Singer looked at the film for a long time before laughing. "Ha! How about that? It sure is something what God can do to keep one of His children on his feet with an injury like that. Can you think of any other explanation, doc?"

Dr. Rush scratched at his chin. "Well, the body is quite amazing. Soldiers have been known to fight for several hours on adrenaline alone, even after suffering massive injuries on the battlefield."

Singer pursed his lips. "Hours, you say?"

"That's right. The phenomenon has been observed and reported to have occurred sometimes up to four hours after the initial injury."

Singer smiled. "Well, in that case, I guess it must've been the adrenaline that got me through those first four hours."

"I'm confident that's the case," the doctor said.

"I'm sure you're right, doc, but this happened over four *days* ago, and in those four days, we held off half a dozen attacks. We even won two gunfights just today. Have you ever heard of adrenaline pulling that kind of overtime?"

Dr. Rush smiled.

"Yeah, me neither," Singer said. "How 'bout checking on Snake? I imagine he's about out of adrenaline, too."

The doctor held up another set of X-rays. As he began detailing Snake's injuries, the description of the damage took me back to the day that shattered my dreams of becoming a major league catcher. It set me on the path that led me into the service of my country, and ultimately up the unrelenting cliffs of the Khyber Pass to rescue the men around me.

"The bones of the wrist and hand make up one of the most complex mechanical structures of the human body." He removed a pen from his pocket and pointed to the center of the X-ray. "This large bone here is the radius, and the smaller one over here is the ulna. Where they met before your accident is called the distal radioulnar joint, or the DRUJ for short. As you can see, that joint is no longer intact. Compared to your other injuries, that's relatively easy to repair for a good orthopedic surgeon, and we just happen to have one of the best in Frankfurt. This area here—where you see the bones that look like pebbles—those used to be the scaphoid, trapezium, trapezoid, and capitate bones. Those aren't as easy to repair, but there have been remarkable medical advances in recent years that have allowed hand surgeons to accomplish some pretty amazing things."

Snake's eyes shifted from the X-ray to the swollen, disfigured form of his wrist and hand. I knew every emotion he was experiencing, and I knew every question he was about to ask. I'd been through it all, and I'd asked all the questions.

I stepped beside Snake, looking at the X-ray. "Doctor, would you mind shooting a picture of my wrist and hand so he can get a glimpse into the future?"

Dr. Rush wrinkled his forehead and assessed my crisscrossed surgical scars. A knowing smile crossed his face. "Yeah, we can do that. Come with me."

Moments later, we returned to the bed where Snake was inspecting his hand as though it were an appendage that didn't belong to him. The doctor held up my X-ray, displaying the bevy of pins, screws, and assorted hardware holding my wrist and hand together.

Snake was in obvious disbelief. "Is that really your hand?"

I nodded. "It really is. And it looked a lot like yours before they put it back together."

Snake's eyes met the doctor's in wordless inquisition.

Dr. Rush said, "It's several surgeries and a few months of rehab, but as you can see, it can be done. So don't give up hope. Just get ready for a little well-deserved time off and a few months of physical therapy."

Snake dropped his head. "It sucked, didn't it, Chase?"

I motioned toward Clark. "Just like he always says...Sometimes you have to learn to embrace the suck."

Other than a few cuts and bruises, the rest of us believed we were relatively uninjured, but the doctor and his staff did full physical exams as part of their protocol.

When he checked me for a hernia—one of my least favorite parts of any physical exam—he never got to the "turn your head and cough" portion. I winced as he probed, and the look on his face maligned his attempts to reassure me that everything was all right.

"It's probably nothing, but we'll want to get an ultrasound and have a urologist take a look when we get to Frankfurt."

I didn't like the idea of an injury to any part of my body, but that particular spot concerned me a little more than most others would have. "What is it? What's going on down there?"

He removed his glasses as if he were imagining anatomical charts of my abdomen flashing in his head. "Do you remember what caused the injury?"

"What injury?"

"There's some swelling and obvious tenderness." He tilted his head. "Do you remember how it happened?"

"I hit the ground pretty hard during a gunfight. I don't know. Stuff just happens. I remember it hurting, but I didn't have the option of calling a time-out to check for groin injuries."

"I'm sure it's fine. Probably just a bruise, but we'll run some tests and have the urologist take a look."

I had enough to worry about with Clark and the rest of the team. I didn't need to be thinking about my gut...or lower.

A man in a green flight suit stuck his head in and announced, "We'll be descending into Frankfurt any minute. Secure the bay for arrival."

Most everyone strapped into one of the seats situated about the bay, and the flight nurse tightened Clark's restraints on the gurney.

We'd flown nearly three thousand miles in the past five hours, but the distance between the world we'd left and the one into which we were descending was greater than most people are capable of comprehending. From tribal territories of Afghanistan and Pakistan in some of the most rugged and hostile mountains on the planet, to the modern civilization of Frankfurt, Germany, the journey was far more than one of mere geographical distance. It was a journey forward in time, ideology, and socio-political stability. The Western world had its share of unrest, but the unthinkable chaos of thousands of years of fighting and the struggle for survival in the Middle East was a scenario I hoped the people I fought to preserve and protect would never have to know.

As the wheels of the C-9 Nightingale touched down with a barely detectible bounce, I watched Clark Johnson's supine form, lifeless except for the tone of his heart monitor, and wondered if he was silently criticizing the Air Force pilots' landing the way he always did when I touched down a little too hot. I wondered what he remembered of the fight that left him broken and near death. I wondered if he'd recover to again be the warrior I'd come to respect and love.

Three ambulances waited on the tarmac of Rhein-Main Air Base, and the ground crew were obviously no strangers to the task of moving patients quickly, carefully, and efficiently. I rode in the ambulance with Clark and Dr. Rush between the airfield and the hospital. Our reception at the hospital was without ceremony, but the immediate attention of the staff was unlike any I'd ever seen. Clark was whisked away with none of the typical bureaucratic nonsense. Snake and Singer, much to their obvious dismay, were wheeled into the depths of the hospital in wheelchairs. Smoke, Mongo, and I stood in the waiting area, uncertain what we should do or where we should do it. We found chairs and tried to make ourselves as comfortable as possible. I believed we were in for a long wait.

"Captain Fulton?" A voice filled the space of the cavernous waiting area. "Is there a Captain Chase Fulton out here?"

I shot a look at Smoke. "Captain? What's that about?"

He shrugged. "I don't know, but she's obviously looking for you."

I stood. "I'm Chase Fulton."

The young lady dressed in blue scrubs and holding a clipboard shot me a look as if I were a prized pig at a beauty contest. "Come with me please."

I followed her through a pair of motorized swinging doors and down a long corridor. She pressed a large square pad on the wall and opened a heavy door into a brightly lit room with a desk and computer in one corner. She pointed toward a pile of cloth on an exam table. "I'm Sergeant Gentry, and I'll be doing your MRI. Please remove your clothes and put on that robe and socks, Captain Fulton."

"Why do I need an MRI?"

She checked her clipboard. "Dr. Rush ordered an abdominal MRI. I just do what the doctors order."

I peeled my sweat-stained, filthy shirt, and let my pants fall to the floor.

"You could have waited until I left the room," the young woman quipped.

"You ordered me to take off my clothes and put on that gown. I'm just doing what you directed."

She laughed. "Touché."

After twenty minutes inside the claustrophobic torture chamber of clangs, vibrations, and humming, I rode the electric sliding table out of the tube.

"How does it look, Sergeant Gentry?"

She took the headphones and squeeze bulb from my hand. "I'm just a radiology tech, not a radiologist. I'm not allowed to make diagnoses."

I scanned the cold room. "That's okay. I'm not really a captain, so we'll keep it between us. What did you see on the scan?"

Just as I had done, she scanned the room as if making sure no one could hear. "It looks like you've sustained some damage to your... um...lower abdomen. There's something going on down there." She subconsciously glanced toward my groin.

"That doesn't sound good."

"I'm sure it's nothing to worry about"—she made air quotes with her fingers—"Captain."

"Thanks, Sergeant."

"It's Tina," she said.

"Okay, then. Thanks, Tina. Can I get dressed now?"

"No, unfortunately not. Follow me."

She led me back down the corridor and into a small room with a hospital bed, chair, tiny bathroom, and television. "Make yourself comfortable, and one of the doctors will be with you shortly. I'm sure you have time to shower if you'd like. It's right in there."

Apparently, I wasn't the epitome of cleanliness, so I thanked her and took her recommendation. I knew enough about the human mind to understand why I checked and double-checked the part of my body the medical staff seemed to be concerned with. Just as Dr. Rush had said, there was definitely some swelling and a lot of tenderness.

After I was sufficiently clean, I donned the robe and socks again and headed back into the room. The bed didn't interest me, but I took full advantage of the chair. It was time to play E.T. and phone home.

Penny answered on the second ring. "Hello?"

"Hello there, Mrs. Fulton. It's your husband."

"Oh, Chase. It's so good to hear your voice. Skipper told me you were off the mountain and you're all right. You are all right, aren't you? How's Clark? Did everything go the way you expected? Where are you? When are you coming home?"

Penny's ability to cram a thousand questions into a thirty-second block of time would never cease to amaze me.

I paused. "Yeah, I'm okay, and Clark is going to be all right."

I could practically taste the concern in her voice. "You took a little longer than necessary to answer my question. Are you *really* okay?"

"Yeah, I'm okay. I hurt my stomach on the mountain, but it's nothing. They're doing some tests, and I'll see the urologist in a few minutes."

"Urologist? What happened? How did you get hurt? Talk to me, Chase."

"I don't know," I admitted. "I'll let you know as soon as I have any news."

"You better."

I ran down the condensed version of the past eighteen hours. "Clark's in surgery now, I assume. They say he broke his back and a few ribs, but the doctor thinks he's going to be okay in time. The rest of the guys are beat up, but they'll be okay, too."

"Okay, so when are you coming home?"

"Probably tomorrow, but I don't know for sure."

She sighed. "I've been worried sick, Chase. I hate this. I hate you being gone and me not knowing where and how you are. It's tough for me."

I wanted to wrap my arms around her and make her forget everything she feared, but from Germany, all I had were words. "I know, and I don't like doing that to you. I'm okay. I promise you that. I'm at an Air Force Base in Germany, and we're perfectly safe here. Everyone is being well cared for.

"Thank you. I know you care, and I know it's hard on you, too. As much as it hurts to be away from you, I love the man you are for putting your life on the line for Clark and the people you care about. I've always wanted a man like you, and now that I have one, I don't want to lose him."

"I can't tell you how much it means to hear you say that. You're everything I could want and so much more than I'll ever deserve. I'll be home soon, I promise."

"Oh, speaking of coming home, you're never going to believe what happened today."

Chapter 17
Make a Decision Now

A woman in a white lab coat over camouflage pants and black combat boots came through the door with a clipboard in her hands. Her glasses had slid down her nose until the entirety of her eyes were well above the rim. She appeared to be in her mid-thirties with short, dark hair and had the look of a librarian with no concept of fashion.

Without taking her eyes off the clipboard, she said, "Hello, Captain Fulton. I'm Major Duncan, and I'm one of the urologists on staff here."

"Penny, I'm going to have to call you back. The urologist is here."

Major Duncan finally looked up as if displeased that I was on the telephone. "So, you sustained a blunt force trauma injury to your groin and testicles. How long ago did this happen?"

"I don't know for sure. Maybe twelve or fourteen hours."

She conducted her examination, and it was somewhat more involved than Dr. Rush's, but there was still no coughing involved.

After removing her gloves, she sat on a short, rolling stool and began scribbling notes onto her clipboard as if she'd forgotten I was in the room. When she looked up, the expression on her face made it clear she realized I was waiting for her diagnosis.

She held up a sketch of how that part of my anatomy should look and then described what the trauma had done. "I'm going to prescribe an anti-inflammatory, some pain meds, and an antibiotic.

We'll give the swelling twenty-four hours and make a surgical decision at that point."

"A surgical decision? What are you talking about?"

"Captain Fulton, you've suffered a significant injury. We'll take another look tomorrow, and if we believe surgery is warranted, we'll talk about the risks and potential for sterility. Do you have any children?"

I didn't understand how diving to the ground could result in the injury she was describing, so I sat in silent disbelief.

"Captain Fulton, are you married, and do you have any children?"

I shook my head. "No, I'm not a captain, and no, I don't have any children."

"And are you married?"

"No. I mean, yes…yes, I'm married."

She made a few more notes and then furrowed her brow. "Did you say you're not a captain?"

I stared at the floor. "Would you mind giving me a moment? I need to call home, and I need to find out if Clark Johnson is out of surgery yet."

She stood. "Of course. You could use some rest. I'll have the nurse bring in your meds and something to help you sleep. And I'll check on Master Sergeant Johnson."

"Who?"

"Master Sergeant Johnson. Clark Johnson."

I blinked as if I were trying to focus. "Oh, yeah. Thank you."

She closed the door behind her, and I sat on the edge of the bed with my phone clamped in my fist. I dialed Penny's number, but what was I going to tell her? How was I supposed to explain what I didn't understand to the woman who'd been my wife for only three days?

"Okay, so tell me what's going on. I'm worried sick, Chase."

"I'm not sure," I admitted, stalling more than being honest.

"What do you mean you're not sure? Just tell me what happened and what the doctor said."

I swallowed hard. "I'm fine. I got hurt, but it's not serious. We were in a gunfight—"

"Oh, my God! Did you get shot?"

"No, nothing like that. None of us got shot, but I hit the ground pretty hard while I was trying to get behind some cover, and…well, I hurt my…"

"What, Chase? You hurt your what? Oh, my. You said urologist, didn't you? Did you break your…"

"Penny, no. I don't think you can actually break that particular body part, but I did get a nasty bruise. I'm taking some anti-inflammatory meds and antibiotics. The doctor says we'll take another look tomorrow."

"I'm so sorry. I wish you were home."

"I know. I wish I was there, too, but I need to wait for Clark to come out of surgery and wake up. I need him to know I didn't let him down."

She was quiet for a moment, then sighed. "I know, and I understand, but please come home soon."

"As soon as Clark wakes up, I'll be on the next flight home. I promise."

A nurse arrived with a hypodermic needle and a paper cup full of pills. My eyes locked on the needle. "Where's that going?"

She looked down at my chart and blushed. "Oh, no. This goes in your arm. It's just a steroid to help with the swelling."

For the first time since I'd left home, I actually laughed. The nurse tried to maintain her composure, but the humor of the moment was too much to overcome.

"Did you really think I was going to give you a shot…down there?"

I caught my breath. "I don't know. It's been a long day."

I rolled up the sleeve of my gown and presented my left arm. She gave me the injection, and I swallowed the pills.

"That was medicine for the pain, an anti-inflammatory, and something to help you sleep. We're moving you up to a room, and

I'll come up and start an IV antibiotic. That's what Dr. Duncan ordered." The comedy hour was over, and the nurse turned to leave.

"Before you go, would you mind checking on Clark Johnson? I guess he's still in surgery, but I'd like to know if he's all right."

She jotted down Clark's name on her pad. "Sure, Captain Fulton. I'll let you know how he's doing when I come up to start your IV."

"One more thing," I said. "Why does everybody keep calling me captain?"

She held up her clipboard and showed me paperwork hanging from the two chrome rings. "Because that's what it says on your chart. Fulton, Chase D., Captain."

I held up my hands. "Whatever you say."

She smiled. "By the way, I'm Captain Becky Clifton, so at least we have that much in common."

I nodded. "There is that."

As she walked out of the exam room, she met a medic with a wheelchair. Captain Becky glanced back at me and then at the wheelchair. "He'd probably prefer to walk rather than sit. He's had a rather delicate injury that may be a bit uncomfortable sitting down."

The medic shrugged. "If you say it's okay, that's good with me. I'm just here to take him up to his room."

Nurse Clifton looked at me inquisitively. "You'd rather walk, right?"

"Yes, I'd much rather walk. One more thing if you wouldn't mind."

"Sure, what is it?"

"There are three extremely filthy and exhausted men in the waiting room. One of them is enormous, and the other two are normal-sized humans. They've been through quite an ordeal over the past few days. Do you think you could—"

She held up her hand. "It's already taken care of. They've been fed and bathed because they were, as you said, filthy. They're being cared for. In fact, you'll probably see them upstairs if you don't fall asleep before they come up."

"Thanks, Captain Becky."

"You're welcome, Captain Chase."

Fifteen minutes later, I was seconds away from drifting off when Becky showed up with an IV bag and the best news I'd heard in years.

"Your soldier is out of surgery and awake in recovery. The doctors said whoever got him here saved his life. Something tells me that was you, so good job. If you're awake enough, you can go down and see him."

I was on my feet before she finished her sentence.

Clark was lying on his back with a hard plastic clamshell brace encompassing most of his torso. When he saw me, his trademark half-smile made its first appearance in days.

"Hey, College Boy. What are you doing here?"

His groggy voice reminded me of the times he'd slept like a child in the backseat of my airplane and awakened only after we'd landed and taxied to the ramp.

"Somebody had to come save your butt. I knew I should've never let you go running off without me."

He squeezed his eyes closed then widened them several times. "It's all a little hazy. Who else got hit?"

"All the good guys are alive."

I didn't see any reason to bring up the pilot's death yet.

The relief flashed in his eyes like a neon sign. "So, I guess that means the bad guys aren't."

I grinned. "Your team is some of the best there is at fighting fire with fire."

Pain replaced relief in his eyes when he tried to nod. "Ooh, who knew moving my head would feel like a lightning bolt down my spine?"

"Yeah, it's probably best if you don't move much. You got beat up pretty good."

He was obviously searching his memory, recalling the events that had put him on his back in an Air Force hospital three thousand miles from his objective. "I remember how it all started, but how I got here is a little fuzzy. We were escorting the train across the pass.

It was loaded with ammo and equipment, none of which needed to fall into the wrong hands. That's why they hired us to ride shotgun."

I fought the sleeping meds and tried to focus on his story as he struggled to piece it together.

As his mind retreated from the anesthetic amnesia, his story came with more confidence. "Brinkwater assigned a Hughes Five Hundred Little Bird to fly airborne scout and air support, and the bird was up when we got hit. The last grade westbound before the plateau is long and steep, so that's where the train was most vulnerable. If we were going to get hit, that's where it was going to happen. And it did."

I moved to the foot of his bed so he wouldn't have to turn his head to look at me.

"Singer was up in the chopper on overwatch. *That* guy behind *that* gun is exactly who you want on overwatch during an ambush."

I remembered the mission in Sol-Iletsk when Singer had pulled off some amazing long-range shots that I'd never attempt.

Clark continued his story. "So, Singer was airborne, and I was high front, just behind the engine. Snake and Smoke were on the right, and Mongo had the left. We figured they'd hit the lead engine to stop the train, so the Little Bird was out front about two hundred meters, and Singer was out the door on a sling. I had the high ground, so other than Singer and the pilot, I was the only one who could see everyone else. We were all focused toward the precipice of the plateau where the train would be at its slowest speed and easiest to board. Everything looked clean, and there was zero ground movement. I was starting to believe we'd made the top."

He began licking his lips and shifting his eyes. "Could you get me some water?"

Clark drank as if he'd spent a month in the desert. He looked like I'd always imagined John the Baptist to look: all wooly and wild-haired, but truly good beneath the animal exterior.

"It's good to see you awake, my friend. You had us all worried."

He smiled again. "It's good to see you, too, kid. No need to worry about me. You know what they say. Old Rangers never die—they just smell that way."

I laughed. "Yeah, well, you came pretty close."

A somber look overtook him. "How about I finish telling you what I remember, and you fill in the blanks for me?"

"I can do that."

"Yeah, so we'd almost made the top, and I was starting to relax a little. That's always when it happens, you know. You lower your guard, and some bastard punches you right in the nose."

I chuckled. "Yeah, I had a pretty good Krav Maga instructor who taught me all about that."

He grinned for the first time. "You should listen to that guy. He's smarter than you think."

In my initial training, I was taught how not to lose a fight, but Clark taught me how to win. I'd never stop learning from him.

"So, when it looked like we were out of the woods, I checked up, expecting the Little Bird to be coming back. That was the routine we'd worked out. The chopper would fly a scouting run in front and down the flanks every hour. When the pilot and spotter were satisfied no one was lying in wait to ambush us, they'd return and land back aboard the train. The pilot was pretty good. We called him Stump. He's a former Night Stalker from 160th, but he got his foot shot off, and they booted him out on a medical."

The 160th SOAR is the Special Operations Aviation Regiment out of Fort Campbell, Kentucky, the Army's most elite aviation unit. Most of their missions are flown under the cover of darkness at incredible speeds, thus earning the men the name Night Stalkers. They're some of the world's most highly respected helicopter combat pilots.

"Are you all right, man?"

I shook my head. "Yeah, I'm fine. They gave me sleeping meds, and they're kicking my butt."

"I'll try to be quick," he said as I made a feeble attempt to suppress a yawn. "Yeah, so I looked up, and the Little Bird was coming back all right, but it wasn't returning to base. It was on a gun run. Singer was pouring lead down on something, and the pilot was flying sideways as fast as that thing would go. I rolled over to see what Singer was shooting at, and my heart sank. We made an unforgivable tactical decision. We'd focused all of our attention out front and ignored our six. There were two squads of bandits on the train and advancing. Singer put down half a dozen while I was low-crawling and laying down as much fire as I could spray. Snake, Smoke, and Mongo were fighting and moving, determined to keep the bandits away from the engine, but they were everywhere...like ants with AK-47s. Stump was dodging rocks and trees and bullets in the Little Bird while Singer kept pouring lead down on the train. We were getting overrun, and there was nothing we could do except keep shooting until the well ran dry."

The sleeping meds lost the fight. I was wide awake and leaning in. "Keep going."

"I don't know what happened after that. I'd taken cover between two freight cars and was down to one magazine. That's when I saw the black smoke pour out of the Little Bird. I figure somebody put an AK-47 round through the turbine, and I watched the chopper disappear just as four Jihadis converged on me. I put two of them down, but I vaguely remember being knocked down between the freight cars. Then the lights went out."

In awe-stricken disbelief, I tried to construct the scene in my mind. A burning chopper, two squads of bad guys attacking a train guarded by five shooters. No matter how hard I tried, I couldn't imagine how it must've felt.

Smoke, showered and in clean clothes that almost fit, rapped on a metal pole holding the curtains. The weariness of battle shone on his face as he looked at Clark. "Welcome back, Baby Face. We missed you."

Clark's half-smile returned. "You too, Smoke. I'm sorry I got taken out of the fight."

"Yeah, we could've used you, but I guess you'd like to hear the rest of the story, huh?"

I answered for him. "Yeah, we would."

He propped up against the foot of the bed and picked up where Clark had left off. "You were giving 'em hell up top. Between you and Singer, I'd say you put down fifteen, maybe twenty before they got lucky enough to down the chopper and send you overboard. I don't know how you survived that fall, man. You looked like a ragdoll when you hit the ground. I've never seen anything like it."

Clark motioned for his cup of water. "What about Singer and Stump?"

"Singer got out as soon as they hit the Little Bird. He jumped with his fifty-cal and hit the ground fifty yards away from the train. He crushed his leg, but the fifty-cal survived."

"So that's how he broke his leg," I said.

"Yeah, that did it, but unlike Baby Face here, Singer wasn't out of the fight."

Clark rolled his eyes. "Thanks."

"Hey, I'm just bustin' your chops. Anyway, Singer started pumping fifty-cal rounds into the track and the wheels of the train, trying to get it stopped."

"He tried to stop a freight train with a rifle?" I said.

Smoke nodded with pride. "Yeah, that's right, and he did it, too. He got it stopped, but only temporarily. He disabled four of the rear cars and the rear engine, so the engineers had no choice but to stop."

More intrigued than ever, I sat wide-eyed in anticipation of what was to come.

"So, we kept fighting, and the bad guys kept going down until they figured they'd lost the fight and headed for the hills. Our best count was about thirty dead and maybe eight or ten who got away. Snake got his arm busted up while he was slugging it out with three or four of 'em. Everybody was out of bullets, and it came down to fist-to-cuffs. He was choking out one of the bastards, and another one hammered his rifle into Snake's arm until he let go. In the process, the jihadi nearly beat his buddy to death with the butt of his rifle."

"That's incredible," I muttered.

"Yeah, well, it ain't over yet. The engineers were pissed. They cut the last four cars and the rear engine loose and chugged off. We couldn't leave him and Singer and the pilot up there to die, so we bailed off. In hindsight, we probably should've taken the train from the engineers, but it was one of those make-a-decision-now scenarios, and we decided to bail out and collect our wounded."

Chapter 18
I Knew You'd Come

The sleeping meds finally won the battle, and I drifted off into the spirit world, imagining how that fight on top of the Khyber Pass must have felt.

"Are you ready for some breakfast, Captain Fulton?"

I dragged myself awake and tried to focus on the tray-wielding young man by my bed. Yawning and rubbing the sleep from my eyes, I said, "Yeah, thanks. Just put it there. What time is it?"

The uniformed breakfast bearer glanced down at his watch. "It's six forty-five, sir."

"Okay, thanks. Wait. What day is it?"

The airman looked at me as if I'd asked him to explain astrophysics.

"I've had a rough week. Can you just tell me what day it is?"

He stifled a chuckle. "Yes, sir. It's Sunday the twenty-seventh, two thousand two."

I lifted the lid from the tray, revealing eggs, sausage, fruit, toast, and coffee. "Looks good. Thanks for the breakfast and date check, but you don't have to call me sir."

"Yes, sir, I kinda do. It's like a rule. You're an officer, and I'm enlisted."

I shook my head. "No, I'm not really..."

His eyes lit up. "You're Special Forces or something, aren't you?"

I took a bite of toast and considered his question. "No, nothing like that. I just fell on a rock, and now I'm here with you." I leaned in to read his name tag. "Airman Griffin. I'm just a dude...just like you."

"Yeah, well, I don't know about that, but enjoy your breakfast, sir."

I'd never liked hospitals, but the Air Force hospital at Rhein-Main Air Base wasn't terrible. I didn't want to make it a long-term stay, but everyone I met made it as pleasant as possible.

I fought back the urge to call home. It was the middle of the night in the U.S., but that didn't stop me from wanting to hear Penny's voice.

After breakfast I showered and went on a quest to find Clark. Unlike most of my quests, that one was quite short. He was encamped in a room directly across the hall from mine and flirting with a nurse. The more she giggled, the more he poured on the charm.

I couldn't resist intervening. "Don't fall for it, ma'am. His wife and four kids—especially the twins—wouldn't approve."

Her giggles turned to scornful reproach. "Married?"

He didn't turn his head, but he shot me a look that would've been threatening if he'd been in any shape to get out of bed.

"I'm just kidding. He's not married, but the four kids thing... well, that's probably true."

Clark rolled his eyes. "Don't listen to him. He's a jerk, and he's just jealous."

"Yep, that's me, jealous. How are you feeling this morning?"

The nurse excused herself. "I'll be back to check on you in a bit, okay?"

Clark winked. "I'll be right here."

She giggled and made her exit.

"I'm doing okay, all things considered. It hurts a little, but now I guess it's my turn to embrace the suck, huh?"

"Yeah, I guess so. It's good to see you awake. You had us pretty scared for a few days."

His joviality was gone. "I guess the pilot didn't make it."

I shook my head. "No. Smoke said he rode the chopper into the side of the mountain. There wasn't enough of him left to bury."

He let out a long sigh. "I thought I was going with him. I was awake most of the first day after the fight, but I knew I wasn't coming off that mountain under my own power. I owe you a big one for coming to get me, brother."

I took his hand. "Is that what we're doing now? Keeping score? You know you'd have done the same if I'd been lying up there."

"Those bastards at Brinkwater left us up there to die, you know."

"Yeah, I know. It was a political decision. I figure they didn't want the repercussions of one of their teams getting shot up—and doing a little shooting of their own—on the wrong side of the border."

He scoffed. "Political decision or not, it was the wrong one. You don't hang good men out to dry like that."

I agreed. "Did you hear what Mongo did on the tarmac in Dushanbe?"

His eyes lit up. "Oh, do tell. There's nothing I love more than a good Mongo story. Well, except maybe that little brunette nurse you scared off."

"He destroyed a gurney, put out Jerry Beard's lights, and beat a landing gear door off the Brinkwater jet."

His smile was textbook Clark Johnson. "That's my Mongo."

"I guess those guys will be looking for work now."

He tried to nod but stopped himself. "Yeah, they're all good operators. They'll find gigs, though they may not be exactly what they want. Guys like that don't make very good security guards at the mall."

I tried to picture Mongo in a rent-a-cop uniform. "I guess you've got a point. Maybe we can find a few things for them to do until something better comes along."

He shot me a look. "You live on a boat with your girlfriend, and I live in a one-bedroom apartment...sometimes. What do we have to offer those guys?"

I pulled up a chair. "A few things have changed since you took your little mountaintop vacation."

He raised his eyebrows. "Oh, let's hear it."

"Try to keep up. A letter from my father showed up in Saint Augustine. I inherited Bonaventure Plantation from the Judge, who turns out to be my great uncle or something like that. Penny and I got married. Bimini, Dennis Crowe's girlfriend from the boat in Greece, is a DIA officer. And we flew you off that mountain in a Russian Hip."

He showed no reaction. "How long was I unconscious?"

"Not long enough for all of that to make sense, but I don't mess around."

He focused on a ceiling tile. "Well, your father has been dead for a long time, so it's weird to get a letter from him. What the hell are you going to do with a pecan plantation? Clearly, the Judge is insane, so it makes sense he's related to you. I knew Bimini was a plant. The Hip was the perfect choice, but I can't wait to hear where you got it. And married?"

I laughed. "Nice job keeping up. And yes, married. The Judge married us the day I flew out to come pull your butt out of the fire. We'll do a real ceremony at some point since I didn't have a best man. You were off getting knocked off a train ten thousand miles away."

"Congratulations, Chase. Oh, and thanks again for coming to get me. I knew you'd come."

We spent the rest of the morning catching up and filling in missing details for each other.

Around ten thirty, Dr. Rush came strolling in. "Well, looks who's awake. How are you feeling, Master Sergeant Johnson?"

Clark raised his hand to shake. "I've had better days, but not lately."

The doctor shot me a glance. "How about you, Captain Fulton? How are you feeling this morning?"

Clark coughed. "Captain?"

I shot him a look. "That's right, Sergeant. Show some respect."

I turned back to Dr. Rush. "I'm in better shape than him, but the urologist says we may be looking at some surgery. I have to be honest. She freaks me out a little."

He patted me on the shoulder. "I'm sure you'll be fine."

Dr. Rush thumbed through the chart hanging on the foot of Clark's bed. "The surgeon who put you back together will be making rounds any minute now. I'm sure he'll be glad to see you in such good spirits." The doctor made his exit.

"Who was that?" Clark said.

"Oh, that was Dr. Franklin Rush. He's a trauma surgeon and emergency med doc. He was the physician on the Air Force medivac flight from Dushanbe to Frankfort."

Just as Dr. Rush had predicted, an Air Force colonel in BDUs strolled into Clark's room as if he were taking a morning walk through the park. "Good morning, Master Sergeant Johnson. I'm Dr. Hatcher, the neurosurgeon who drew the short straw last night and had to slice into your back."

Clark reached up to shake his hand. "I'm sorry you drew the short straw, but I'm thankful you were here. From what I heard, I was in a mess."

The colonel turned to me. "And who might you be?"

Clark beat me to the punch. "Apparently, he's Captain Fulton, the commando who led the expedition to get us off that mountain."

I stood and offered my hand. "Nice to meet you, Dr. Hatcher. Thank you for what you did for Clark...I mean Master Sergeant Johnson."

He waved a dismissive hand. "Ah, don't thank me. Mine was the easy part. It's you who deserves the thanks"—he motioned toward Clark—"especially from him."

I glanced at my partner and then back to the colonel. "Anybody can do what I do. You're the lifesaver."

"Well, I don't know about that, Captain, but would you mind giving us a few minutes?"

I hurried toward the door. "Not at all. I'm just across the hall if you need me."

* * *

Penny answered as if she'd been holding the phone, anticipating my call.

"Good morning, Mrs. Fulton."

She giggled. "Good morning to you, Mr. Fulton. How is your, um, injury?"

"Sore," I admitted, "but I'll survive. How are things there?"

"Things are good. Maebelle brought some orange juice she squeezed last night, and it's the best I've ever had. I just wish you were here to enjoy it with me."

"I'll be home soon. Clark's doing great, so I should be headed home tonight after I see Dr. Duncan again. You said you have some news I'm not going to believe."

"Yes! Chase, it was the weirdest thing. I took one of the horses out for a ride by the river, and I saw two guys who I thought were fishermen in a boat up by the old paper mill. You know how sound travels on the water? I could hear them talking, but they weren't speaking English."

There were a lot of people who spoke a lot of languages other than English, so that wasn't particularly intriguing, but Penny's level of excitement over the event had my attention. "Okay. What language were they speaking?"

"If it wasn't Russian, it was something a lot like it."

My interest was piqued. Men speaking Russian, or something like it, less than three miles from Naval Submarine Base Kings Bay was definitely interesting.

"Did you tell anyone?"

"Yeah, I told the Judge, and he called a guy he knows at the base."

"What guy?"

"I don't know. A security guy or something. He's coming to talk to me today."

I closed the door to my room. "Are you sure it was Russian?"

"No, but you know I'm learning to speak a little Russian because you think it sounds sexy. It sounded a lot like the CDs I've been listening to."

"I don't think it's sexy," I argued.

"Oh, come on, Chase. I'm smarter than that, and I know what you like."

I tried to get us back on track. "Just be careful what you tell this security guy, even if he is a friend of the Judge. He doesn't need to know what I—what *we*—do. Did the guys in the boat see you?"

"Yes, but like I said, I was on the horse and pretended not to see them, and we galloped away."

"But you're sure they saw you?"

"Yeah, I'm sure. They looked right at me and immediately stopped talking."

There was no reasonable explanation for a pair of Russians to be in a boat on the North River at Bonaventure. The more I thought about what it could mean, the more I knew I had to put my feet back on the ground in Georgia before Penny found herself neck-deep in more trouble than even I could get her out of.

"I'm on my way!"

Chapter 19
Baby, I'm Coming Home

There was no way I could know what was happening in Saint Marys all the way from Frankfurt, so getting on a plane suddenly became my priority. If Penny was right about two men speaking Russian in a boat downstream from a nuclear submarine base, I needed to be there.

Clark's visit from the surgeon lasted longer than my phone call with Penny, so I was chomping at the bit to get back in his room. When the doctor finally emerged, I pushed by him like a fat guy at a buffet.

My partner looked up. "Wow. Miss me that much?"

"Sorry, I just got off the phone with Penny, and there's something going on at home. I need to get back to the States as soon as possible."

Even in his narcotic euphoria, he frowned in concern. "What is it?"

"I'm not sure yet, but she thinks she heard a couple of guys speaking Russian in a boat near Kings Bay sub base. I'm not sure what that means, if anything, but it's probably best I get home tonight."

He sucked air through his teeth as he considered what I'd said. "I don't see how that could be anything good. Did she call the cops at the base?"

"No, she didn't, but the Judge called a friend who works in security at the base, and he's coming out to interview Penny today."

He sighed. "You should definitely be there for that interview."

I looked at my watch. "I don't think that's possible."

He rolled his eyes. "Come on, Chase. How many things are truly impossible? Between Skipper and my dad, they can probably find a way to teleport you home."

"I can't believe I haven't called either of them since we've been in Germany. Skipper's going to kill me."

He almost smiled. "Go make some calls and let me know before you leave. Maybe they'll let me go with you."

I laughed. "Yeah, I'm sure they'll discharge you any minute now. What did the surgeon have to say?"

"Go make the calls. I'll tell you about it later."

I had my phone to my ear before I made it back to my room.

Skipper's tone made it clear she was unapologetically furious with me. "Where are you? Why haven't you checked in? This is completely unacceptable, Chase."

"I'm in Germany at the hospital on the Air Force base, and—"

She giggled. "Yeah, I know. I talked to Penny, and I can track your sat-phone, remember? How's Clark?"

"That's what I need…my analyst busting my chops."

"Hey. I'm not *your* analyst. You're *my* operator."

"Oh, is that how it is?"

"Yes, it is. Now how's Clark?"

"He's going to be fine. The surgery went well, and he's awake and in good spirits. I have to leave him here and fly home as soon as possible. That's part of the reason I'm calling. Penny—"

She interrupted again. "Yeah, I also know that. We girls stay connected, unlike you good-for-nothing men in the field."

"I'm not sure I'm comfortable with you knowing every move I make."

"Get used to it, operator. You're booked on Lufthansa from Frankfurt to Miami, leaving in two hours, so you better find a doctor to sign you out of there, and then get your butt to the airport."

"You're the best analyst I've ever had, Skipper."

"Hey, I thought we talked about that. I have you—not the other way around."

"Whatever you say. Oh, and did you—"

"I'm on it. I don't have any answers yet, but I can't think of any non-sinister reason anyone would be speaking Russian on the North River in Saint Marys, Georgia."

"Okay, I should've known you'd be way ahead of me. I'll see you soon. Or maybe not. Where are you?"

"I'm still in Maryland, but I'm coming to Bonaventure, so yeah, you'll see me soon. Don't miss your plane."

I hung up and pushed through the door back into Clark's room. "Skipper booked me a..."

A pair of doctors in white lab coats turned to face me.

"I'm so sorry. I didn't know you were in here."

Clark spoke up. "It's okay, Captain. Come on in. These are two more of the surgeons who had their hands in me last night. I can't remember their names, but one of them is an ortho guy, and the other is the lung guy."

They introduced themselves, but I didn't listen.

"Look, I'm sorry, but we have an operational movement to discuss. Can you give us three minutes?"

The two doctors looked at each other as if I'd asked them to eat a frog. Apparently, they weren't accustomed to having people ask them to wait. I liked the turning of the tables.

I held the door open. "Thank you. We'll only be a couple of minutes. Of course, if both of you have top-secret clearances, a need to know, and a signed nondisclosure agreement, you can stay."

The surgeons stepped into the hallway, shaking their heads.

"Skipper has me booked on a flight in less than two hours, so I have to go, but I'll be back if this Russian thing turns out to be nothing. The rest of the team is still here. When you see them, ask if they'd be interested in doing some work for us until they get a better offer. We can't offer anything permanent, but offering short-term work is the least we can do since Brinkwater crapped on them."

He focused on me, obviously trying to overcome the effects of the painkillers. "Okay, I'll talk to them. Call me when you get home."

"It'll be the middle of the night, but I'll call you when I'm sure you'll be awake. I'm sorry I have to run, but there's no other option."

"No, no. Go. I understand. But, hey, before you leave...thanks again for coming to get us. We were in a heap of trouble up there."

I put my hand on his shoulder. "You never have to thank me... ever."

* * *

The Lufthansa flight lifted out of Frankfurt International Airport, and I pulled down the window shade, hoping to get a few hours of sleep. I should've known my brain wasn't going to let that happen. Instead of sleep, I plowed through hundreds of possibilities why two men would be speaking a Russian-sounding language in Saint Marys.

"*Bist du Amerikaner?*"

I turned to the lady in the next seat. She appeared to be in her fifties, trim, and quite attractive, with dark hair falling across her shoulders in the style of a much younger woman.

"*Ja, ich bin Amerikaner. Und Sie?*" I answered in German before realizing I'd done so.

The woman smiled. "Your German is quite good for an American."

I blushed. "Thank you, and your English is quite good, even for an American."

She continued her bright smile. "That's funny."

"It's true."

She placed her hand on my arm. "Forgive me for intruding, but are you a soldier?"

"No, ma'am. Why would you ask?"

Her smile faded. "You sit and move like a soldier, and you wear the scars on your skin and in your eyes."

I shifted my body to face her. "How do you know so much about soldiers, ma'am? I'm Chase, by the way."

"I am Gretta. A soldier once loved me, and I have loved him always."

Intrigued, I let my eyes ask the question without voicing the words.

She ducked her head. "He died in the war, or so they tell me. I've never seen his body, so until I do, I'm still his wife."

Suddenly, the woman became Penny thirty years in the future. I could almost hear her telling some stranger on a plane that she still loved a man whose slain body she'd never seen.

Taking her hand, I said, "I'm so sorry, Gretta. May I ask how long ago?"

Gretta wiped a tear from her eye. "Thirty years ago tomorrow is when the men came to my door to tell me Lawrence was missing in action and presumed dead."

The psychologist in me wanted to console and encourage her to move on after spending half of her life in grief, but the soldier in me wanted to know how it felt to be the wife of a combatant. The soldier won the internal battle. "How long were you married?"

She held up her left hand and displayed a simple silver band. "It'll be thirty-two years in June of this year. Would you like for me to tell you the story of how we met?"

I couldn't suppress my smile. "Yes, I'd like that very much."

Gretta raised her hand, signaling for the flight attendant. "I'm going to need a drink before we start. I hope you don't mind."

"Not at all," I said.

The perky young flight attendant leaned down, and in beautiful German, asked, "What would you like, ma'am?"

"I'd like a nice champagne and a good scotch for my new friend."

"Yes, ma'am. Of course," came the reply in perfect English.

Gretta turned to me with concern on her face. "You are a scotch man, no? You look like a scotch man to me."

I grinned. "Yes, ma'am. Scotch is always a good choice."

"I thought you might need a drink, too. I can't promise I won't cry a little."

"I can't make that promise, either," I said to reassure her.

The drinks arrived before Gretta began her story, and we touched glasses.

"To new friends," I offered.

She held up her glass. "*Prost!*"

With her champagne flute held delicately in her hand, she stared into the golden wine as the tiny bubbles made their way to the top. "He was the most beautiful man I'd ever seen, but of course I'd never seen too many. I was a silly girl just after my first year at university. It was May of 1969, and I was in Paris studying language." She paused, almost giggled, and placed her hand on my arm. "Who am I kidding? I was drinking French wine, eating cheese, and dancing with every charming boy who'd ask. Have you been to Paris?"

I could see the beautiful nineteen-year-old German girl in her eyes. "No, ma'am. I've not seen Paris yet."

"Go in the springtime, and for God's sake, stop calling me ma'am."

I nodded and enjoyed another sip of my relatively good airline scotch.

"I was at a sidewalk café with a platter of cheese, a bottle of Bordeaux, and a book in my hands when this beautiful American man came strutting down the street with four of his friends and five French girls hanging on their arms and every word. You can always tell the American boys anywhere in the world. They have that look and that confidence like Russian men, but with manners. You American boys always have the manners. Forgive me for getting off track, won't you?"

"There's nothing to forgive. It's your story, and we have five hours left together. I'm not going anywhere."

She continued holding my arm as she became animated. "Lawrence was the boy doing the talking and strolling down the Rue Pierre Charron. I'll never forget it. I lowered the book I'd been pretending to read and let my eyes find his. Imagine my delight when I found he was looking straight back at me. He was so tall and strong, like you, and he walked like a movie star…until a child chasing a balloon managed to trip him, sending him stumbling and tumbling like a circus clown. I covered my mouth so he couldn't see me laughing. I just knew he would climb back to his feet, dust himself off, and never look back at me again. But that's not what he did. He hopped up, chased the boy's balloon until he'd caught it, and delivered it back to him. Oh, my schoolgirl heart fluttered, and I couldn't take my eyes off him. There was this big beautiful man with a heart for children and a smile like the sun. I was instantly and helplessly in love with him. And you'll never believe what he did next."

I was mesmerized and hanging on every word of her story. "What? What did he do?"

"He came over, tipped his hat, and in the worst French I've ever heard, said, 'I hope you enjoyed my act. I'll be doing a juggling show on the corner later tonight. You should come.' Oh, I giggled with such delight and first replied in French, saying I'd loved his act and I would pay at least a franc to see him juggle. Well, he stuffed his hat in his pocket and sat down at the table across from me. Then he stuck up his finger for the waiter to bring another wine glass. His friends were clamoring for him to rejoin them in the street, but he waved them away. We drank wine, ate cheese and baguettes, and talked until the sun sank into the trees. He took me dancing long into the night. Then we held hands and strolled along the River Seine, counting the stars and falling in love."

She finished her champagne and waved for another. I'd been so wrapped up in her story I noticed I'd only taken one small drink. She seemed to notice as well, and the smirk on her face said she liked that I was more interested in her story than in my drink.

Gretta accepted another flute of champagne from the flight attendant and quickly turned back to me. "I hope I'm not boring you."

"Not at all. Quite the contrary, in fact. I'm fascinated."

"In that case, I'll continue. I fell in love with Lawrence a thousand times that first night together and a thousand more every night after that. He was so kind and attentive. When I asked why he was in Paris, what he told me both terrified me and immediately broke my heart."

Chapter 20
The Warrior in Me

If Gretta had merely been holding my attention before that powerful statement, she was in absolute possession of it afterward.

"What did he tell you that was so devastating?"

She tried to smile. "Lawrence told me he was a soldier...or would soon be a soldier. He was enrolled in the ROTC and had one more year of university before he'd become an officer in the Army. Falling in love with an American soldier in 1969 was the equivalent of playing Russian roulette with a fully loaded gun. The only thing I knew about American men was they were drafted or volunteered, and then they died in Vietnam. Do you know why there are so many beautiful Russian girls looking for husbands all over the world?"

I shook my head but didn't speak.

"All the Russian men died in World War Two. Well, of course not all the men, but the number was around twenty-six million, leaving twenty percent more women than men in the former Soviet Union. I just knew marrying an American soldier would be the worst thing a girl could do, but I was so much in love with Lawrence."

She paused, again staring at her champagne. I don't know where her mind took her at that moment, but I suspect it was back to the banks of the River Seine in 1969.

"I'm sorry," she said. "I was just remembering how badly I was torn between loving a man who'd surely be dead in a year and finishing my studies at university. In the end, I decided that loving

Lawrence for a single hour would be worth more than anything I could ever do without him. So, I followed him back to the States, and we were married before Christmas. My parents were furious, but I'd never been happier. And I didn't think any girl had ever been as much in love as I was.

"Lawrence graduated in the spring, and they commissioned him as second lieutenant in the Army. He looked so dapper and beautiful in his uniform. I know men aren't supposed to be beautiful, but oh, he was handsome beyond the wildest dreams of any girl that age. The Army ordered him off to Camp Rucker in Alabama to learn to fly helicopters. Growing up in Germany, I'd never heard of Alabama, and I certainly didn't know anyone who could fly a helicopter. We packed up what few belongings we had and drove to Camp Rucker in our 1956 Chevrolet. It was all such an exotic and exciting adventure for me.

"Lawrence and I both knew he'd be going to Vietnam as soon as he graduated from flight school, but neither of us would mention it. We lived our lives as if we'd be together forever. He taught me how to fish in the Pea River near the tiny house we rented on what little money the Army paid him. Sometimes, when he didn't have to fly on the weekends, we'd go to Panama City on the Gulf of Mexico and play together on the beach. He even took me sailing twice. It was the best time of my life. I can't tell you how grand it was."

I finally took another sip of my scotch. "It sounds absolutely delightful. I'm so glad you had that time with him."

"Oh, me too. The joy I knew in those days was worth all the pain and loneliness I've known since then."

She took another drink of her champagne. "Would you mind raising the shade so I can look outside?"

"Of course not." I slid the white shade back into its notch, and she stared through the thick glass for several long minutes.

A tear escaped the corner of her eye. "He graduated on a Tuesday afternoon, and they let me pin his wings onto his uniform. I was so proud of him, and those wings made him look ten feet tall.

"When the graduation ceremony was over, the somber reality of what would come next overtook the forty-five new pilots and their families as they left the hall with heavy hearts burdened with what each of them knew all too well. That was true, of course, for everyone except Lawrence and me. It was raining that afternoon, and he held the umbrella for me as we walked outside and onto the flight line, where there must have been a thousand helicopters. We climbed inside one of them. It was a Huey. Do you know what that is?"

I nodded. "Oh, yes. I know exactly what that is."

She held my arm even tighter. "Well, Lawrence let me sit in the pilot's seat, and he took my finger in his hand and told me what every knob and switch did as we touched each of them. I didn't understand anything he was telling me, but I loved the feel of my hand in his and the excitement in his voice. He loved that helicopter, and more than that, he loved me."

She grew quiet and let a conspiratorial look come across her face before scanning the cabin around us. Most of the passengers were asleep, but the ones who weren't obviously had no interest in Gretta's story. She leaned in and whispered, "When he finished showing me the cockpit, we made love in the back of that Huey with the rain pouring down all around us—right there on that airport in the middle of the afternoon. Can you believe that?"

I lowered my head. "At this point, Gretta, I can believe anything."

"After we'd done, well, you know—that—we drove back to our little rented house by the river. I knew it would happen, and it did. We were sitting on the front porch swing, watching the rain and holding each other like young lovers do, when he said, 'I've got orders.' I pretended not to hear him, but the words echoed in my head like a ringing church bell, and I held him ever tighter. When I finally gathered the courage to speak, I whispered, 'When?'"

I could see the anguish of that day playing in her eyes as she sat stoically beside me. I expected her to burst into tears, but she kept talking as if the story were someone else's.

"He said, 'Monday,' and I was over the moon. That meant we had the rest of the week and the weekend—five whole days together before he'd have to leave. We spent every second together, loving each other as if we'd never see each other again. For two days, we walked a thousand miles on the beach and counted every star in the sky, just like we'd done in Paris the night we met.

"As much as we both didn't want it to happen, Monday came, and he had to go. I cried myself to sleep that night and every night after for as long as I can remember. Occasionally, a letter would come, and he'd tell me about the men in his unit and how good they were and how much he was learning from them. He'd reassure me that he wasn't in any danger like the infantrymen on the ground. He tried to keep me from worrying, but it was no use. I worried and cried every day. And I wrote to him every night.

"The last letter I wrote to him was the one I knew would make him the happiest of all. I told him when his tour was over and he came home, I'd look very different than I did when he left. I told him I'd be as fat as an elephant and he'd be a father soon thereafter."

I almost dropped my glass. "You were pregnant!"

She beamed. "Oh, yes, I was pregnant, and it was the best thing that could ever be. Lawrence wanted a dozen children—six boys and six girls—and he wanted to fly for Pan Am when the war was over. We'd talked about how glorious our life would be after the war and how we'd see the world together, and how we'd take the kids everywhere."

Suddenly, her beautifully animated smile dissolved into sadness. "He never read that letter. He never knew I was pregnant. Eight days after I'd licked, stamped, and mailed it, two Army officers knocked on the door of our little house. There was only one reason two officers came to anyone's house in those days. Lawrence had been shot down near the border of Vietnam, Cambodia, and Laos. No one could've survived the crash, they said, but they didn't know Lawrence. They didn't know how strong and brave he was."

The flight attendant apparently sensed what was happening and delivered another glass of champagne.

Gretta nodded her thanks and turned back to me. "I cried for days without stopping. I couldn't eat or sleep. All I could do was cry.

I loved him more than anyone had ever been loved. I thought it was the worst pain anyone could endure until I lost the baby a week later."

My stomach churned in agony for her, but she kept talking.

"They never found Lawrence's body, and there was never a report of him being in a POW camp. I never believed he was dead. I've believed for thirty years that he survived the crash and evaded being captured. Sometimes I still believe he's living in the jungle, waiting for someone to come find him, and praying every night that he'll get to come home to me."

Silence hung over us for what felt like hours. I was without words, and Gretta silently sobbed.

She took my hand. "Are you married, Chase?"

The question pierced my heart. "Yes, ma'am, I am."

"What's her name?"

"Her name is Nicole, but everyone calls her Penny because when she was a little girl, her father said she wasn't big enough to be a nickel, so she must be a penny."

She looked into my eyes as if she could see into my soul. "War is the worst thing there is, and love is the very best. The Army forgot about Lawrence. They gave me a flag, and now they send a pension check every month, but the Army let him die in their minds. They forgot about him, but I never did."

Gretta traced the scars on the back of my hand with her fingertip. "Whatever you are, Chase, soldier or otherwise, never forget what I've told you. Cling to and cherish the ones who truly love you, for they will never let you die. No matter how dense the jungle and how remote the odds, they'll never let you die."

Maybe the world is utter chaos and nothing happens for any reason at all, but sitting beside Gretta and hearing her story on a plane I should've never been aboard, made me believe an angel with the slightest German accent had been sent to help me understand what truly had meaning. Suddenly, the warrior in me wanted to beat his sword into a plowshare and have a dozen babies with the woman who loved me—the woman who'd never let me die.

Chapter 21
Going to be Fun

Dominic met me at the arrival gate at Miami International. "It's good to see you home, Chase. How's Clark?"

"He'll be okay. His back was broken, but the team kept him stable on the mountain, and we got him to the hospital in time. He's got a few pounds of metal in his back now, but apparently the nerves survived."

Dominic exhaled a sigh of obvious relief. "That's great news. I'll never be able to thank you for getting him off that mountain. How's the rest of the team?"

"They're okay. One of them has a badly broken leg, but it'll heal, and another has an injury like mine. His wrist and hand are in bad shape, but"—I held up my right hand—"that's a wound that can be overcome."

Dominic's shoulders relaxed, and the tension in his face dissolved. "It sounds like it could have been a lot worse. I'm serious, Chase. I owe you for what you did to get my son and keep him alive, and I have no idea how I'll ever repay you."

"He's as much my brother as your son. I'd wade through Hell or climb any mountain for him. You don't owe me anything, but I'd love a ride to Saint Marys if you know anybody going that way."

His mouth curled into the half-smile I'd seen a thousand times on his son's face. "I think we can handle that."

Forty-five minutes later, I was asleep aboard a King Air, north-bound off the east coast of Florida. I didn't know who owned the plane or who the pilots were, but I was thankful for the ride. Through the small round window, I saw Penny standing on the ramp at Saint Marys Airport. I carefully descended the stairs from the plane, the pain in my abdomen more pronounced than I wanted.

"It's so good to have you home."

Feeling Penny in my arms was home for me. It didn't matter what time zone or even what country as I was in, she was what home would always feel like for me.

"It's good to be home."

I thanked the pilots and offered to have the King Air fueled, but they refused.

The older of the two pilots said, "It was a pleasure, sir. Everything is taken care of. Is there anything else we can do for you before we go?"

I shook both of their hands. "You've done more than enough. Thanks, guys."

We rode back to Bonaventure Plantation in a car Penny borrowed from the Judge.

"So, you go first. Tell me everything. Is everybody okay? Is Clark okay? When's he coming home? Are you okay? You're moving kinda slow. I've been so worried about you."

The day I met Penny in Charleston, a year before, the second thing I noticed about her was her energy. She talked fast when she was excited, and it always seemed like she had more to say than her mouth could spit out. It amused me then, and it never stopped making me smile.

"Well, you're wound up," I said through a tired smile.

"Yeah, well, my new husband just ran off on some mountain climbing expedition the day of our wedding, and a lot's happened while he was gone. You know how it is."

"That guy sounds like a real jerk. Who would run off on his wedding day?"

"No, he's not a jerk…most of the time. Actually, the reason he ran off is why I love him the most. He cares more about other people than about himself." She grinned. "You're pretty special, Chase."

"I'd rather stick to being a jerk. There's less pressure that way."

She rolled her eyes. "Cut it out. Tell me what happened over there."

"We'll talk about that later. Let's get back to *Aegis*. I want to hear about your Russian-speaking boaters and your interview with the security guy from the base."

We pulled into Bonaventure Plantation as the Judge came ambling down the steps. "Welcome home, son. Is everybody okay?"

"They will be, Judge. Thanks for looking after Penny while I was gone."

"That girl doesn't need anybody to look after her. She's more capable of taking care of herself than most men I know."

"You're right about that," I said. "We're going to hang out on the boat for a while. We'd love to have you join us."

"No, no. You two have a lot to talk about, I'm sure. I just wanted to welcome you home. Come see me at the house later if you'd like."

"We'll do that, Judge. It's good to be home."

My boat was a different kind of home for me. I was comfortable and relaxed aboard *Aegis*, and I wondered if I'd ever feel the same on land.

Penny poured two glasses of tea, and we sat on the upper deck. Even in late January, the coastal Georgia low country was warm enough to enjoy the midday sun and light breeze.

"Okay, let's start with what you saw when you went riding."

She slid forward on the settee. "It's like I told you on the phone. I went for a ride on one of the horses, and through the trees I saw two guys in a boat near the old plant. The horse noticed them, too, and stopped. He looked at the men for a moment and then started eating some grass. That's when I heard them talking, and it sounded Russian. I don't know enough yet to know what they were saying, but it was definitely Russian—or something like it. Does that make sense?"

"It makes perfect sense," I said. "I only wish you knew what they were saying."

"Yeah, that's what Agent Hunter said."

"Who's Agent Hunter?"

"He's the security guy from the base. The Judge knows him and says he's the guy I needed to tell about the men in the boat."

I nodded. "Okay, so this guy, Hunter…. Tell me about him."

She pursed her lips. "I don't know. He seems like a nice enough guy. He's no-nonsense, though. He asks questions, and he's quick to let you know if you don't give him the answer he wants."

"I like guys like that. At least you always know where you stand."

"Yeah, he seems like a straight shooter. Anyway, he wanted to know what time it was when I saw them, and he wanted a description of their boat. And he wanted me to try repeating what they said, but I couldn't."

"And you're pretty sure they saw you?"

"Oh, yeah. I know they saw me. It's hard to hide on a horse in an open field."

"Did they try to chase you?"

She shook her head. "No, that would've been a waste of time. They'd never catch me. They just started the boat and motored away."

"How close were they? Did they get a good look at you?"

She focused up the slope toward the plantation house. "Maybe a little farther than from here to the house."

I surveyed the two-hundred-foot expanse of lawn between *Aegis* and the house. "That's a long way. They might have trouble picking you out of a lineup, and that's a good thing."

"That's exactly what Agent Hunter said."

"Could you ID either of the two men if you saw them again?"

She laughed. "You and Hunter must've gone to the same school. He asked the same questions."

I wanted to meet Hunter. "Okay, so could you?"

She thought about it for a few seconds. "I might recognize their voices, but I'm not sure. I told Hunter the same thing."

"Did Hunter ask what you're doing here?"

She took a long drink of her tea. "Yeah, he did, and I didn't know what to say. I'm a terrible liar, so I decided to be vague. I told him we were guests of the Judge and we'd be here a few days, maybe longer."

"What was his response?"

"He just said, 'I see.'"

I laughed. "I like this Hunter guy already. What did you tell him about me?"

She wrinkled her nose. "That's the part I really sucked at. I said you were unexpectedly called away for work and you'd probably be back today."

"Let me guess. He wanted to know what kind of work I did."

"Yes, he did, and I told him you were a consultant overseas. That's when he looked at *Aegis* and said that the consulting business must be good."

"I'd better talk to Hunter. Did you get his card?"

She reached into her pocket. "Of course."

I read the blue and white official-looking card.

United States Naval Criminal Investigative Service
Special Agent Stone W. Hunter

Other than learning about Hunter, Penny didn't reveal anything I hadn't already known, so we headed up the pathway to talk with the Judge.

"Oh, yeah. I've known Hunter for two or three years now... maybe longer," the Judge said. "He's not really a cop. He's more of a security specialist, you might say. He draws a disability retirement from the Air Force. I think he's been with NCIS since the Air Force retired him. I'm not sure how old he is, but to me, anybody under seventy is still a kid. I reckon he's around thirty or something like that, wouldn't you say, Miss Penny?"

Penny nodded. "Yes, sir. I'd say that's about right."

I was making mental notes. "What did he do in the Air Force?"

The Judge made a pistol with his thumb and index finger and aimed it directly at me. "Now you're asking the right questions, son. Have you ever heard of the Air Force Combat Controllers?"

Hunter just became a lot more interesting. "I've read and heard a little about the CCTs. If I'm not mistaken, they're air traffic controllers who've been through most of the same schools as the SEALs and Green Berets. They deploy with the special operations forces and call air strikes and manage battlefield airspace. Isn't that right?"

The Judge shrugged. "You know more about them than I do. I've never been able to get him to talk much about it. He did tell me he got shot up in Central America on some drug interdiction stuff and that's why the Air Force sent him packing. It sounded like he'd rather still be out there with the air commandos."

I tried to take in what the Judge was telling me, but it was clear I was going to have to talk with Hunter. "Do you think he'll talk to me?"

The Judge laughed. "No, but he'll listen to you talk."

"I thought that might be the case. I believe I'll give good ol' Agent Hunter a call."

* * *

Hunter took my call and agreed to meet me for breakfast. "Do you know where Spencer House is?"

"I can find it. We're staying at Bonaventure, and Maebelle has a friend who works there."

"Yeah, I know where you're staying," Hunter said. "And Seth is Maebelle's...friend. I'll meet you there at seven thirty tomorrow morning."

Penny was right. No nonsense.

Hunter wasn't what I'd expected. Instead of the six-foot-four-inch linebacker I'd envisioned, he was around five-foot-eight and maybe one-ninety with a neatly trimmed beard and sandy red hair. He wasn't a physically imposing figure, but he wore an air of confidence that left little room for doubt that he was in charge.

"Good morning, Mr. Fulton. I'm Special Agent Stone Hunter."

I stuck my hand in his. "It's nice to meet you, Agent Hunter. I've heard a lot about you in the last twenty-four hours."

"You can drop the *agent*. Hunter is fine."

"Okay, then. Hunter it is."

We had a seat at an antique oak table in a beautifully decorated dining room inside Spencer House.

A bearded man about my age stepped through the door from the kitchen. "Good morning. I'm Seth. Help yourselves to the coffee, hot tea, and juice. There's fresh banana bread made by a friend of mine. I think you guys might know Maebelle." He finished describing what was on the buffet and then took our omelette orders.

Penny whispered, "Yep, Maebelle was right. He's gorgeous."

I elbowed her. "You're a married woman. Behave yourself."

"Yeah, but my husband ran off on our wedding night. Remember?"

"Touché."

With no one else in the dining room, Hunter's interrogation began. "So, you're an overseas consultant, I hear. What do you consult on?"

I glanced at Penny. "Well, that's not entirely true, but I suspect you already knew that."

"Actually, Mr. Fulton, I'm having trouble finding anything at all about you other than you used to play baseball at UGA. After that, you've become a ghost."

"You can drop the Mr. Fulton and just call me Chase."

He nodded. "Fair enough, Chase. So, what is it that makes your wife Penny so sure she can recognize the Russian language? Congratulations, by the way."

I considered how far to take the conversation in public. "I speak a little Russian. It helps with my work. And Penny's learning a few words just for fun."

"Fun. I've never heard of anyone learning Russian for fun."

Instead of responding, I dug into my omelette.

Apparently sensing I wasn't going to continue playing his game about learning Russian, Hunter said, "So, this consulting work of yours. Tell me about that."

"What do you want to know?" I asked through a mouthful of steaming eggs.

"You just came back from one of these consulting trips, right?"

I nodded.

"Then you probably wouldn't mind showing me your passport?"

Ah, Hunter was good. I was going to have a lot of fun.

Chapter 22
A Nonanswer

We finished our breakfast, and I invited Hunter back to the boat, ostensibly to have a look at my passport. He accepted.

"This is quite a boat, Chase. We don't see many like this up here."

"Thanks. It's home for us. We do a lot of traveling, and we like this area. You'll probably be seeing quite a bit more of us around."

He ignored my comment. "So, your passport?"

I pointed into the main salon. "Let's go inside. Would you care for some more coffee or maybe a mimosa?"

He strolled through the doorway. "Sure, another cup of coffee would be great."

Penny set three mugs on the table. "Are you two dogs going to keep circling and growling at each other, or finally sniff each other's butts and decide you're friends?"

For the first time, Hunter laughed. "Well now, that's quite a way to put it."

I joined the laughing. "I'm not much of a butt sniffer, so why don't we cut to the chase, so to speak?"

Hunter took a sip of his coffee. "Okay, I'll go first. Retired Air Force, early retirement, got hurt. Went to work for NCIS and ended up here. That's my story. Now let's hear yours."

"That's a short story," I said. "Are we still circling and growling?"

"Still circling, but not growling."

"Okay, then. Played ball, got hurt, changed careers, spend a lot of time overseas."

Hunter smiled. "I should've expected that. I've got an idea. As a show of good faith, let's go for a boat ride."

"I'm always up for a boat trip," Penny said. "We'll take our dinghy."

Hunter surveyed our rigid hull inflatable boat hanging from the davits at *Aegis's* stern. "Perfect. Let me get my bag, and I'll be right back."

Penny and I lowered the RHIB into the water and started the engine.

Hunter came back with a heavy mesh bag and a scuba tank across his shoulder. "Mind if I drive?" he asked, climbing aboard the RHIB.

I stepped from the wheel, clearing the way for him. "She's all yours."

We idled away from the dock and picked up speed as we turned south for Cumberland Sound.

Over the roar of the engine and wind, Hunter said, "Nice boat."

Penny didn't give me a chance to respond. "Thanks! We try not to buy crappy boats."

As we continued northward up the sound, Cumberland Island came into view on the right and the Naval Submarine Base Kings Bay on the western bank.

Hunter pointed our bow toward the island. "Toss out the anchor and get ready for the show."

I hefted the anchor overboard and let out enough line for the anchor to hold in the muddy bottom. "What show?"

He pulled on a wetsuit and set up a military-grade scuba rig. "You'll see. Just keep an eye on the entrance to the Navy base. I'll be back with a couple of friends in just a few minutes." With that, he rolled backward and disappeared beneath the surface.

Penny was obviously as confused as me. "What in the world is he doing?"

I leaned against the steering console. "I have no idea, but I suspect we're about to find out."

Ten minutes later, a bottlenose dolphin surfaced inches from the port stern of our RHIB and chirped at Penny.

Penny grabbed my arm with one hand and excitedly pointed toward the dolphin with the other. "Look at that!"

I gripped the console to avoid being pulled into the water. I'd seen thousands of dolphins, but I'd never seen one show up and say hello. While we were still in awe of the dolphin, another friendly creature surfaced less than three feet away.

"Chase! That's a sea lion! They aren't supposed to be here."

Penny was right. There was no reason one would be in Cumberland Sound.

Hunter surfaced between the dolphin and sea lion and spat out his regulator. "Penny, Chase, meet Petty Officer Second Class Stinky and Chief Petty Officer Prowler. Prowler, the dolphin, likes to find people and things that don't belong in the water around the entrance to the base. Stinky likes to attach buoys to those people and things so we can yank them out of the water and find out why they won't show us their passports."

He rubbed the heads of his friends and patted the side of our boat. Stinky and Prowler laid their heads on the tube and allowed Penny and me to slide our hands across their skin.

"Chase, this is amazing." She couldn't stop grinning. "It's the best thing ever."

Hunter slapped the water. "Come on, guys. You've got work to do."

The dolphin chirped and slid gracefully beneath the dark surface, but Stinky made a show of frolicking about before racing off toward the base.

Hunter was back aboard the RHIB and climbing out of his wet gear before we knew it. "So, what do you think? Pretty interesting pair, wouldn't you say?"

I helped him pull the wetsuit across his foot. "Do they really patrol and tag divers in the water?"

"Yeah, they really do, and that's just one of the multiple layers of security we have here that most people will never see. Even sitting right here under everybody's noses, Kings Bay is one of the most secure waterfront facilities you'll ever see."

"Remarkable," I said. "I had no idea."

Penny flicked water from her fingers then combed them through her hair. "Are you supposed to be telling us this kind of stuff? Isn't it classified?"

Hunter pulled a towel from his bag and draped it around his shoulders. "The dolphins and sea lions used to be classified, but word gets out about things like this, and most people write it off as urban myth. The way I look at it—truth, fiction, urban myth—who cares as long as it keeps the subs safe. That's my job—to keep the submarines safe while they're in port. That's when they're vulnerable. Out there, at sea, they don't need me. That's their world… where they're silent and deadly."

With the engine started, I hauled the anchor aboard while trying to understand why Hunter was giving us a peek behind the curtain. I used the corner of his towel to dry my hands. "So, all of this falls under the purview of NCIS?"

He looked up with feigned confusion. "Is that what my business card says?"

* * *

Back aboard *Aegis*, Hunter rinsed his gear and changed into dry clothes. I refilled his scuba tank with our onboard compressor and helped him hang up his wetsuit and BCD to dry.

Penny emerged with mugs of piping hot coffee. "I thought you could probably use this. You've got to be freezing."

Hunter took the mug. "Thanks. The water's not bad, but I never turn down a cup of coffee after a dive."

I excused myself and made a trip to the safe in my cabin. Back on deck, I tossed my passport on the table. "You're welcome to look, but you're not going to find anything interesting. When I travel for work, my passport rarely comes along. I suspect the same is true for you."

He slid the blue passport back across the table without opening it. "It used to be true for me, but I don't spend much time overseas for work anymore. I'm stuck here, but I'm proud to be able to do whatever I can. This is important work, even if I'd rather be out doing what you do. You know...consulting."

I chuckled. "I guess that means we're officially past the butt sniffing."

He took another swallow of coffee. "Yeah, I guess so. Does that mean you work for Brinkwater or one of those outfits?"

I quickly shook my head. "Absolutely not. I work for...."

He placed his mug back on the table and eyed me. "Go on."

"Well, the truth is, I'm not completely sure who I work for. Congress signs my checks most of the time."

"Congress, you say?"

"Yeah, I do freelance work from time to time, but generally, I go where I'm told and do what I'm told to do...within reason."

"And this most recent trip. Was that freelance or an assignment?"

"A little bit of both. Friends of mine got themselves in a bind in a part of the world where people like us aren't always welcome. Someone had to go pluck them out."

"So, that's what you do. You're a plucker. Like a PJ...a pararescueman?"

I laughed. "No, not exactly. I don't spend much time dangling from a helicopter on a cable."

"Oh, those pararescue boys are a lot more than just wire hangers. They'll get in there and rough it up with the best of them."

"Is that what you did in the Air Force?" I asked.

He let a knowing smile come across his face. "No. If you are what you say, you already know what I did in the Air Force."

"You were CCT, right?"

He looked across the marsh. "It's a beautiful day for January, don't you think?"

Sometimes a nonanswer is more of an answer than the truth.

In response to his blatant desire to change the subject, I asked, "What do you think the guys speaking Russian in the boat were up to?"

"I don't know yet, but I'll find out," he said. "I need to talk to the Judge about putting some eyes and ears on the ground out here."

"I think he'd be more than happy to help any way he can. He's one of the good guys."

Hunter looked up the slope toward the house. "He is. He helped me get my stuff right with the VA and made sure I was getting everything I'd earned when the Air Force retired me. He wouldn't take a dime for all the legal work he did for me."

"That sounds like the Judge."

He stood and stuffed his still-wet gear into the bag. "I've taken up enough of your time this morning. I'm sure I'll be seeing you again, but you've got my number. Call if you see anything that doesn't look right."

As he stepped from my boat and onto the dock, Jeff, one of the Judge's clerks, tossed a rolled newspaper up to me.

"What's this?"

"The Judge thought you might find the story on page seven interesting. Give it a read when you have time."

That caught Hunter's attention, and he glanced back up at me.

I motioned toward the dock. "Drop your gear there. It'll be fine. Come on back up."

I unrolled what turned out to be the *Washington Times* and opened it to page seven. The headline read "Top Al-Qaeda Leaders Captured near Jalalabad."

The story by an embedded reporter detailed the operation to capture the terrorist leaders outside the eastern Afghanistan city, but the most interesting piece of the article was in the closing paragraph. It was a quote from Jerry Beard, the senior Brinkwater official in the region: "I'm proud to have been part of the mission to safeguard the equipment necessary for the accomplishment of this mission. Brinkwater's invaluable experience and capabilities continue to prove that we are America's premier security contractor, doing things no other civilian agency can do in support of our military across the globe."

I tossed the paper to Hunter and dialed Smoke's sat-phone. He answered nearly a minute later. "Yeah."

"Smoke, it's Chase. Have you seen today's *Washington Times?*"

"No. Why?"

"You need to hear this."

I read him the article, concluding with the quote from Jerry Beard.

"That son of a bitch! He left us up there to die, and now he's taking credit for saving that trainload of gear."

"That's what it looks like to me," I said.

"Clark told me you offered to give us a nest until we could find some work. If you're serious about that, we could all use it right now. There's no chance Brinkwater is going to pay us for this job, and somebody has to cover the medical bills that are going to fall out of this tree we're shaking. I'm coming home and bringing Mongo. It makes me a little nervous to think what he's going to do when he sees that article, but I can't let Beard get away with what he's trying to pull. The world needs to know the truth."

Chapter 23
My Doorstep

When I hung up the phone, Hunter was folding the paper and shaking his head. "Look, Chase. I'm a simple guy. If you want me to butt out, I'll walk away." He held up the paper, shaking it in the air between us. "I've got to pursue the Russians in the boat, but this is clearly something else."

"Give me a minute." I walked inside the main salon, trying to put all the pieces together. The Russians had to be unrelated to what happened on the Khyber Pass, so I needed to separate the two issues.

What would Clark do? When am I ever going to grow up, step out of his shadow, and start thinking for myself?

I poured a scotch over five ice cubes in my favorite tumbler and yelled down the stairs into the cabin. "Penny, I need you to come up. I've got some things to tell you."

Hunter was on his phone with his back to me as he looked out over the marsh. When he pocketed his phone, I leaned through the doorway. "If you've got a few minutes, come in and have a seat."

He followed me inside as Penny was coming up the stairs.

"Is everything okay?" she said. "What's going on? Is it Clark?"

There was that energy of hers I found so beautiful. "Clark's fine. Come sit down. I don't want to have to tell this story twice. You'll both probably have questions to which the other would like to hear the answers."

Penny and Hunter sat on the settee as I lifted my drink from the counter. "Hunter, would you care for a scotch?"

He eyed my drink. "No, but I could go for a Miller Lite if you've got one."

Having no idea if we had a beer onboard, I glanced at Penny. She pointed toward the pull-out cooler and smiled. "I don't know what you'd do without me."

"I don't either," I said, handing a beer to Hunter. "Can I get anything for you?"

She shook her head. "No, thanks. I'm good. Let's hear what you have to say."

Penny and Hunter sat silently for twenty minutes as I poured out the story of what happened in Afghanistan. Occasionally, Penny would cover her mouth when I described the injuries Clark and the others had suffered. Hunter showed less reaction but grimaced when I detailed the firefights.

I paused to have a drink and catch my breath, trying to make sure I hadn't left out anything important. Believing I'd covered everything, I said, "So now we've got Jerry Beard claiming to have run the operation that safeguarded the delivery of ammo and equipment, when in reality, he was never on that mountain, and he left the dead body of the chopper pilot and five survivors—all of them good men—up there to rot."

Penny's eyes met mine. "What are you going to do?"

I stared into my glass and then at Hunter. His slow returned gaze made me a little uneasy.

"What?" I said.

He shrugged. "I'm just trying to figure out if you're going to ask me what *I'd* do."

"Okay, let's hear it. What would you do?"

"I'd piss in Beard's canteen and beat him to death with it. That's what I'd do."

Maybe it was the stress of the whole conversation, or maybe she actually found it funny, but Penny burst into uncontrollable laughter. When she finally caught her breath, she pointed at Hunter. "That sounds like something Clark would say."

She was right. Maybe Hunter and Clark were cut from the same cloth.

"Are you suggesting we go straight at Beard?"

He helped himself to another beer from the pull-out cooler, twisted off the cap, and took a long pull. "I'm not suggesting anything. I'm just telling you what I'd do. People like Beard think they're above the law and every moral code the rest of us live by. To me, it's simple. A man should do what's right, no matter who's watching, and then be willing to sign his name to what he's done. That's the way I see it."

I thought Hunter must've been older than me but younger than Clark. That measure of wisdom and clarity from a man of that age was rare, but perhaps he'd seen enough while carrying a warrior's shield to learn a lifetime's worth of lessons most men twice his age would never know.

He was right. There was only one way to deal with Beard and men like him. I had to charge him like a bull elephant and watch him back down. Anything less would be a slap in the faces of the men I'd pulled off that mountain.

My phone chirped the instant before I dialed Smoke's number. "Yeah, this is Chase."

"Chase, It's Smoke. I just got off the phone with Beard."

I punched the speaker button and laid the phone on the table. Pressing my finger to my lips, I motioned for Penny and Hunter to stay quiet. "Did you call Beard, or did he call you?"

"He called me trying to make nice. He had some spiel about how he was amassing a search and rescue force to get us off that mountain, but you beat him to it. He went on about how he was going to tell Congress how reckless you were rushing in and risking more lives, and how he had an entire rescue mission planned down to the letter. He says we'll all be paid handsomely for our bravery. All we have to do is cash the check and stand by our nondisclosure agreement not to discuss what happened up there."

"And what did you tell him?" I asked.

"I told him he could shove that check and nondisclosure agreement right up his ass. We all knew the truth, and soon, the rest of the world will know, too."

Hunter's grimace returned, this time more pronounced and painful than before.

I sighed. "That may not have been the best play, Smoke. It might've been better to let him think you'd go along. That would have at least bought us some time to figure out what to do."

"Yeah, I'm sure you're right, but it hit me the wrong way. And guys like us don't do much going along to get along, if you know what I mean."

I spun the phone around so the microphone was pointed between Hunter and me. "Listen, Smoke. I briefed a trusted friend on what's going on, and he's going to help. He's former CCT, and now he's with Navy security. His name's Hunter. He's been listening in."

"Chase, I wish you hadn't done that. This thing is on the verge of getting out of control already. The more people we involve, the worse it's liable to get."

I cleared my throat. "I understand, and I know what you mean, Smoke, but with Clark out of commission for who knows how long, we can use Hunter's help. Like I said, he's former CCT and a solid guy."

Smoke exhaled on the other end of the line. "Yeah, I've worked with some of those combat controllers. They're bulletproof and as solid as they come. If you say this guy's good, he's good with me. Put him on. Let's hear what he has to say."

Hunter looked at me as if asking permission to speak. I nodded. "Smoke, my name's Hunter. Check me out. I went down with Delta in Columbia a couple years ago on a drug interdiction thing. You may remember the op."

Silence filled the air, and I could almost hear Smoke rewinding his memory. "You must've been with Garcia and Thibodaux."

Hunter frowned. "No. It was Garza, not Garcia."

"Yeah, I know, but now I know that you know, too. I've heard of you, but I don't think we've ever pulled any triggers together."

Hunter almost smiled. "Not yet."

Smoke's tone relaxed, but he was still all business. "So, Chase read you in on this. Is that right?"

"Yeah, he brought me up to speed, and I've seen this kind of thing turn political in a snap. Once that happens, it takes more than a bunker buster to shut it down."

I felt like I'd been pushed aside, but perhaps that was for the best. Smoke and Hunter had more operational experience in their toenails than I had in my whole body.

Hunter asked, "So, are you guys still in the hospital in Frankfurt?"

"Yeah, I'm coming home on the first flight tomorrow morning with one of my men. Well, more like one and a half. We call him Mongo, and he's a lot more than just one man."

"I've known some guys like that," Hunter said. "They tend to break a lot of stuff, but they sure come in handy when you need them."

Smoke laughed. "Yeah, we all need a Mongo in our life."

It was my turn to jump back into the ring. "Smoke, you should get those guys out of the hospital as quickly as you can. The more I think about it, the more I'd like them tucked away somewhere Beard and his guys can't get to them. I don't want him shoving cash under their pillows and looking for favors."

"That's good thinking, Chase. I'll see what I can do to get them out of here, but I don't think they're going to let Clark fly for a while. He's got a lot of healing to do, and a flight to the States would be tough on him."

I closed my eyes and considered our options. "You're probably right, but he doesn't have to come all the way to the States. We've got a lot of friends all over the world. I'm sure we could find some-place nice and warm for him, and maybe even a nurse or two to flirt with."

"Okay," Smoke said, "you get to work finding a place to stash him, and I'll see what I can do about springing the rest of the crew out of here and getting them headed west. Any ideas where we can hole up while we're working the issue?"

I glanced up the slope toward Bonaventure Plantation. "Yeah, I think I know just the place."

* * *

The Judge heartily agreed to let the team camp out at Bonaventure. "There's an elevator at the Spencer House, and we don't have one of those here. If your boys are as beat up as you say, they may not like climbing that old staircase, no matter how charming it is."

I turned to Hunter, but he held up his hand as he pressed his phone to his ear. "I'm already on it."

I liked having him on my team. A man who knows how to get things done before anyone has to ask is an asset by anybody's definition.

Hunter placed his hand over the mouthpiece. "Somebody has to pay for them, but Mary says she has three rooms on the second floor that are yours as long as you need."

"Tell her we'll take them," I said, "and I'll cover the bill. Judge, I'm sorry to bring this to your doorstep, but these guys are in trouble, and I'm their best hope for coming out of this alive."

The old man narrowed his eyes. "Son, you're not dropping anything on my doorstep. It's your doorstep now. I'm a temporary tenant 'til the Lord calls me home. Just don't put Maebelle in any danger, okay?"

"I wouldn't dream of it, Judge."

Our pup, Charlie, came bounding down the stairs of the antebellum mansion, stumbling and falling every other stride. I reached down and scratched at his ears. "I've been wondering where you were, boy. What are you doing in the house?"

Maebelle leaned across the banister from the second floor. "He's been keeping me company, and I've been keeping him fed. I think I've made a new best friend."

I looked up at her. "Maebelle, with the way you cook, you'd be hard-pressed to find a man—or beast—who wouldn't be your best friend."

She waved me off. "Stop it, Chase. You'll embarrass me. Did I hear you say Clark was coming here?"

Every woman who encounters Clark Johnson falls instantly in love with him for reasons I'll never understand.

"I'm working on getting him home, but it won't be anytime soon."

She pretended to pout. "That's too bad. I'm sure I could nurse him back to health."

"I'm sure you could, Maebelle."

Charlie sat motionless in front of Hunter, looking up at the man as if hypnotized.

Hunter whispered, "Down," and pointed toward the floor. Charlie obeyed instantly and laid his head between his front paws. I was impressed, but the show wasn't over. Hunter held out his palm toward Charlie and spoke softly. "Stay...stay...stay..." Then he threw his hand into the air and commanded, "Up!"

Charlie leapt from his belly and into the air, wiggling and squirming like a Tasmanian devil.

"That's amazing," I said. "I can't get him to do a thing I say."

Hunter patted Charlie's side. "The only two things I know anything about are bad women and good dogs, and as far as I can tell, there's none of the first and one of the latter around here."

That got a good chuckle just as my phone chirped.

I excused myself into a hallway before answering. "This is Chase."

"Chase, it's Smoke. We've got a big problem."

The steel in Smoke's voice sent chills down my spine. "What is it?"

"You were right about Beard trying to get to the team, but he wasn't shoving cash under their pillows."

Chapter 24
The Warrior's Fire

"Tell me what happened, Smoke." The anger in my voice echoed in my ears as if I were listening to someone else; someone trying to hide their fear amid a determination to settle the score.

"Snake is dead."

My heart pounded, and bile rose in my throat. "How?"

Smoke cleared his throat, and his voice softened. "We're not sure yet. It looks like a heart attack brought on by an overdose."

I let myself land on the second step of the grand staircase. "An overdose of what?"

He sighed. "I don't know, but somebody got to him and put something in his IV. Who did you say Hunter was with?"

"He's officially with NCIS, but he's assigned security at Kings Bay."

I could hear the relief in Smoke's voice. "That's what I thought. That means he'll be able to get some answers. Get him on the phone with Air Force OSI in Frankfurt, and start a file. I'm getting Singer out of here. Mongo is on Clark until you can find a safe place to stash him."

"I'm on it. Does Mongo have a sat-phone?"

Smoke gave me the number and hung up. I briefed Hunter, and he was on the phone before I finished talking.

Seconds later, I was on the line with Dominic.

"Dominic, listen. I need a safe place to put Clark in Frankfurt, and I need it fast. Do we have a safe house or a contact? Anything?"

"Uh…what? Slow down, Chase. What are you talking about?"

"There's no time to slow down, Dominic. Clark's in grave danger."

"What do you mean, grave danger?"

"Dominic, we don't have time for this. I need you to think."

"Okay, okay. Give me a minute. Frankfurt…um…I'm trying, Chase, but I'm coming up empty."

I needed to calm down and think rationally, but they'd gotten to Snake inside a hospital on a secure Air Force base. That meant they could get to Clark, too. Mongo, the human brick wall, would hold them off in a fight, but what if they'd already gotten to my partner, just like they'd gotten to Snake?

Right on time, Hunter looked up. "I've got a pair of ambulances and a Marine security escort en route from the embassy to pick up the rest of the team. I need names and numbers."

I pressed the phone back to my face. "I'll fill you in as soon as I can, Dominic, but for now, read page seven in today's *Washington Times*. You'll get the picture."

As soon as I held up my hands in a catching motion, Hunter launched his phone across the room. I told the Marine every detail I knew about Smoke, Singer, Mongo, and most importantly, Clark Johnson.

"We're on it, sir," came the crisp reply, and I tossed the phone back to Hunter.

Penny stood in silent awe, a condition quite rare for her, so I shot her a reassuring look and a quick wink. The look in her eyes told me she wanted to smile, but I saw concern and worry over everything she didn't understand.

I rose from the stairs, gently kissed her cheek, and whispered, "We've got this. It's what we do."

She grabbed my hands. "No, Chase. This isn't what you do. You kill people."

I did my best impression of Clark's half-smile. "Exactly."

Hunter was scribbling feverishly on a legal pad he'd retrieved from atop a two-hundred-year-old barrister's bookcase. I looked over his shoulder, desperately trying to read his hasty shorthand and listen in to his conversation with the Office of Special Investigations agent in Frankfurt. He shoved me away and kept writing.

Moments later, he told me what little he'd learned. "They don't know much yet. They're sure it was a homicide, but nobody's in custody. Your friend Snake, whose real name was Rodney Blanchard, suffered a massive heart attack from an overdose of epinephrine."

I shook my head in disbelief. "What about—"

My phone chirped before I could finish my question, and I shoved it to my ear. "Yeah."

An ominous voice filled my head. "You might want to get your little pack of rescued dogs under control before we have to put the rest of them down."

As quickly as the line had come to life, it was dead again. The look on my face must've given away my shock and surprise.

"What was that?" Hunter's eyes were full of suspicion.

"It was a warning. Somebody told me to get my pack of rescued dogs under control before they have to put the rest of them down."

I'd seen the same fire in Clark's eyes when a high-ranking Russian officer decided to take potshots at us in the upstairs bedroom of his home on the Moscow River. We left his corpse smoldering in the ashes of that house.

The same fire burned in Hunter's gaze. It was a warrior's flame and a drive so powerful nothing could quench it. The warrior would keep fighting, moving forward, and he would prevail. Until that moment, I had no idea how deeply Hunter was willing to dive into this pit with me, but after that look, I knew he'd be bringing a shovel in case we needed to dig deeper than our foe was willing to.

"You really know how to start a fight, Chase."

I took that as a compliment from Hunter. "I have a knack for derailing trains."

"I see that," he said, "and I've got a lot of respect for it. I've got work to do, so I'm going back to the office to bring myself up to speed. You don't know anybody at the Agency who can play analyst on this one, do you?"

"The Agency" had long been the name used by field agents for the CIA.

"Nope, I don't have anybody at Langley, but I've got the best analyst you've ever seen on my payroll."

He grinned. "Well, I guess you better get him to clock in. We're gonna need him."

I shook my head. "It's no guy. She's young, has plenty to prove, and she happens to be my little sister."

"The more I learn about you, the more I like. I'll be in touch every two hours, if not sooner."

With that, he was gone. I don't know what rock he crawled from beneath, but I was thankful to have him on my team. There was little left for me to do besides getting Skipper on a plane and coming up with a plan.

* * *

Getting Skipper on a plane turned out to be the easy part. Coming up with a plan proved to be a little more challenging.

Back on the boat, Hunter called and reported that the Marine security escort had relocated Smoke, Singer, Clark, and a reluctant Mongo from the hospital on the air base to the U.S. Embassy. They were safe, at least for the time being, but we still had to get them home and deal with the upheaval.

I paced, trying to devise a plan to get them home without shining a light on ourselves. "That's it!" I must've yelled out.

"What's it?" demanded Penny.

"The spotlight!"

"What are you talking about? You freak me out when you get like this." Penny looked as scared as she was intrigued.

I brushed the hair from her face in an effort to calm her down and to give me an opportunity to focus on anything other than life and death, if only for a few seconds.

"The last thing, and also the primary thing Jerry Beard wants is the spotlight. He wants it to shine on him when he's telling his version of events, but he doesn't want anyone else to see the truth."

Penny smiled. "I like when your brain goes to work."

"There has to be a way to make Beard think he's won so he lets his guard down."

Penny listened intently without interrupting. Her interest in the mayhem of my life reminded me how intertwined our lives had become, and that realization both thrilled and frightened me. I loved having her by my side, but I feared the exposure to the darkest side of humanity would leave her bitter and jaded. I should've known she was stronger than most and could withstand the worst humanity could bring to bear while still coming out smiling on the other side.

"We've got to pick Skipper up from Jacksonville in two hours."

I was about to suggest a method of getting my car back up to Saint Marys, but Penny beat me to the punch.

"Let's get one of the Judge's clerks to drive us down to Saint Augustine. You bring the plane up here, and I'll drive the BMW back and pick up Skipper."

"That's a great idea," I said.

Penny smiled. "I try not to have crappy ideas, you know."

"Yeah, I know. Let's get on the road."

Ben Hedgcock drove us to Saint Augustine, dropping me off at the airport and Penny at the municipal marina where my car was parked.

I easily beat them back to Saint Marys in my Cessna 182, but not by much. Skipper had her equipment, including the satellite uplink, set up and running in less than thirty minutes after arriving aboard *Aegis*, and she was anxious for a briefing. Hunter arrived just in time for that event.

He started with what little he'd learned from the OSI at Frankfurt. "Those guys have no idea what's going on, and I wasn't about to tell them. I think it's better if they're running around in the dark for a while. Don't you?"

I agreed.

We briefed Skipper on everything that had happened over the previous twenty-four hours, and she took everything in without saying a word. When our briefing was over, she asked a few questions for clarification, but otherwise kept her head buried in her laptop.

An idea hit me as we were waiting for a situation report from Smoke. "What if we could give Beard the stage he wants so badly and then beat him at his own game?"

Hunter, Skipper, and Penny all leaned in, waiting to hear my idea.

"What if I could get television coverage of the CIA handing Beard some sort of citation for service to his country, and then bust his chops right there on national TV?"

The three looked at each other and then back at me with looks of incredulous interest.

"How do you plan to do that?" Hunter asked.

"I'm still working out the details, but if I plant a big enough bug in the Agency's ear, I don't think they'll pass up a chance at some good publicity."

Skipper turned back to her laptop. "Keep working it, Chase. I see a plan coming together."

Hunter's eyes lit up. "That reminds me. I ran the call log from your phone trying to figure out who called you with that message about your pack of rescue dogs. The call originated from the Raleigh-Durham, North Carolina area, but that's as far as I've been able to get."

"It doesn't matter who made the call," I said. "We know it was somebody working with Beard, and that's all that matters."

Hunter screwed up his face. "I'm not so sure about that, Chase. You're right about whoever it was working with Beard, but it does matter where he made the call from. If he called from Brinkwater operations, that means the whole company is as stinky as an outhouse rat. If not, that may mean Beard has gone rogue, and a rogue is a paranoid, timid animal. Either way, we can use it to our advantage. We just have to figure out which scenario it is."

"I have a feeling it's the whole company," I said, shaking my head.

"You may be right, but it's too early to jump to that conclusion. We'll let it play out and see where it goes. A guilty fox always runs back to the henhouse. We'll keep an eye on Beard and see if he goes looking for eggs."

"You're a pretty good cop, Hunter."

He scowled at me. "Don't put that on me, Secret Agent Man. I'm no cop. I'm a combat controller…first there. That's our motto: First there. We crawl into places the enemy never expects us to be, and then we call down hell from above onto our foes from danger close."

I nodded, silently absorbing his battlefield philosophy. "Is that what you plan to do here? Call down hell from above?"

He pursed his lips. "Well, maybe not from above, but we're going to cause some hell to show up for our friend Jerry Beard."

Chapter 25
Penny's Question

I paced the deck of my boat, replaying the plan in my head and searching for the pitfalls. There were too many to count. On the surface, the plan was simple enough. I needed to get the attention of somebody in Washington focused on Jerry Beard and what a hero he is. Second, I had to get Smoke, Clark, if he was capable, Singer, and myself in the same room with Beard during his fifteen minutes of fame. I'd have to find a way to leave Mongo outside. He'd likely tear the roof off the place, and I needed a much subtler approach—at least initially.

Walking back into the main salon, I saw Penny with a pencil in her hair, holding up a loose bun atop her head. My eyes lit up.

"What's that look all about?" she asked.

I pointed at my beautiful, brilliant wife. "You're a screenwriter. I need you to write a scene, and I need Skipper to get it in front of an agent."

Penny lowered her chin. "You're not making any sense."

"Sure I am. Just listen."

I explained what I had in mind to Skipper and Penny, and the pair immediately went to work.

Hunter nodded his approval. "Have you got a minute to hear what I've learned?"

"Absolutely."

He spent the next ten minutes laying out what the Air Force OSI agents had accomplished, and one particular piece of news sounded promising. "It's a long shot, but they pulled a syringe out of a sharps disposal receptacle on the wall of Snake's room. It didn't have a needle attached. Just a syringe."

"I don't understand what that means."

Hunter sighed. "Patience. I'm getting there. When a nurse administers a drug using a hypodermic needle, she deposits the syringe into the sharps disposal receptacle. But when she injects medication directly into an IV with a syringe with no needle attached, she almost always throws the empty syringe into the bio-hazard disposal bin—not the receptacle."

I was still lagging, but Hunter continued. "That means whoever put that needleless syringe in the receptacle either wasn't a nurse or made a careless mistake."

It hit me. "Maybe both."

"Maybe both, indeed. Maybe whoever put that syringe in that receptacle is the same person who dosed Snake. He must've thought it was the perfect place to dispose of the murder weapon."

"Did they find any prints?"

"We'll know soon, but I'm still working other angles in case this one turns out to be a dead end."

I looked over Penny's shoulder. "How's the script coming along?"

"Almost finished," she said. "And Skipper's found the perfect mail chute to drop it down."

"Is that so?" I asked.

"Yep, sure is," Skipper said. "Look at this."

Skipper's computer screen was split into two side-by-side displays. The picture on the right looked like a photocopy of a to-do list with several items lined out. The other was a list of flights scheduled to depart Frankfurt and arrive on the East Coast of the U.S. They appeared to be commercial flights, but seven lines down the screen, amid a few other meaningless plans, was a flight leaving Dubai, UAE, and arriving at RDU—Raleigh-Durham International Airport.

I grabbed Skipper's arms and kissed her squarely on top of her head. "I've said it before, and I'll never stop saying it. You're a genius!"

She squirmed away from my grasp. "Yeah, yeah, I know, but the flight is the boring part. Look at the calendar."

The picture wasn't clear enough to make out every line, but it appeared to read "PDB—Brinkwater re: J. Beard."

"Skipper, if that's what I think it is, you're far more than a genius. Is that the prep notes for the President's Daily Briefing?"

"No, even I can't get those on such short notice. I mean, I can probably get them, but not this quick. This is in the basement at Langley. It's a shot of an aide's assignments for the day."

"How did you get that?"

"You don't need to know that." She pointed both thumbs at herself. "You just need to know that I got it."

"Okay, so now what are you going to do with it?"

"I'm going to make sure the story Penny's writing ends up in the hands of that aide and then in the hands of the aide's boss. And then, for the grand finale, in the President's Daily Briefing. It'll take some luck, but I happen to have the inside scoop on this particular aide. He's ambitious, not too bright, and most importantly, he's coming off an embarrassing goof that has him in hot water with his boss. That means he's anxious to find a way to get back in her good graces, and a juicy little morsel like Penny's creative writing project is just the ticket he's looking for."

I kissed the top of her head again. "Stop doing that. I haven't washed my hair in like, days."

"Okay, I'll stop, but you're still brilliant!"

I turned to Penny. "Let me see what you've got so far."

She held up one finger and kept scribbling. "Wait a second. I'm almost done."

When she handed me the sheets of paper and I'd finished reading, I couldn't believe my eyes. Penny got her own kiss on the head.

I slid the pages in front of Hunter, and he leaned back, making a fist at me with his right hand. "So help me, God. If you kiss me on top of the head, I'll knock you out."

I pointed toward the pages. "Read that, and tell me what you think."

He shook his fist. "I mean it. I'll knock you out."

A few minutes later, he walked across the salon and leaned toward me. "Okay, you can kiss my head now. This is brilliant."

I shoved the former combat controller and snagged the pages from his hand. "Oh, no. You shunned my love once. It won't be offered again."

He huffed. "I don't know what kind of outfit I've stumbled into here, but I'm starting to think I've found my people."

I stared at the compact, confident NCIS officer—or whatever he was. "I'm starting to think the same thing about you."

Penny feigned a cough to get my attention. "I don't mean to break this up, but do I need to make any changes to the script?"

In unison, Hunter and I said, "None."

In an exaggerated display, she yanked the pages from my hand. "Thank you."

Two minutes later, the notes were scanned and landing in the inbox of the CIA aide somewhere in the bowels of a nondescript building in Langley, Virginia.

A phone chirped and I reached for mine, but there was no one calling. Hunter chuckled and pulled his phone from the pocket of his khakis. "Agent Hunter."

I watched as he listened intently.

"Okay. Can you keep that under wraps? We have an op here that's going to require some discretion." After a few seconds of listening, he said, "That'd be great. Just sit on him for twenty-four, and I'll let you know. If he rabbits, don't freak out. If his prints are in the system, we can find him no matter where he runs. Let him think he's in the clear." He shoved his phone back into his pocket. "Bingo!"

"What?"

"We got a hit on the prints we lifted from the syringe. They belong to a guy named Harold Grimes. Goes by Hal. Ever heard of him?"

Thinking back to Dubai, I said, "Yeah, I think I have. He's a supervisor or team leader at Brinkwater."

Hunter cocked his head. "This just keeps getting better and better. It looks like we've found our killer."

The thought of one of the world's biggest security contractors being behind the murder of one of their own operators to cover up a political embarrassment sickened me. I didn't want to believe it, but the pieces kept falling into place, making the likelihood more plausible by the minute.

Clark's team fought off an attack on a supply train on top of a mountain between Pakistan and Afghanistan, leaving bodies strewn everywhere. Then, instead of taking responsibility for the incident, the company they were working for made the calculated decision to leave their own men to die on top of that mountain. Now it seemed that company was going to outrageous lengths to not only cover their own tracks, but to kill the operators involved and suck up the glory for the safe arrival of the munitions and equipment. And Jerry Beard appeared to be at the center of the whole thing.

I swallowed the disgust in my throat. "How long can you get them to hold off before they pick him up?"

"They're not going to pick him up. They're an investigative force with no arresting authority outside the Air Force base. It's not their job to arrest this guy. It's their job to report what they know to the appropriate authorities. And that's where I come in."

"What do you mean?"

"My position as a senior security officer at the nuclear submarine base on the East Coast gives me access to the phone numbers of the appropriate authorities. With one phone call, two at the most, I'll have every allied police force in the world looking for Hal Grimes and waiting for my order to slap the cuffs on him."

I rushed toward Hunter and grabbed him in a bear hug. It took all of my strength to hold the tree stump of a man, but I finally got him still enough to kiss him squarely on top of the head.

Like Jacob wrestling the angel in the Old Testament, I knew I hadn't really won the battle. Hunter had allowed me to hold him still long enough to insist on a blessing.

I felt it coming, and I knew there was nothing I could do to stop it. His knee landed exactly where I'd taken the impact with the ground on top of the Khyber Pass a few days earlier, and my eyes rolled back in my head.

* * *

This time, there was blood. The on-call urologist at the medical center in Saint Marys confirmed the diagnosis of the emergency room doctor who declared that my serious condition required immediate surgery to stop the bleeding and repair the tissue damage.

When I awoke in the recovery room, Penny, Skipper, and Hunter were waiting with pained expressions.

The nurse holding my hand listened intently to my heart through her stethoscope and smiled when I opened my eyes. "Everything went fine, Mr. Fulton. Your wife and friends are here, and the doctor will be in to talk with you in a few minutes. On a scale of one to ten, how's the pain?"

I shook the sleep from my head and rubbed my eyes, still confused and groggy. "I'd have to say seven."

Penny rushed toward my bed. "Are you okay?"

"Yeah, I'm okay. I survived three gunfights ten thousand miles from home and then ended up in an O.R. after a knee shot from a Navy cop. I'm not sure what that says about me, but I think I'm okay."

Hunter's eyes fell to the floor. "Man, I'm sorry. I didn't realize you were hurt. I assumed you were sore from the mission, but—"

"It wasn't your fault, Hunter. I'm just bustin' your chops. You couldn't know. We were horsing around."

Penny stepped in. "No, Hunter. It wasn't your fault. The doctor said the blood clot was just waiting to burst."

The nurse returned with a paper cup filled with ice chips and encouraged me to eat them. Seconds behind her, the surgeon strolled in wearing his green surgical scrubs and paper booties.

"It went really well, Mr. Fulton. We repaired all the damage and stopped the bleeding. You'll be pretty sore for a few days, so take it easy and get plenty of rest, but all in all, I'd say you were quite lucky. If your wound had ruptured away from a hospital, things could have been much worse. How would you rate your pain?"

I shot a glance and Hunter and we answered in perfect unison, "Seven."

He spent the next several minutes describing the damage I'd sustained and what he did to repair the wound, but it was Penny's question that left me breathless.

"Will we still be able to have children?"

Chapter 26
Frozen Peas

"Chase, he said rest and frozen peas."

Penny's priorities were slightly different than mine. I had a team of men who needed me to help keep them alive so they could tell their story, and those men were being pursued by a company that had the desire and means to shut them up by stopping their hearts. Penny thought I should be in bed snuggled up with a bag of frozen produce.

"I'll take it easy. I will. But I can't go to bed. There's too much at stake right now. We have to get Clark and the team back home."

"I know. It's just all so much. I don't know how you do it. I'm worried about Clark and the guys, you know I am, but I'm more worried about you."

I spun around and took her in my arms. "I know, but right now, the worst thing that could happen to me is melting peas. Clark, Smoke, Singer, and Mongo are seven thousand miles from home and running for their lives. I don't have a choice."

She ran her hands through my hair. "I know, and that's one of the things I love about you. You care more about other people than you care about yourself. Nobody will ever know the sacrifices you make, Chase Fulton."

I offered an abbreviated smile. "No one has to know. That's part of the point. What I do—what *we* do—isn't something that shows up on page seven. And it never can be. The politicians get to puff out their chests and gloat. We get to rub dirt on our wounds, embrace the suck, and move on to the next mission. That's kinda what I signed up for."

She tried to smile. "I'm not sure what I signed up for, but I know it'll never be dull."

It occurred to me that my handler, Dominic, wasn't in the most recent loop, so I dialed his number.

After a short briefing on the murder, the continued attempts at a cover-up, and my plan to set a trap, he declared, "You have absolutely anything you need. You can pull out all the stops."

Until that point, I hadn't given much thought to the finances of the operation. I was just trying to keep the team alive and get Clark home, but I was relieved to know somebody else would be writing the check.

"Thanks, Dominic. I'll be in touch. For now, start working on getting a ride for Clark and the remaining team. We need to get them stateside as soon as possible."

"Consider it done."

I headed for Skipper's workstation, but as my foot left the deck on my second stride, it felt like I'd been hit by a bolt of lightning. Back onto the seat I went, with frozen peas in place.

I squeaked out, "Let's hear it, Skipper."

"Are you okay?" She had a look of terror on her face.

"Yeah, I'm fine. I just moved too quickly. Tell me what you've got."

"Basement Boy took the bait. He's been at it since three this morning, and it looks like his efforts are picking up steam. Penny's story is going to be front-page news all over the world if this keeps up."

"No, that's not what we want," I said. "We want her story to get lost in all of this. We want Jerry Beard's face on the front page with the word *traitor* stamped across it in big, bold letters."

Skipper shook her head. "That part's up to you and Hunter. I'm setting the trap. You're the ones who have to deal with what we catch."

"That we can do. Keep monitoring, and let me know when a timeline starts coming together."

She spun back around, anchoring her fingertips back to the keyboard. "You got it."

Maebelle delivered breakfast, and Penny delivered pain meds. It didn't take long for the effects to set in. Fatigue—mental and physical—and the painkillers sent me into the spirit world with my bag of peas.

The team let me sleep, although I suspect they did so because Penny threatened to kill them if they disturbed me. As much as I hated to admit she was right, sleep was the best thing for me. I awoke clearheaded and ready to work.

Hunter had taken the lead in my absence. His briefing was concise and efficient, just like everything else I'd seen him do.

"Your man, Dominic, will have a Gulfstream G550 on the ramp in Frankfurt in less than two hours. That means we'll have your team on U.S. soil inside of sixteen hours."

I listened intently, creating a mental timeline as he spoke. "That's a good start. What else?"

He scowled. "Shut up and listen. Hal Grimes is back in Dubai, but Skipper intercepted an email from his wife telling her mother that Hal would be home in the next twenty-four hours. Beard checked out of Dubai and will be on the ground at Raleigh-Durham late this afternoon."

"It looks like the guilty foxes are running back to the henhouse," I said.

Hunter frowned again. "Do you want to hear the rest of what you missed while you were napping, or do you want to keep talking?"

"I'm sorry. I won't interrupt again."

He flipped through his legal pad. "Good. So, that covers the flights. Next, Skipper has been snooping around in the Brinkwater server, but that's slow going. Their network is pretty secure. We need to find some internal documents implicating more than Beard and Grimes. This thing has to run deeper than just those two." He glanced up, apparently expecting me to comment, but I didn't.

"Skipper has been watching her snowball grow as it rolls around at Langley, and it's turning into quite the boulder. Apparently, your old friend Michael Pennant, the deputy director of operations, is up for a promotion. I can't wait to hear how he became your buddy, but we'll deal with that later. It looks like he wants to be the director of clandestine services, and this little victory might be his ticket. Egos can be fun to watch. It's too early to know when it'll happen, but there will be a press conference, and that's where we should spring our trap."

I had a thousand questions, but I silently waited for Hunter to finish.

He finally nodded. "Okay, that's it."

I emptied a bottle of water down my throat. "You're right. This thing does have to run deeper than just Beard and Grimes. Beard has some rank in the company, but I think Grimes is a mid-level knuckle-dragger, and essentially Beard's enforcer. I can't prove any of it yet, but that's the impression I get."

Hunter nodded. "Yeah, that's the beauty of this kind of thing. We don't have the burden of proof. We just have to get close enough to the right tree and shake it hard enough for the truth to fall out. Gravity is on our side."

"Are *you* going to listen, or do you want to keep talking?"

He chuckled. "Okay, I deserved that. Go on."

I tried to picture what the dog and pony show would look like when the bureaucrats and bad guys started patting each other on the back. "You and I have credentials that'll get us into a press conference, but we need to get Penny in the crowd."

Skipper slowly turned from her workstation. "Way ahead of you, boss."

In her hand was a lanyard with a laminated press pass identifying Nicole Thomas Fulton as a reporter for the Houston Chronicle.

"Where'd you get that?"

She lifted her chin with pride. "I made it. That's what we geniuses do. I deserve a raise."

"Indeed, you do."

I repositioned in my seat, careful to avoid another lightning bolt. "So, what else is there to do right now?"

Everyone in the room expected someone else to speak.

Finally, Hunter said, "I guess I could go catch some Russians in a boat."

Everyone except Penny laughed. "I forgot all about those guys. Do you think they have something to do with this?"

I locked eyes with Hunter, waiting for his opinion.

Before making his exit, he said, "Nothing I've come up with ties this to the Russians, but I've had a couple guys on the case since you made the report. I'll check in with them and see where it stands."

Skipper looked up. "It's my turn to get some rest. I've been staring at this screen way too long. Wake me up in two hours or if anything happens." She disappeared down the stairs to what used to be her cabin.

That left Penny and me alone in the main salon.

I turned to look at my beautiful new wife, who was stooped over and wringing her hands.

Gingerly, I moved to sit beside her. "Are you okay?"

She nodded quickly, obviously trying to suppress the tears, and I held her tight as she trembled. It broke my heart to see her like that, but there was nothing I could do other than let her cry.

"I wanted children so badly," she breathed between gasps.

My heart plummeted into my stomach. "I know, Penny, and I'm so sorry. I wish...."

I didn't know what else to say, and historically when I found myself in that situation, I said the most ridiculous things. My track record wasn't going to change that day.

"Penny, if children are the most important thing to you, I understand, and I love you. I want you to have everything you want. If I'm not the guy—"

She jerked away and sent her open palm across my face in an attack I never saw coming. I've been hit by men of every size, shape, and color from all over the world, but Penny's assault felt more violent than that of any man I'd ever fought. The strike wasn't the limit of her venom. The cold anger and hurt on her face were as painful as the blow.

"Chase Fulton, look up there. Look at that house! That's where I stood one week ago and vowed to love you forever. I didn't put any conditions on that love. Yes, I want children. That's never been a secret. But I want you first. All of you. Whole or broken or anything in between, I want you. So help me, if you ever *think* of saying anything like that to me again, I'd rather you put one of your bullets in my chest, because that bullet would hurt a hell of a lot less."

The weakest words in the English language escaped my lips before I could stop them. "Penny, I'm sorry."

She stuck her finger to my lips, her tears drying and staining her flawless face. "Don't be sorry, Chase. Just love me. Love me the way you want me to love you. I'll never ask for more than that."

Chapter 27
Time Traveler

Twenty-four hours later, Clark Johnson sat up in bed and cursed the clamshell brace the doctors were forcing him to wear. "Where am I *now?*"

"You're home," I said as I stood from my chair in the corner of the room.

"I don't have a home," came his weak reply.

"Sure you do. You're in Saint Marys at Bonaventure."

He squeezed his eyes closed several times and tried to focus on his surroundings. "Man, this is all too much. I was on a train, then I was under a train, then I was in a hospital, then an embassy, and now I'm in a plantation house. Is it eighteen sixty again?"

"I thought you said you liked to travel. Do you have something against time travel?"

He slowly shook his head. "You're something else, College Boy. How 'bout telling me what's going on?"

I caught Clark up on the events of the previous three days, including Snake's murder, Beard's claim, Grimes's involvement, and what we planned to do about it.

"How can I help?"

I laughed. "You can stay in bed and get better. They say you've got a long road ahead of you. Between the ribs, the punctured lung, and the broken back, you'll have plenty of time to catch up on your needlepoint."

He wrestled with the cover. "Yeah, well, I don't do too good laid up in the bed, and I suck at needlepoint. I need to get up."

Arguing with Clark Johnson was like wrestling with a pig. I knew both of us would end up muddy, tired, and smelling terrible, but the pig would be the only one to enjoy it.

"I'll help you up if you want, but I don't know where you plan to go."

"I'll take that help," he said, "and we'll figure out where we're going after I make it to my feet."

The progress was slow and involved several words that I can't spell coming out of Clark's mouth, but we finally made it to the back porch where he gently put himself on a well-padded chair. "Whew, that was an adventure. Where is everybody?"

I eyed him carefully, wishing I'd insisted on him staying in bed. "Singer's leg is too badly broken to climb stairs, and he's too stubborn for a wheelchair, so I've got him tucked away at the Spencer House. Mongo's on his door and won't move. Smoke is doing what Smoke does…drifting around and watching over everything."

He looked out over the marsh and the North River. "How about this Hunter guy? What's his story?"

"Like I told you before, he's a former combat controller and now works for Navy security in some mysterious capacity. He's sharp, and Smoke says he checks out."

Following a long inhalation, pain flew across Clark's face. "Yeah, those combat controllers are a rare breed. They're fearless, almost bulletproof, and nobody on the battlefield is more dangerous than they are. They've got wave after wave of fighters and bombers itching to do whatever the controller orders. What does he drink?"

"What difference does that make?" I asked, trying not to laugh.

"Just tell me what the man drinks."

"Okay, he drinks Miller Lite."

Clark smiled. "In that case, I feel okay about Hunter looking out for you 'til I get out of this thing." He tapped the hard plastic shell encapsulating his torso and abdomen.

"I don't need anybody looking out for me," I protested.

"That's it, kid. Keep on believing that. So, when do I get to meet your new guardian angel?"

I'd spent most of the day preparing Clark's room and getting the team settled in after Dominic's Gulfstream delivered them safely back to the States, and I realized I hadn't seen Skipper or Penny in several hours. I was on the verge of starting an expedition to find them when a powerboat pulled up to the dock beside *Aegis*.

Penny, Skipper, Hunter, and Charlie climbed out of the boat and started up the path toward the home. Charlie beat everyone else to the house and completely ignored me, choosing instead to pry open the door with his nose and tumble inside, no doubt searching for Maebelle, who always had something for him to eat.

Skipper threw herself on the ground in front of Clark and went into a performance of how good it was to have him home and how much she wished he hadn't gotten hurt.

Penny made no performance and instead kissed Clark on the cheek. "You could use a bath and a shave."

"It's good to see you, too, Mrs. Fulton."

She held up her left hand, displaying the simple wedding band.

I stood from my rocking chair and motioned toward Hunter. "Clark, this is Stone Hunter. Hunter, meet—"

"Oh, we've met." Hunter stuck out his hand. "Stone Hunter. You're Baby Face with Fifth Special Forces Group. We did an op together with the tenth mountain in ninety-three. It was my first real-world op. You carried a sandbag full of dirt around for two days to prove how silly it was for me not to ask for help carrying radio batteries when my pack was fifty pounds heavier than everybody else's."

Clark almost laughed. "Yeah, that sounds like something I'd do. Did you ever ask for help with those batteries?"

Hunter shook his head. "Nope. It's tough enough being the only Air Force troop in a gang of Green Berets and SEALs. I wasn't about to let them think I couldn't carry my own gear."

Clark looked at me. "See, College Boy? I told you those combat controllers were the real deal."

Any man who could impress Clark Johnson was more man than I'd ever be. Hunter was quickly proving to be more than meets the eye.

"Where have you guys been?" I asked.

Penny blushed. "You're never going to believe it. I'm such an idiot. Hunter found the mysterious Russians in the boat."

I turned my gaze to Hunter, who was making a limited attempt to stifle his amusement. "Oh, yeah. We found them, all right. On the scale of threats to American security, they fall somewhere between a stuffed bunny rabbit and a ladybug."

He produced a business card from his shirt pocket and handed it to me. I examined the card, written in Cyrillic on one side and English on the other.

Aleksandar Kipelov, Ph.D.
Environmental Sciences
Sofia University St. Kliment, Ohridski, Bulgaria

"What are Bulgarian environmentalists doing in Saint Marys?" I asked.

"They're studying broadleaf wetland grasses, believe it or not. It's some kind of program through Florida State University, and it all checks out. There's a whole team of 'em staying in Fernandina Beach."

I grinned at Penny. "So, it wasn't Russian."

She continued blushing. "Nope, not at all. It was Bulgarian, but hey, I've been around you guys long enough to think the whole world is one big den of would-be threats."

As if we'd practiced, Skipper, Clark, Hunter and I said, "It is."

Penny held up her hands in surrender. "See, my point is proven. Besides, if I hadn't seen and heard those guys and told you about it, you wouldn't have come home, and we'd have never met Hunter. Everything happens for a reason."

I'd never subscribe to that theory, but I was thankful to have met Hunter, regardless of the cause.

"Okay," I said, "so that mystery is solved. Now we can get back to work on the real mission."

Skipper hopped up from the porch. "While you were building a nest for Clark, the rest of us were working, and you're going to like what we've done."

It was becoming clear that I'd built a team, quite accidentally, that was capable of almost anything.

Penny's eyes lit up. "Oh, Chase. You're going to love it. Michael Pennant is holding a press conference tomorrow afternoon in Georgetown with none other than Jerry Beard. Good ol' Jerry is expected to talk about how he and his team safeguarded that supply train full of munitions and equipment across the Khyber Pass. Pennant is going to give him a civilian service medal. That's supposed to set up a great photo op, I'm sure. What it's actually going to do is give me, a reporter from the Houston Chronicle, a chance to get Jerry Beard on the record about his so-called heroics."

Hunter perked up. "Penny's being modest. She's going to do more than just get him on the record. This is the best part. She's going to get him to go on the record in front of two of the five men who were actually on that mountain when the train was attacked."

"Why only two?" asked Clark.

Hunter looked him over. "Well, Smoke and Mongo are the only two fit enough to travel and deal with the crowd. I'd love to have you and Singer there, but if it gets weird—and it will get weird—getting the two of you out in a hurry would be quite the challenge. And, of course, the fifth man would've been the pilot of the Little Bird who didn't survive."

Clark sighed. "All right. I'll buy that, but you better light up the sky with those guys. If you don't, then you wasted a lot of time carrying those batteries all by yourself."

Hunter nodded in acknowledgment of Clark's expectations.

"You guys were right," I said. "I do like this plan. It sounds like all we need now is a ride to Georgetown, and I know just the guy." I dialed the number and waited for him to answer. "Hey, Dominic. I've got a member of your bloodline here who'd love to see you.

How about you hop on the G550 of yours and get up here to Saint Marys?"

"I'm on my way, Chase."

I continued. "Good. You can babysit while the rest of us borrow that Gulfstream for a little field trip to D.C."

He didn't balk. "I told you, all you have to do is ask. Whatever you need is yours for this one. Can I talk to Clark?"

I turned to toss the phone to Clark, but I thought handing it to him gently would be a better idea.

"The Gulfstream will be here tonight," I said. "Dominic will stay with Clark, and we'll be wheels-up at dawn."

Hunter held up a finger. "There's one little thing I forgot to mention."

"What's that?"

He pulled a folded sheet of paper from his pocket and held it toward me.

When I read the cover sheet of the federal arrest warrant for Harold "Hal" Grimes, I knew the press conference couldn't come soon enough. "You're going to need a tranquilizer gun."

Hunter laughed. "I can handle a dozen Harold Grimes."

I shook my head. "It's not Grimes who'll be the problem. Somebody will have to keep Mongo from killing that guy before you get him into custody."

Catching on, Hunter said, "That might save the taxpayers some money. I think I'll leave the tranq gun at home and let Mongo run his course. After all, he does seem to be a force of nature."

* * *

Dominic and the G550 arrived before dinner, and Maebelle couldn't have been happier. The thought of feeding nearly two dozen people at Bonaventure was a dream come true for her. Like always, she didn't disappoint.

Although he should've stayed in bed, Clark wasn't about to miss the festivities. Maebelle paid particular attention to him while the

Judge regaled the group with story after story. Some of them may have even been true.

As the evening was winding down, Smoke pulled me aside. "Chase, everything you've done has been remarkable. There was a time, twenty years ago, when I was a lot like you, but those days are gone. This is a young man's game, and I'm almost forty-five. I got a good pilot killed. My sniper—the best I've ever seen—destroyed his leg. I got Clark run over by a train. And Snake…I got him murdered. It all happened on my watch. I'm responsible for it. I was responsible for those men. They trusted me, and I let them down. I'm done, Chase. The team is yours now, and they're the best team of operators I've ever known. Care for them better than I did. Thank you for what you do, and don't ever forget that there's nothing more valuable to any living thing than freedom. The day we let that truth die is the day humanity reaches its doom." He stuck his hand in mine and locked eyes with me. "Don't let that happen on your watch."

I opened my mouth to speak, but Smoke stopped me. "Just take care of your men, Chase."

I watched him waft through the front door of the antebellum mansion like the mist his moniker implied.

Chapter 28
On Hallowed Ground

The early morning snow flurries came to an end as the wheels of our Gulfstream touched down at Ronald Reagan Washington National Airport.

Smoke's words from the previous night kept ringing in my ears: "Don't let that happen on your watch."

Hunter broke my trance. "Don't you think it's funny they named the national airport after the president who fired all the air traffic controllers back in nineteen eighty-one?"

"You're a strange guy, Hunter."

"Thanks, boss. I'll take that as a compliment."

We disembarked and loaded into the ubiquitous black Suburban Skipper had arranged for us. Mongo mounted the front seat since he couldn't fit anywhere else except on the luggage rack. Hunter and I sat in the second row of seats while Skipper and Penny climbed into the third row. Our driver was a man I never thought I'd see again.

He turned and watched me slide into the seat. "Hello, Chase Fulton. Remember me?"

The first time I rode in a vehicle with the man I knew as Grey was day one of my training at The Ranch. That seemed like a thousand years before, but it had only been half a decade. On that first day of training, Grey intentionally ran our truck into a filthy black lake in an obvious attempt to drown me. I survived that and a few dozen other close calls, including an infiltration and exfiltration from Havana Harbor with Grey at the wheel.

"You keep popping up, and you always seem to be driving something. How've you been, Grey?"

He made a jovial, round-faced grin. "It's good work if you can get it. And I've been great. How about you?"

"I've had my hands full lately, but I can't complain."

Grey turned back to the wheel. "It wouldn't do any good if you did."

We wound our way through the streets of D.C., dodging traffic cones, bicycles, and every manner of vehicle imaginable, but it soon became obvious we weren't heading for Georgetown.

"Where are you taking us? The press conference is in Georgetown."

He shook his head. "No, the press conference *was* in Georgetown. Now it's at the Pentagon. Pennant wanted to use it as a 'hallowed ground' backdrop for his speech. Bureaucrats, huh? What are you gonna do?"

"I'm gonna make 'em wish they stayed home in bed."

Grey chuckled. "That sounds like the Chase Fulton I remember."

I turned to Hunter. "Does the venue swap change anything on your end?"

He shook his head. "A few things, but I'm good. I'll make some calls so my people know where to be."

"How about you, Penny? Are you okay with the change?"

"What difference does it make? Pentagon, Georgetown…it's all the same to me."

I leaned forward. "Grey, you said Pennant is using the Pentagon as a backdrop. Does that mean we'll be outside?"

"I drove by this morning, and they've got a huge tent set up. They'll run heaters and power for the lights and cameras and stuff. It'll feel like you're inside, but it'll be on the Pentagon lawn."

We had lunch and went over every last detail of our plan. "We'll let Pennant speak without interruption and then listen to the BS coming out of Jerry Beard's mouth for as long as we can stand it.

Penny, I don't want you to be the first reporter to ask questions. Let some of the others throw him a few softballs before you start bringing the heat."

"Yeah, I get that," she said. "We'll let him enjoy the limelight and believe he has everything under control."

"Exactly. Hunter, when do you plan to arrest Grimes?"

Hunter situated himself in his typical relaxed posture. "I'll play it by ear, and we'll get the most dramatic value out of it we can. But I won't let him slip away. He'll be in cuffs when we leave. I have seven other agents who'll be in place throughout the event."

I slapped our resident giant on the shoulder. "How about you, Mongo? Do you have your speech ready?"

He nodded nervously. "I'm not real good at speaking in public, so I might screw it up a little, but he'll get the point. If he doesn't, I can always climb up on the stage and—"

"No, Mongo. That's not a good plan. I'd rather you stand up and tell everybody what happened on that mountain when Penny gives you the signal."

"I think ripping his arms off would be a good way to get him to listen."

"It's not Beard we want to listen to you, Mongo. It's the crowd of reporters and journalists."

"Yeah, I know, but I'd still like to do it."

I laughed. "Well, maybe you'll get the chance before it's all over."

By all indications, we were ready for the show, but I couldn't get Smoke off my mind. I wanted him with us, but since he'd walked away the night before, Mongo would have to be enough. If Singer and Clark were medically fit, their presence would have gone a long way, too, but sometimes you gotta work with what you've got.

Security was tight, but Skipper's counterfeit press passes got Penny and Mongo through the gates. Hunter's NCIS creds did the trick for him, and my Secret Service ID swung the gates open wide.

Our seats were five rows from the podium and right of center stage. Perfect. A team of technicians conducted sound checks and realigned some lights. It was going to be a media event Washington D.C. wouldn't soon forget.

A bright-eyed young woman from the CIA's public relations office took the podium. "Ladies and gentlemen, please stand for the posting of the colors by the United States Army's…The Old Guard."

The crowd rose as one as we watched the polished, crisp motions of the honor guard marching in with the flags, flanked by recruiting-poster-quality soldiers armed with ninety-year-old M-1 rifles. The Army band played the national anthem, and well over half the crowd saluted in military tradition while the rest of us proudly held our hands over our hearts.

"Ladies and gentlemen, the deputy director of operations for the Central Intelligence Agency, Mr. Michael Pennant."

Pennant, dressed in a two-thousand-dollar black suit, approached the podium. "Good afternoon, ladies and gentlemen. I have something I want you to see." He turned away from the podium. "Please raise the curtain."

Mechanisms attached to an enormous white panel began to whir, slowly raising the panel above the roof of the tent in which we were seated. Through the now open end of the tent, with the cold D.C. winter air pouring in, everyone sat captivated by the sight beyond. Sighs and groans went up from the crowd as we stared at the destruction.

"I apologize for the cold, ladies and gentlemen, but what you see before you is only one small example of the scar left upon our nation following the unthinkable acts of terrorism committed against us less than four months ago. The scars you see behind me on the building that represents our very beacon of security in this country —as devastating as they are—pale in comparison to the scars left on the hearts of the thousands of families who lost loved ones on that horrific day, September eleventh, two thousand and one. Those scars are left not only upon the hearts of the families affected by the cowardly and unthinkable acts of a few, but also on the heart of every American who loves and values the freedom this great nation represents. Fellow Americans, today we stand on hallowed ground."

A round of applause filled the tent as the curtain was lowered back into place.

Penny leaned over. "He's good."

I whispered, "If you shovel enough of it long enough, that happens. Don't get sucked in."

Pennant spoke for fifteen minutes about the resolve of the greatest nation to ever exist and her will to fight back against the perpetrators of the events of 9/11.

Finally, he came to the part of his speech that would usher in my troops. "Furthermore, ladies and gentlemen, Americans of every race, creed, color, and religion, we are fortunate today to have with us one of the men who is spearheading this fight against the forces of terror. This man is more than a leader in the modern definition of the word. He is a warrior in the ranks of the greatest warriors throughout history. But before I introduce him, please indulge me a moment longer while I tell you about a tiny village—nothing more than an outpost, really—where Taliban and Al-Qaeda leadership thought they were safe...just like the two thousand nine hundred seventy-seven innocent victims believed on the morning of September eleventh when they arrived at work or took their seats on those doomed airliners.

"On that fateful morning, one hundred twenty-five brave Americans perished behind me inside those scarred and burnt walls of our Pentagon. Every one of them believed they were safe and that they'd see their families again at the end of the day. Only nineteen of the lives that ended that day belonged to people who knew they'd seen their last sunrise. Those nineteen lives belonged to the cowardly hijackers who despised freedom so badly that they gave up their own lives in the name of terrorism. Those are not the lives that bear remembering. Those are the names you'll not hear me utter today. Those are the cowards, the forces of evil, the implements of an ideology that has no place in a world of freedom. Those cowards were the weapons of even more cowardly men...the men in that small village I mentioned south of the city of Jalalabad, Afghanistan.

"On January twenty-seventh of this year, a contingent of forces made up of infantrymen of the One Hundred and First Airborne Division Air Assault from Fort Campbell, Kentucky, led by a platoon of U.S. Army Rangers, stormed into that camp, where they initially met resistance by the poorly trained, yet well-equipped Taliban and Al-Qaeda fighters who were charged with protecting their leaders.

"The actions of the brave men of the Rangers and the One Hundred and First Airborne Division resulted in the deaths of over two hundred enemy militants and the capture of nine key Taliban and Al-Qaeda leaders, all of whom believed they'd struck a mighty blow against the infidels of the 'evil America.' These are some of the first—and most certainly not the last—of the men who will pay a dear price for striving to enslave the world with their ideology and archaic fearmongering.

"We celebrate these brave young men who raided that camp, that outpost, where Taliban and Al-Qaeda leadership believed themselves to be safe. Most of those brave young men are still in the region continuing to strike back at the enemies of freedom. While you and I shiver over the slight chill I allowed into the tent, those warriors—your warriors—are living in conditions harsher than you and I are capable of understanding, yet they fight on, and they do so believing that you and I will ensure they receive the support they need—the food, the ammunition, and the emergency medical supplies that are crucial to their operation.

"I'd like to read a brief excerpt from a letter we recently received from the nine-year-old daughter of one of the infantrymen who raided that village. 'Thank you to all of you who made sure Daddy got what he needed to win in the war and then come home to me and Mommy and my baby sister...'"

Penny elbowed me. "Yep, that was me. I wrote that."

I smiled as Pennant continued.

"Part of the responsibility we have as the greatest nation on Earth is to put some of our best forces—many of which are comprised of former military servicemen and women who now serve as civilian security contractors—on the task of safeguarding the arrival of those much needed supplies and equipment. I'm proud today to introduce a man who represents the tip of the spear in this effort. A man who not only talks the talk, but also walks the demanding walk of escorting supplies and equipment to our fighting men and women. Ladies and gentlemen, an American hero...Mr. Jerry Beard."

Beard took the stage to a thunderous ovation. "Thank you so much. You're great Americans, and I appreciate your applause. I'm humbled and proud to serve. Let me begin by saying I am not alone in this effort, despite Director Pennant's introduction. I'm merely the man who had the good fortune to lead the amazing team of men who put their lives on the line to protect that train—a train that carried the ammunition and supplies that made it possible for the Rangers and infantrymen to accomplish their challenging mission. My team, as I'm sure you can understand, deserves and requires anonymity. It would be irresponsible of me to parade those fine men out here on this stage and tell you each of their names so you could take their pictures. As much as I'm sure the American people would love to see the faces and hear the names of these brave men, it isn't possible. The reasons for this are obvious to most of you, but for those of you who don't understand, they will be continuing to fight for you and serve you. Putting their faces and names in the public eye jeopardizes not only them, but also their families. I am not willing to do that to men who routinely put their lives in my hands."

Mongo's face looked like the inside of a watermelon, and I patted his knee. "Easy. You'll get your chance."

Beard spoke for seventeen minutes on how he led his brave team through the Afghan mountains and across the Khyber Pass in some of the most treacherous conditions on the planet, protecting that train without incident. Every word of his speech was a lie, and every second of it was being captured by no fewer than two dozen television cameras and a hundred audio recorders.

When he finished, he almost bowed before saying, "I have a demanding schedule, but I feel I owe it to the American people to take a few questions before I must return to the warzone."

Chapter 29
Showtime

Mongo grabbed my arm in his vice-like grip. "Can I rip his arms off and beat the truth out of him now?"

I was tempted to let him do it, but we'd come too far to screw up a good plan, so I encouraged Mongo to stay in his seat a few more minutes.

Several reporters, obviously caught up in the emotion of the performance, lobbed softball questions at Beard, and he graciously poured out a heaping helping of BS while crushing each question right out of the park. He was a dynamic speaker, almost on par with Pennant, but he hadn't faced Penny and Mongo yet.

Finally, Penny stood with her hand in the air, and Beard pointed at the beautiful blonde. "Yes, ma'am. In the blue. Go ahead."

The other reporters grumbled and reclaimed their seats, impatiently waiting their turn.

"Mr. Beard...Nicole Fulton with the Houston Chronicle. Let me start by thanking you for your bravery and such refreshing honesty. It isn't always what we get from these sorts of events."

Beard smiled. "Well, Ms. Fulton, thank you. Bravery and honesty are what the American people deserve most of all in times such as these, but please go ahead with your question."

Penny cleared her throat. "Mr. Beard, how many men did you say were on the security team you led across the Khyber Pass, and was anyone injured during the crossing?"

Beard checked his watch. "Well, there were ten men on my team, and because of our presence, the train was not assaulted; therefore, we suffered no casualties. Not even so much as a hangnail, I'm proud to say."

"And no equipment losses, either?"

"No, Ms. Fulton. We lost no men, suffered no injuries, and lost no equipment. Thank you for your question."

"But Mr. Beard, are you forgetting about the Hughes Five Hundred D Little Bird helicopter crash that killed your pilot, on your payroll, following the attack on the train, during which five rail cars were lost, over two dozen Taliban fighters were killed, and three American contractors were wounded?"

A stir made its way through the crowd of reporters, and all eyes turned to Beard standing alone on the stage.

The man looked again at his watch. "I'm sorry, Ms. Fulton, but I'm afraid you've been misinformed."

One of the broadest smiles I've ever seen came across Penny's face as she reached down and encouraged Mongo to stand. The giant of a man pulled himself from his seat and stood to his full height, towering over everyone in the immediate area.

Penny pointed toward Beard. "Go ahead, Marvin. Tear his arms off."

Mongo swallowed the lump in his throat and wiped beads of sweat from his brow. "My name is Mongo."

The crowd chuckled, but he continued, unfazed. "Well, my real name is Marvin Malloy, but the men I serve with call me Mongo because…well, I guess you can figure out why."

Nervous laughter continued, and Beard pulled the microphone to his lips. "I'm sorry, Mr. Malloy, but I really must be going. I've got important—"

"You can stand right there and listen to me, you liar. You were never on that train, and you were never on that mountain. But I was. I was there with five of my brothers when that supply train got hit by dozens of Taliban fighters."

Beard practically yelled into the microphone. "This man is clearly deranged. Can we get some security to escort him out? He should be showing some respect for an event of this magnitude."

That was the last straw for Mongo. He bounded over three men and two women and headed for the stage. I tried grabbing him, but stopping three hundred pounds of warrior is a task better suited for a battleship. Beard let his microphone fall to the podium and turned to make his exit. Mongo was still charging the stage as I began scanning the area for Hunter. He'd been beside me when Penny stood up, but he was nowhere in sight.

Watching my plan fall apart before my eyes sickened me and sent my brain into overdrive, trying to come up with a way to save it. As I'd succumbed to the realization that I'd failed, Mongo froze, and awe fell over the crowd.

Special Agent Stone W. Hunter was at the edge of the stage with his hand in the center of Jerry Beard's chest. He was walking the man backward toward the podium with two men in full military Class-A uniforms following close behind. Hunter held up his badge for the gathered crowd to see and then "encouraged" Beard to have a seat. Beard resisted, so Hunter encouraged him more aggressively.

The first uniformed man, his leg cast from ankle to mid-thigh, stepped to the podium and picked up the microphone. "My name is Sergeant First Class Jimmy Grossmann, but the men I serve with call me Singer. I'm a born-again Southern Baptist and Airborne Ranger sniper. I was one of the six men hired by Mr. Beard's company to protect the train he claims to have been aboard. He was not aboard that train. The detachment commander aboard was my friend, retired Major James "Smoke" Butterworth, U.S. Army Special Forces. The remainder of the team was comprised of Sergeant Rodney "Snake" Blanchard U.S. Marine Corps Force Recon; Sergeant Marvin "Mongo" Malloy, Airborne Ranger, whom you've already met; Chief Warrant Officer Billy "Stump" Carter, the pilot of Little Bird who did not survive the crash during the attack; and this man." Singer stepped aside, allowing the next soldier to take the podium.

"My name is Master Sergeant Clark "Baby Face" Johnson, U.S. Army Special Forces, and I was second-in-command of the operation to protect the supply train during its crossing of the Khyber Pass during the third week of January. Here is the truth of what happened on that mountain *without* Jerry Beard.""

I'd never seen Clark in his uniform. His chest full of medals, ribbons, and decorations reflected the beams from the lights overhead. The green beret perched on his head looked like a crown from where I stood, and his polished jump boots reflected like black mirrors on his feet.

"During the attack, Stump, the pilot, was killed. Singer broke his leg while leaping from the failing helicopter, but stayed in the fight and killed at least six men after breaking his leg. Snake's hand and arm were destroyed from repeated blows from Taliban fighters, yet he also stayed in the fight and dispatched multiple aggressors that afternoon. I was knocked from the train during a multi-combatant hand-to-hand battle. I broke my back, five ribs, punctured my left lung, and badly damaged multiple internal organs. Snake could not be here because an associate of Mr. Beard's named Harold Grimes murdered him in an Air Force hospital in Frankfurt, Germany, earlier this week. Grimes is now in the custody of the NCIS, and is, no doubt, telling all his secrets to the interrogators as we speak."

The crowd erupted with applause, and everyone in the tent took to their feet, but Clark held up his hand.

"There's more. The most important thing you need to know about what happened on that mountain is that we did our job. We protected that train, and when it got ugly, Jerry Beard left us up there to die. It took a man with more honor in his little finger than Jerry Beard ever dreamed of having in his whole body to put an operation together at his own unimaginable expense and pull us off that mountain. Had he not done so, the world would've believed Beard's lies, and we would've perished at the top of the Khyber Pass.

"The final statement I'd like to make is this. The commander of our detachment, Major "Smoke" Butterworth, was found dead by apparent suicide early this morning with this letter pinned to his sleeve. 'I have failed both the men under my command and the nation I have devoted my life to serving. Men of valor and honor and strength trusted me with their lives, and I lacked the constitution to live up to the role of the leader they deserved. Cowards in pursuit of personal glory and financial gain have defeated me when armies of thousands could not. Low-life bastards bent on self-aggrandizing and political power have gained positions they exploit, and that exploitation cost the lives of good men who loved their country. I'm ashamed of my weakness, and I go to my grave knowing all I have fought to protect and defend for two-thirds of my life is quickly falling into the hands of those who lack both the wisdom and willingness to respect and defend our freedom. James Butterworth, Major, U.S. Army Retired.'"

Reporters threw their hands into the air and yelled questions at Clark and Singer as I melted back into my chair. Smoke was dead, and I could've prevented it. His speech to me the night before was a desperate cry for help, and I didn't heed it. I let him walk away. I was a trained psychologist and seasoned operative, but I let him walk away. I was the one who failed Major Butterworth. It wasn't the other way around.

The roar of the crowd dissolved into the air as I felt the weight of Smoke's words collapsing upon me. I had turned twenty-eight years old the day all of that began, but I had aged a lifetime in the two weeks since then.

I felt Penny's arm across my shoulder and her hair falling beside my face. The mission I'd undertaken had cost the lives of two good men and had robbed Penny of the family she so desperately longed to have. Part of me died, too. I suppose that's how ambitious young men who believe they can change the world become men of determined pessimism. Maybe I'd turned a corner from believing in the good of mankind to expecting everyone I encountered to be the next Jerry Beard.

A pair of strong hands gripped each of my shoulders. "Mr. Fulton, you need to come with us."

The next sound I heard was the owners of those strong hands collapsing to the floor with Mongo's hands gripping their throats.

"No, Mr. Fulton doesn't *need* to do anything of the sort. You two *need* to leave my friend alone."

The two men clawed at Mongo's wrists but finally gave up and withdrew credentials from their jacket pockets.

I recognized the cred-packs. "Mongo, let them up. It's okay."

The two men climbed to their feet, cautiously remaining well clear of Mongo's hands, and straightened their ties. "We're with the Secret Service, and the president would like to speak with you, Mr. Fulton."

Chapter 30
My Number

I was in no mood to be toyed with. The men may have been Secret Service agents, but wherever they intended to take me would be far away from the president. I'd been dealt a blow I wouldn't soon overcome. Smoke's death rested as much on my shoulders as anyone else's, and I wasn't interested in playing hide-the-spy with the Secret Service.

"Are you okay, Chase?"

I had no idea why Mongo felt such loyalty to me. He'd spent far more time than me in forgotten corners of the world conducting missions no one would ever hear of. He'd endured military training I'd never see, and he possessed skills I'd never develop, yet he stood by me as if I were solely his responsibility.

"Honestly, Mongo, I don't know yet. Why don't you stick around and see what this is really about?"

The huge man folded his arms across his chest and stood inches away from me, staring intently at the two agents.

The younger of the two was the first to speak. "You can call off your dog, Fulton, or we can take him down for you."

I took a step toward the two men. "You're the second person to call these men dogs. The first is in handcuffs and will never again see the light of day. I don't care what kind of badges the two of you carry, you'll show these men some respect."

The older agent shrugged. "Makes no difference to me. Our instructions were to tell you the president wanted to talk with you and then escort you to the White House. If you choose not to come, that's up to you."

I still didn't know the rules of the game we were playing, but I was certain of one thing: like the previous six years of my life, I was in way over my head.

"Okay, fine. We'll come with you to the White House. What are you driving?"

The two agents looked skeptically at each other. "A Suburban. Why?"

I nodded sharply and took Penny by the elbow. "Perfect. So are we. We'll follow you there."

Obviously unaccustomed to having anyone refuse a ride to the White House, the younger agent immediately began making radio calls. Controlling the environment is a skill learned and developed over decades of practice. I was practicing.

Behind me, my partner was sitting on stage, erect in a chair, with a horde of reporters gathered around him. The look on his face was one of physical pain and disgust with the absurdity of the questions he was being asked. Although I'd never wear one, it made me proud to see Clark in his uniform, even if it was stretched over the plastic clamshell back brace his body required.

Whoever was on the other end of the agent's radio calls must have approved the convoy. When we reached the gate, we were granted access after nothing more than a cursory glance by the armed guards and thirty seconds of sniffing by an explosives dog.

"Chase, is this really happening?"

The look on Penny's face was priceless. It was an amalgamation of fear, disbelief, and innocence.

I took in the sight of the Eisenhower Executive Office Building on our left and the majesty of the White House on our right. "I think it is."

Grey looked over his shoulder. "Is this your first time here, kid?"

I laughed. "Yeah, you could say that."

"Relax. I've been here a bunch of times. You'll get used to it eventually, but it's pretty cool at first. It just turns into a big hassle after a while, though."

His nonchalance somehow made me feel more at ease, but Mongo had yet to say a word. I looked forward to hearing what he had to say if and when he ever opened up.

We pulled under the portico of the West Wing and were hustled from our Suburban, through a set of heavy double doors, and to a security station. Grey stayed in the truck. After a pass through a metal detector and the confiscation of twenty pounds of gear from Mongo, we were issued visitors' passes on lanyards and instructed to not remove the passes from around our necks for any reason.

Penny was still wearing her Skipper-provided press pass and seemed amused to add another around her neck. "What the heck is about to happen in here?"

"I have no idea, but it's gonna make a great story for your newspaper."

"Oh, you're funny."

The same two agents who'd escorted us from the Pentagon stayed with us as we continued down a long hallway. I had a lot of questions, but something told me none of them mattered at that point.

I'd seen it on television, but the Oval Office was not what I expected. It was cavernous and sparsely furnished. It was an impressive space on its own merits, but when the president of the United States stands up to shake a man's hand, everything else in the environment pales.

"Good afternoon, Mr. Fulton. It's a pleasure to finally meet you. Welcome to the White House. Is this your first time?"

I've stood toe to toe with men trying to kill me with knives, sticks, guns, and even hand grenades, and I held my own, but putting my hand in the president's was not something I was prepared to experience. Words wouldn't come, and I couldn't blink.

The president smiled and even chuckled a little. "After what I saw on television, I didn't take you as the shy type, Chase. May I call you Chase?"

Realizing I was still shaking his hand, I released it and withdrew mine before shooting Penny a disbelieving glance.

"This is Penny, Mr. President."

It was one of those moments I'd love to be able to rewind and try again. The first words out of my mouth to the president of the United States were, "This is Penny."

The president, still smiling, offered his hand to her. "I thought your name was Nicole. At least that's how you introduced yourself at the press conference. And you're not a reporter from the Houston Chronicle. We know that much."

She said, "It's an honor to…"

The president waved off the formality and motioned toward the sofa. "Have a seat, won't you? And you're Mr. Malloy. Is that right?"

The president's small hand disappeared inside my protector's meaty grip. "Call me Mongo, sir."

The chuckle became full laughter. "Mongo it is, then. Have a seat."

I was sitting in the Oval Office, across from the president, with a giant on one side of me and my beautiful wife masquerading as a reporter on the other. Nothing could've prepared me for anything so surreal or absurd.

The president pushed a button on a panel beside his chair. "Betty, send in Tommy and Gene, and maybe something to snack on. We may be awhile. Oh, and get Gail for us, would you?"

"Yes, of course, Mr. President."

A door I hadn't realized existed opened into the office, and a pair of uniformed men strolled confidently into the room. Both addressed the president respectfully and stood, apparently awaiting instruction.

Simultaneously, another door swung inward, and a young lady rolled a cart of pastries and coffee into the room. As if there were a never-ending line of people waiting outside invisible doors, a woman came into the room wearing a dark blue suit, carrying leather binders in her arms.

She handed the stack to the president and turned toward the sofa. "Mrs. Fulton, Mr. Malloy, would you follow me, please? We've arranged for a private tour of the White House."

Both Penny and Mongo immediately turned their attention to me as if awaiting permission, though no one in the room was less in charge than I was. Even the pastry-cart lady had a more command-ing presence.

"Yeah, yeah, go. Have a tour. I'll be hanging out in here with the president and these guys."

I had no way to know if the president was always in such good spirits or if he found the three of us amusing, but he had another hearty chuckle as Mongo and Penny were led from the office.

"Chase, meet General Tommy Beaufour, director of Central Intel-ligence and Admiral Gene Galloway, the chief of naval operations."

I stood, shook hands, and kept my mouth shut.

The president passed a binder to each of us. "Gentlemen, have a seat. Let's get right down to business."

I still had no idea what I was doing in the Oval Office with the CNO, the DCI, and the president.

"Chase, do you know General Beaufour?"

"Of course I know who he is, Mr. President, but we've never met," I managed to say.

"Well, he knows you, and there are two more things he knows better than anybody I've ever met. Those two things are tactics and people. When Tommy called me this afternoon and said I needed to see this slider on TV, I thought I was about to watch somebody throw one hell of a pitch, but then I remembered it's wintertime and Tommy must be talking about some other kind of slider. Turns out, he was talking about you, Chase."

It was apparently my turn to talk, but I was still lost. "Mr. Presi-dent, I have no idea what you're talking about, and in fact, I have no idea what I'm doing here at all."

The president motioned toward the DCI. "Go ahead, Tommy. Tell Chase what's going on."

General Beaufour said, "Chase, *slider* is a term we use to describe an operative who can move in and out of official assignments and positions, as well as those sorts of missions we don't necessarily want to leave our fingerprints on. Does that make sense to you?"

I tried to keep my mouth shut as much as possible. "Sure."

"You've been a no fingerprint kind of guy for us for some time, but when you packed up and headed to Afghanistan, and especially when you showed up in D.C. today, you slid into a spotlight that is hard to douse."

So, that's what this is about. I'm on the verge of being spanked for stepping out of my lane. But why would my spanking come from the President and not Dominic?

General Beaufour wasn't finished. "Don't worry, Chase. You've done nothing particularly wrong. In fact, you've done quite a few things exactly right. As far as I'm concerned, you exposing Michael Pennant's involvement with Jerry Beard is enough to call you a friend of the Agency. We've had our eye on you for some time for something special. You've moved up the timeline a little."

The president had just become the second most interesting person in the room for me. Tommy Beaufour had my attention.

"Chase, we have a proposition for you. You're young, bright, fearless, and uniquely situated to staff, equip, house, and deploy a force of men who are sliders, like you."

He opened his binder and laid it on my lap. "Sign this."

I read through the nondisclosure agreement in front of me and signed the bottom.

"Good," he said. "Now we can talk. There are twenty such teams situated throughout the world, all led by graduates of The Ranch, and none officially on the government payroll. Yours is to be number twenty-one. I understand you have a particular affinity for the number twenty-one."

He pulled out a seven-year-old black-and-white photograph of me being hefted into the air in Omaha, Nebraska, after winning the 1996 College World Series, my number twenty-one clearly visible on the back of my University of Georgia jersey.

I held the picture between my fingers, trying to relive the inno-cence that was my life back then. I could smell the field and taste the sweat on my face. The agony of my demolished right hand pounded through my head as if it had happened all over again. A flood of memories poured through my mind: The Ranch where I walked away from my life and became a covert operative. Havana Harbor, where I eliminated my first target. Miami, where I'd watched Anya take a bullet to the back. The Shenandoah Valley, where I took down a rogue Russian SVR colonel. Panama, where I'd lost my family and dealt a nasty blow to the Chinese Ministry of State Security. Moscow and Sol-Iletsk, where I pulled off the only successful escape in history from the infamous Black Dolphin Prison. And the Khyber Pass, where I rescued my brothers.

I tossed the picture back to General Beaufour. "I'm not that guy anymore."

"Precisely," said the president. "Admiral, I believe it's your turn."

Admiral Galloway spoke with the confidence of a man who'd taken incoming fire and shot back. "Chase, you probably have no idea why I'm here."

I released a burst of nervous laughter. "Admiral, I have no idea why *I'm* here, let alone you."

"Fair enough," the admiral said. "I'm here because in a few days you're going to have your name on a deed for a massive piece of property next door to my submarine base in Saint Marys. That makes us neighbors. You know the old saying about good fences making for good neighbors? Well, that's not the case with us. I'm here to give you a set of keys to every lock on my fence. Anything the United States Navy can do for you is at your disposal…short of launching a volley of intercontinental ballistic missiles, of course."

The president cleared his throat. "Um, we may be able to negoti-ate that should it become necessary."

I had no idea if he was joking. "So, let me get this straight. You want me to build a team of covert operatives based out of Saint Marys, Georgia, and sit around waiting for orders. Is that what I'm supposed to do?"

The president smiled. "Not at all, Chase. You're going back to Georgia to build your own little private army, and you'll do exactly what you're doing now—saving the world, one bad guy at a time. The only difference now is when you need a favor, you'll have all three of our private numbers. You pick up the phone, and you get what you want from us. Any time, day or night. And all we ask is that we get the same from you."

The three men—the chief of naval operations, the director of Central Intelligence, and the president of the United States—stared directly at me, awaiting my answer.

Chapter 31
What About Penny

Answering a question with a question can be a frustrating and end-less cycle, but that's what I did.

"What about Penny?"

Admiral Galloway spoke up. "We thought that might be your first question. That's why we've arranged for the two of you to spend at least part of your honeymoon at Langley."

"Langley?" I said. "Nobody wants to go to Langley on their honeymoon...or any other time for that matter."

The DCI grinned. "Well, your honeymoon is a time when you're expected to disappear and be left alone by friends and family. We want the two of you to do that, but under that guise, you're also free to ask all the questions you want while everyone in your life believes you're basking in the sun someplace tropical."

"I do have one more question," I said.

The three men looked unconcerned.

"Why me?"

The president stood. "That's easy, Chase. We chose you because of the question you did *not* ask."

"What *didn't* I ask?"

The leader of the free world put his hands in his pockets and sucked in through his teeth. "You didn't ask what it pays. That's precisely why we know you're our man. The world is full of motivations. You demonstrated yours are based in loyalty to your country and to your men. Why else would you have done what you did in Afghanistan and at the Pentagon? Hell, son, I don't know which of those places is more dangerous for guys like you."

* * *

Perhaps I didn't fully understand the limits of the nondisclosure agreement I'd signed in the Oval Office, but the flight back to Saint Marys was one long briefing session. The six of us would become the foundation of Team Twenty-One to be housed at Bonaventure Plantation on the banks of the North River, right next door to the U.S. Navy.

* * *

In the weeks following my meeting with the president, the world changed. We were at full-fledged war with Al-Qaeda and the Taliban. America remembered what it was like to, once again, be one nation under God, as we put away our petty differences and started thinking of each other as family instead of strangers. Not since the Japanese bombing of Pearl Harbor on December 7, 1941, had America felt its collective heart break in an instant, the way it did on September 11, 2001. The skyline of Manhattan wasn't the only canvas with a void. We Americans felt the emptiness in our hearts and on our freedom-kissed soil that had been occupied by the 2,977 innocent victims who lost their lives in the worst terrorist attack in modern history.

The world would never again be the same.

Author's Note

Although the characters in my novels are fictional, most are based on the personalities, actions, attitudes, and sometimes physical traits of real people I've known throughout my life. Many are based on warriors I've been fortunate to know, work alongside, and respect through the years. Men and women like those quiet heroes depicted in my novels are not the exception to the rule of the American spirit; they are the embodiment and epitome of that spirit. They go about their daily lives—sometimes next door and sometimes in our own homes—without asking for recognition, praise, or financial gain. They are strong, independent, capable, and loyal. They don't want medals or their names up in lights. They simply want to defend what they believe is the greatest nation that has ever existed on this planet.

We don't get to see their heroics; those deeds are done in the shadows and under the cover of darkness so you and I can sleep peacefully every night. Something else we don't see are the ghosts and demons that haunt the minds and bodies of those warriors who keep us free. Just like my characters, many great American heroes are suffering silently right in front of us. They lie awake through the night, sweating and trembling, as they relive what they've seen and heard and done for the rest of us. On those long, lonely nights, they pray for the dawn so they can rise, pull on their boots, and keep doing the things that make our way of life possible—things most Americans will never know—things most people could never understand.

Some of our warriors, like the fictional Major James "Smoke" Butterworth in this novel, lose their final battle to the demons they cannot overcome. Those men and women deserve better than to die alone, ashamed, and believing themselves failures.

In these times of political turmoil and petty bickering, I ask that you stand with me in supporting the brave men and women who proudly stand between us and the wolves at the gate. Those wolves will only be held at bay as long as our warriors believe that what they are standing in front of is worthy of defending and worth dying for.

—Cap Daniels

About the Author

Cap Daniels

Cap Daniels is a former sailing charter captain, scuba and sailing instructor, pilot, Air Force combat veteran, and civil servant of the U.S. Department of Defense. Raised far from the ocean in rural East Tennessee, his early infatuation with salt water was sparked by the fascinating, and sometimes true, sea stories told by his father, a retired Navy Chief Petty Officer. Those stories of adventure on the high seas sent Cap in search of adventure of his own, which eventually landed him on Florida's Gulf Coast where he spends as much time as possible on, in, and under the waters of the Emerald Coast.

With a headful of larger-than-life characters and their thrilling exploits, Cap pours his love of adventure and passion for the ocean onto the pages of The Chase Fulton Novels series.

Visit www.CapDaniels.com to join the mailing list to receive newsletter and release updates.

Connect with Cap Daniels

Facebook: www.Facebook.com/WriterCapDaniels
Instagram: https://www.instagram.com/authorcapdaniels/
BookBub: https://www.bookbub.com/profile/cap-daniels

Made in the USA
Monee, IL
09 March 2024

54762565R00136